Heartless

A Regency Romance

by

Jaimey Grant

Heartless

A Regency Romance
by Jaimey Grant

Cover design by Laura J Miller
www.anauthorsart.com

Published by TreasureLine Publishing
www.treasurelinepublishing.com

First published September 2008
Third Edition
EAN13: 978-1-61752-145-4

Author's Note

Dear Readers,

Heartless debuted in 2008, one of my four self-published titles. It was contracted to TreasureLine Publishing in 2011 and underwent a makeover, inside and out.

I never felt completely at peace with the earlier edition. There were parts untold, things unexplained, and maybe a few things that could have been better explained. I tried to do that in this new revised edition.

If you've read *Heartless* before, I hope this edition brings you as much pleasure or more. If this is your first time reading this particular story, I hope you enjoy it. I am deeply grateful to you, my readers, old and new, for your continued support.

Jaimey Grant

Dedication

This edition is dedicated to my beta readers, past and future. I cannot express the depth of my gratitude for your time and effort.

A special thank you goes out to Rachel Rossano, Linda Boulanger and Jennifer Lyons. I can never repay you for all your support. Thank you.

Chronological Regencies
~Honor~
(the story of Connor and Verena)
~Betrayal~
(the story of Adam and Bri)
~Deception~
(the story of Levi and Aurora)
~Spellbound~
(the story of Tristan and Raven)
~Heartless~
(the story of Hart and Leandra)
~Redemption~
(the story of Darius and Jenny, and Miles and Gwen)

Short Stories
~Assassin's Keeper~
(Regency fiction in *Unlocked*)
~Survival~
(fantasy fiction in *Unlocked*)
~Eliza's Epiphany~
(Regency romance in *Whispered Beginnings*)
~The Dragon's Birth~
(fantasy fiction)
~My Lady Coward~
(serial Regency romance at www.jaimeygrant.com)
~The 11th Commandment~
(serial Regency romance in InD'Tale Magazine)

Heartless

TreasureLine Publishing

1

London
October 1820

THE third Duke of Derringer slammed his fist on the solicitor's desk. An inkwell, a pen, a tea cup and Mr. Grimsby jumped.

The black-haired, black-eyed duke gave him a searching look. Did the little man jest? If so, he was less intelligent than Derringer had thought. But Mr. Grimsby looked more terrified than amused so he decided that the bespectacled gentleman was not lying.

"Indeed?"

"Just so, your grace. I can only apologize that we did not find this until recently," he added with a nervous swallow. His large Adam's apple bobbed and Derringer found himself distracted. The man was not blessed with any amount of good looks, the duke thought. He pushed his thoughts back to his present problem.

The Duke of Derringer had just been informed that he could not have his inheritance unless he married by a certain date. He'd always had whatever money he wanted, been given free rein with his finances. Then, after the death of the senior member of the solicitor's office, a clause to the late duke's will was discovered.

Now Derringer sat across from this spindly-legged little man awaiting the date of his life sentence.

"How long do I have?" Derringer snapped.

The solicitor looked down his long nose at the papers before him, squinted once, sniffed twice, and squinted again before answering. "By your thirtieth birthday, your grace."

Before the last word had left the man's mouth, Derringer was on his feet and leaning over the desk. With one hand braced for leverage, the duke held the other man aloft by his jacket lapels.

"What did you say?" he demanded in silky tones.

The man of business gulped. "By the time you're thirty?" he squeaked.

Derringer shook the whiny little creature like a terrier shaking a rat. "Do you realize what day this is?" he barked at the frightened little man.

The lawyer managed to croak, "The twenty-second?"

"It's the twenty-second of October, you bloody clunch! My birthday is a sennight from now. Seven days! How the bloody hell do you suppose I can marry in a sennight, you mangy whoreson? It takes that long just to get a special license!"

The solicitor released a petrified squeak and the duke dropped him in disgust. He paced about the tiny chamber. Seven days. He had seven days to find, woo, and marry some chit just so he could have complete access to his rightful inheritance. He hoped his father was burning in a particularly painful corner of hell for this one.

And what had possessed the late duke to draft such a codicil when his son was still in leading strings?

He turned his dark gaze on the cowering little man. "Is there anything else?"

The solicitor shook his head vigorously. He cowered even lower when the duke approached the desk and leaned toward him. "I will marry before the twenty-ninth, Grimsby, even if I have to ask the first girl I come across to be my duchess." He stood up straight, still glaring down at the solicitor from his superior height of six-foot-three. "Prepare yourself, Grimsby. I trust you won't be disappointed in my choice."

Derringer left the office of Lehman, Grimsby, and Bimm with a determined stride. He would find a damned female and drag her to the altar if he had to.

As if his day could possibly get worse, Derringer thought as he entered the inn near Maidstone. He wasn't even sure why he had decided to return to Derringer Crescent after nearly two years. He hated the drafty castle and preferred to avoid servants who had known him since he was in leading strings. They had a way of knowing things about a body that one would rather not have commonly known.

Logic insisted that London was the place to find his bride. But he had avoided London for nearly two years as well. The last time he'd graced the capital with his august presence, he'd been shot helping Lord Levi, Earl of Greville. He'd fled the country just as soon as he could stand, leaving Levi to take care of an injured wife by himself—Lady Greville had thrown herself in the path of a bullet to save her husband in the single most brainless act of selfless courage Derringer had ever witnessed.

Those events and his already dangerous reputation would prevent even the most daring of females from marrying him, however.

So now he was on his way to Folkestone to take a look at his childhood home—and any young woman who may have not heard that he was the devil's right hand. He didn't want to stay there; the place had too many horrible memories for comfort. But he should at least check in to see if there was anything that required his personal attention. And perhaps he should send his cousin Martin to look after the place, he thought with an inner sigh. He didn't particularly like the other man but he was willing to give him a position since their grandfather had not seen fit to leave any of his vast wealth to his second son, Martin's father.

And how the devil did the wheel of his curricle break? He was fortunate he wasn't killed in the resulting accident. Thankfully, he'd been traveling at a relatively slow pace due to the poor quality of the roads and the growing dusk— an unusual circumstance since he had a habit of racing along the English countryside at breakneck speeds regardless of weather or road conditions. It was said he had the devil's favor; hence, his amazing good health after a lifetime of near-death experiences not all due to his own negligence.

But now, mere hours from home, he was stranded at the Black Bear hostelry late enough that he probably couldn't get the blacksmith there for a good few hours. Damn it all to hell if he had to stay the night there!

Derringer slapped his leather driving gloves against his buckskin-clad thigh and surveyed the taproom, taking in the number of men watching him surreptitiously over the rims of mugs. Did they realize how transparent they were in their curiosity?

A commotion near the door distracted him from his inspection of the locals. He turned to see a very small, very plain, and very young woman in a drab brown cloak and ugly black bonnet arguing with the landlord.

"We don't serve yer kind 'ere, girl, so git," the man ordered gruffly.

Her kind? Derringer's lips twitched. Was the man blind?

"But you don't understand," the girl pleaded, her soft voice rife with sincerity. "I'm not one of those kind. I have a little money, so I can pay, I assure you. And it's only for one night. I have nowhere else to go." A note of desperation trembled on her final word.

"No, now off with you," was the innkeeper's implacable reply.

The girl stared at the landlord through a pair of hideous spectacles and somehow managed to look down her nose at the man while looking up at him. The duke found himself admiring her tenacity. The sensation surprised him.

As she turned to leave, Derringer called her back, his mind racing with possibilities even as he opened his mouth. Despite her hideous clothing and plain features, he wasn't appalled at the idea of her in his bed. Quite the opposite, actually. Strange thought, that.

And she was desperate. Desperate women were known for all kinds of unusual actions, such as marrying a complete stranger. He almost smiled.

She eyed him warily, spine straight and fingers clenched before her. "Yes, sir?"

"A moment, if you will." Derringer turned away, catching the landlord's eye. With a tip of his head, he indicated his immediate need of a private parlor. When no objection was forthcoming—how could there be when the man was far too busy with two drunks who were intent on spilling each other's blood?—Derringer offered his arm to the young woman, just as if he were in the habit of such gentlemanly behavior, and led the way.

At the doorpost, she paused, clearly unwilling to enter a room alone with him. She had a care for her reputation then, a further indication of her breeding.

Derringer settled his dark gaze on her. "Follow me," he ordered, gentling his tone. Yet she hesitated still. "Come, girl, I won't eat you," he muttered in exasperation.

"That's not what I'm afraid of."

Her candor caught him unaware but only for a moment. Then he leaned down. She stared up at him suspiciously, her hazel eyes huge behind her spectacles. "I will not ravish you either, my dear," he murmured. Her suspicious look did not waver one whit. "I only ravish blonds and I only eat redheads," he couldn't resist adding, though he couldn't tell exactly what color hair she possessed.

The girl released a giggle and clapped a hand over her mouth. She nodded once and Derringer led her to a chair. "Are you hungry?" he asked brusquely.

"Famished," she replied.

"Springs!" Derringer bellowed. The landlord appeared before him as if by magic. "Dinner immediately. And brandy. Your best, Springs, from that personal stash I know you keep. None of that bilge water you foist on your other customers. Now!"

Springs scurried off without a word to do the duke's bidding. Derringer sat down at the table.

The young woman sat stiffly on the very edge of the chair opposite. She folded her gloved hands demurely in her lap and bowed her head meekly, giving him a great view of the top of her ugly bonnet.

"Take off the hat and the cloak," Derringer commanded. Her eyes flew up to meet his. She had a stubborn chin. "Trust me. We have much to discuss and you will be more comfortable. And none of this false meekness, my dear. I won't stand for it."

She hesitated before complying with his demand. She smoothed her hands over her dull brown hair, tucking a few straying locks back into the severe knot at her nape. Then she sat with her hands folded in her lap and her head up, watching him.

Silence reigned until the landlord returned with their meal. He bowed and scraped as usual and Derringer studied his companion while she studied him with equal curiosity.

Being a connoisseur of beauty, it came as something of a surprise to Derringer to realize that the girl sitting opposite him was not plain. Her features were not fashionable, true, but he'd never found fashionable beauty very appealing. Her regular, ordinary features were somehow pleasing. If not for the spectacles perched on her *retroussé* little nose, she'd even be pretty.

Her hair he couldn't help but wonder about. Would it be long and straight or curl in riotous abandon? The sudden image of silky brown curls spread over his pillow and streaming over a pair of naked breasts taunted him. Which only led to the obvious contemplation of her form under all that sensible dark wool she sported as a gown. His imagination caused him some distinct discomfort. It took some considerable willpower not to shift his position in his chair.

It was too long since he'd visited his mistress, he thought with a measure of disgust.

"I have a proposition for you," Derringer began as soon as their meal was laid out before them. He waved Springs from the room before the man could even open his mouth. Obsequious pandering was tedious at best.

He poured himself a glass of brandy and swirled it around, watching the ripples in the liquid. "How old are you?"

"I am twenty," she replied softly.

"Blast," the duke muttered. "I don't suppose you will turn twenty-one within the next six days?"

"No," she said. "Not until February."

"Damn and blast," he muttered. He studied her round little face. What the devil was she doing at an inn alone? "Are you an orphan?"

"Yes," she answered immediately.

"Are you a lady of gentle birth or merely an upper servant with aspirations above her station?"

The girl set her fork carefully beside her plate. She took a sip of wine and smoothed the hair back from her face. He realized she was trying to compose herself.

"That was rather blunt, I must say. I am not a servant. I am of gentle birth but I would not be considered a lady," she finally said evenly.

A whore? He looked her over carefully and decided she was not a whore. Fallen from grace perhaps, but not an actual courtesan. "Who is your father?"

"The late Earl of Harwood." She picked up her fork and began to eat steadily again.

"The late earl? When did Harwood die?"

"Almost a sennight past."

A week ago? The devil. "Oh. Is the countess dead as well then? You said you were an orphan," he pointed out as he refilled his glass. He was quite sure the countess was not, but he hadn't known about Harwood, damn his spies, so it was conceivable that yet another useless detail had slipped his notice.

"The countess is alive and well. My mother, however, died nearly one-and-twenty years ago."

She was a bastard. Perfect, Derringer thought with a certain amount of glee. That should set Grimsby on his ear. The wealthy, powerful, and handsome Duke of Derringer throwing his life away on a penniless bastard would give that milksop something to fret about. Marvelous!

"You sound like a gentlewoman," he remarked lazily.

"I was raised in my father's house. I was sent to Miss Forester's Select Seminary for Young Ladies when the time came and given every benefit of a daughter of the house. Then Papa died and his wife threw me out after the will was not found. Everything of Papa's went to his son, the new earl." All this was said in the most prosaic, matter-of-fact tone Derringer had ever heard.

Her voice changed subtly as she continued. It might have gone unnoticed by anyone but him. "I was told he left nothing for me but I refuse to believe my father would not take care of me. We were very close and he assured me I would always be taken care of, that I need never fear poverty. Well," she shrugged fatalistically.

"And you had no one else to turn to when you found yourself in straitened circumstances?"

She hesitated. "I first went into the village to see my beau, Mr. Hubbard," she confessed, a shade of reluctance coloring her tone while an embarrassed pink colored her round cheeks. "He had heard about the lack of will and let me know that he was no longer interested in marrying me. But he was more than willing to give me a much different position." She shook her head and shrugged. "So now I am alone and apparently at your mercy, sir."

"So you are," he agreed with an assessing look, uncomfortably surprised at his sudden desire to tear Mr. Hubbard limb from limb. "Marry me."

Leandra dropped her fork. It clattered onto her plate and her eyes flew up to stare at the crazy man sitting across from her. "Are you daft, sir?" she asked with her normal candor. "I mean, are you an escaped Bedlamite?"

She didn't give him a chance to reply. "You are kind, sir. I thank you for the meal and the sympathetic ear, but you needn't feel that such desperate means are called for in helping me. I'm certain you like to help people, but marriage? Is that not going much too far, my lord? I assume you are a lord of some sort based on the landlord's attitude but perhaps you are escaped from your keeper? I mean, even lords can lose their minds. The newspapers overflow with such stories..." Her voice drifted to silence.

He didn't smile, but she didn't expect him too, either. He just gave her that same blank look that he had been giving her since the first time she had seen him. It was a probing look that made her uneasy. As if he was trying to read her mind.

"I assure you, I am not mad nor do I jest," he said in a tone that supported his avowal. Then, with a look that was almost amused, he admitted, "And helping people is not something I am known to do."

"I don't even know who you are. Everything about you suggests that you are a peer. Yet, you know I am baseborn and you still ask me to marry you. Why?"

He shrugged one broad shoulder and then unashamedly contradicted what he had told her no more than a few seconds earlier. "You need help; I need a wife. It sounds like a fair exchange to me."

Leandra's eyes widened. The gentleman was very handsome in a non-fashionable way, very elegant…and very dark. Everything about him was dark. He wore a black cloak over a black jacket, a black shirt, and black buckskins with black topboots. Even his cravat was black. His gloves, tossed on the table beside his plate, were black leather. His black hair was worn long and tied back with a black velvet ribbon. His eyes were black and his skin was tanned dark. She wondered a trifle breathlessly if his handkerchief and smallclothes were black as well. He quirked a black brow at her even as she assessed his appearance.

"Do I pass muster on a purely physical level?" he asked, voice tinged with sarcasm.

"Do you have a black horse?" Leandra heard herself asking before she could stop herself.

A sharp bark of laughter escaped him. "As a matter of fact, I have several black horses as well as a black cat and a black dog."

"Oh, my," she murmured.

Silence.

"Are you going to marry me or not? I have no time to persuade you to change your mind," he said as he tired of the novelty of baiting someone new. He was sick of the inn, sick of being stranded, and sick of her odd silence.

She thought quickly. He could be one of those depraved lunatics that preyed on young defenseless women. Or he could be sincere in his need for a wife. Leandra wondered how many more times an opportunity like this would come her way. She stared into the gentleman's eyes, looking for…something.

And then she saw it. It flashed through his dark eyes and she actually saw it. He was human after all, she thought with satisfaction. She saw a glimmer of uncertainty in his gaze.

"I have one question, sir," she said determinedly. "You have not mentioned whether you need an heir."

Derringer gave her a benign look. "I will eventually. I see no reason to force you to do anything you find distasteful," he added dryly.

She blushed. "I did not mean to imply that I find you distasteful, sir," she replied, thinking quite the opposite. "I merely wondered if you wanted a true marriage or one in name only. You do not know me after all and I would be very much surprised should you find me in the least attractive."

She met his gaze squarely and had not the least bit of self-pity on her round face. She appeared…accepting.

"Truly?" was all Derringer drawled in reply to her self-deprecating comment. He could have told her that there was something about her that attracted him like a fly to honey. He remained silent on that score and allowed her to think what she would. "Are you accepting my proposal, then?"

Leandra took a deep breath. "Yes."

Springs tapped on the door, not allowing the duke any time to actually be surprised at her relatively easy capitulation. He snapped distractedly at the landlord to enter.

The slimy little man bowed low and said obsequiously, "The blacksmith is 'ere, yer grace. Shall I send 'im in?"

"No, I will take him to my curricle myself in a moment. Leave." The man was gone before the command had fully left Derringer's mouth.

"Your grace?" Leandra whispered. "Oh, dear God."

"Did I not mention I hold a dukedom?" he asked far too innocently.

"No," Leandra breathed, feeling just a trifle put out and more than a little unsure of herself. "I'm sure the fact just slipped your mind, *your grace.*"

"Do not be a shrew," Derringer remarked, his own nerves frayed to the breaking point from his hectic day. He stood to take his leave.

She inhaled, the movement swelling her chest and drawing his grace's eye to her not insignificant bosom.

Ignoring his ungentlemanly reaction, she asked, "Which dukedom do you hold?"

"Derringer."

He stared at her as if expecting some sort of reaction but all she could do was stare back. She'd never heard of the Duke of Derringer.

He straightened, his fingers tightening around his black gloves. "My mother's cousin is a bishop. I'll see him tonight about a special license. We'll marry tomorrow."

He was a wee bit irked that she didn't seem to know who he was. Everyone knew of the Duke of Derringer. He was infamous and feared throughout the kingdom. Where had she been that she'd not even made the connection that he was Lord Heartless?

"Tonight? Tomorrow?" she sputtered. "How is that possible?"

"I have to marry by the twenty-ninth, my dear. We will marry tomorrow just to make sure everything is legal and legitimate. And cousin Horace has been after me to marry this age so getting the license will not be difficult to obtain. I am a duke with connections, after all."

"Oh," she said in a small voice. She stiffened her spine. "Very well, your grace. We shall marry tomorrow."

"Good. I'll arrange a room for you tonight. We'll marry from here and I will escort you to the Crescent after the wedding." He walked to the door and turned the knob.

Then he paused and turned back to the young woman at the table.

"By the way, what is your name?"

2

LEANDRA Merrily Harcourt married the third Duke of Derringer one early morning in late October. Shivers threatened to send her to the floor, the enormity of what she'd just done closing in on her. She knew so little about this man she now called husband.

The local vicar ended the ceremony. Leandra barely managed a full breath when the duke suddenly pulled her against his tall form and pressed his lips to hers. Shocked gasps came from the vicar and his curate.

For Leandra, time slowed. The embrace shocked her as much as their audience but for a very different reason. This man she'd known for mere hours manhandled her and she felt...excitement. She gasped and he released her with a mocking grin.

"Thank you, vicar," the duke said as he escorted Leandra from the room. He tossed a few gold coins at the man as payment for services rendered and then handed the curate several pound notes as a donation to the church. "I have money to spare now," he said carelessly to Leandra's questioning look. "Thanks to you, wife."

His voice held a note of something that made Leandra shiver uneasily. Oh, Lord, what had she done?

She knew exactly what she'd intended. She had leapt at the chance to become somebody's—anybody's—wife. Seduced by his manner, all ease and power, she'd craved the same feeling. She wanted to be able to act in any way she pleased without fear or threat. The penniless bastard daughter of a deceased earl had very little actual freedom.

Derringer settled his wife into his repaired curricle. He pondered the conversation he'd had with the blacksmith just moments ago.

"Been cut, yer grace," the large man said confidently.

"What the devil do you mean it's 'been cut?'"

The blacksmith didn't even blink at the duke's anger. "That there wheel's been cut, yer grace, sawed near through. I would say as 'ow someone ain't wishful of yer safe return."

"Of all the…" the duke muttered. First, he had to marry to get a fortune that rightfully belonged to him and now that certain someone who was trying to kill him had struck yet again. "The devil!"

"Are you quite well?" his wife asked suddenly, ripping him back to the present.

He glowered at her bespectacled face. "Yes," he growled as he swung himself up onto the seat next to her.

The girl nodded in apparent satisfaction. "Why have you no valet, your grace?" she asked, eyebrows raised in avid curiosity.

"What the devil do I need one of those whiny, sniveling creatures for? Bleeding milksops, all," he muttered as he urged his perfectly matched blacks into motion. Personal servants knew a man's every secret, he reminded himself.

"Perhaps you should try for a little calm, Lord Derringer," she suggested, her mild tone having the opposite effect.

He pulled back on the reins, bringing the horses to a standstill. They had yet to leave the innyard and he saw they were drawing a crowd of curious onlookers. He didn't care.

"And what good, *wife*, will calm do me, hmm?" he inquired silkily. "I have not the least reason to restrain my temper and no Friday-faced shrew of a wife is going to convince me otherwise!"

Leandra stared at her husband with rising indignation and dismay. He really was as devilish as his black garb suggested. This was not a very promising start for their married life.

"You are behaving like a child, your grace," she retorted with the same unruffled calm she'd endeavored to display every moment since she had met him.

The duke's mouth dropped open. He made as if to say something, snapped his mouth shut, and gave the horses the office to start moving. The first ten minutes of their journey was accomplished in silence. Leandra used the time to study her husband with unabashed curiosity.

His facial features were really too harsh for actual handsomeness but she was sure that he was very popular with the ladies despite his looks. The thought of her husband in the arms of some other lady caused a strange stirring of disquiet in her stomach. She didn't want to imagine any such thing but she was nearly positive that he had a mistress tucked away somewhere.

"Do you have a mistress, your grace?" she asked with a benign look. She met his gaze, one brow tilted slightly.

"Pardon me?" His wife's candor was going to be a constant trial, he suspected. "That is not a topic for gently bred females," he snapped. Perhaps he should have married a woman who had at least heard of him. She'd not have the courage to talk back.

"You are a one to talk about propriety," his wife scoffed. "Besides, illegitimacy is not a topic suitable for drawing room conversation and yet that's precisely what I am."

"That has nothing to do with my mistress," he snapped. Really, why did the chit want to know something like that?

"Very well, your grace," she returned equably. "I will desist from questioning you about her. Perhaps I will meet her one day," she mused.

"Over my dead body," Derringer muttered.

"Oh, never say such a thing, your grace!" Leandra exclaimed with feigned horror. "I would hate to see you die just so I could meet your light-o'-love."

Derringer's eyes narrowed. His bride of only a few hours gazed back with wide-eyed concern, but he thought a twinkle of mirth lurked behind her thick spectacles.

"Why do you wear those ugly things?" he grumbled.

"What ugly things?"

He pointed his whip at her face and nodded.

"My spectacles, sir?" She laughed delightedly, a dimple peeking out of her left cheek. "I can't see without them, your grace."

"But they're ugly," the duke insisted stubbornly.

"What is that to the point?" she asked with a twinkle. "It is not as if my own looks will be improved overmuch with their swift removal. And I find I much prefer to be able to see where we are going and where we've been."

Derringer looked around at the boring pastureland through which they were currently passing and wondered if perhaps she needed stronger lenses in her spectacles. He glanced at her again and was a trifle disconcerted to realize she watched him very closely. He frowned at her. She smiled back.

He went on the attack as he always did when he felt cornered. He let his dark eyes slide over her insolently until her smile disappeared and she flushed. How he managed this and kept his team on the road had everything to do his exceptional skill as a first rate whip.

With just the right amount of contempt in his deep voice, Derringer inquired, "And the ugly bonnet and cloak? I noticed your dress is about as becoming as a flour sack. If you were raised as Harwood's daughter I would have thought he would dress you as such."

Leandra experienced more hurt by his slur on her father than his assessment of her appearance. She knew she was a drab goose compared to the beautiful swans her new husband was probably used to in Society, but he implied that her father didn't love her enough to outfit her properly. It brought tears to her eyes.

Damming the torrents that threatened to destroy her carefully maintained composure, Leandra replied, "I was told to leave my pretty frocks behind, your grace. The countess would not allow me to take anything given to me by my papa." She paused and took a deep breath. "Not even the locket with his picture and my mama's. It is the only thing I had that showed how he loved my mama." Her voice broke pitifully and she turned away from the duke lest he think she was trying to win sympathy from him.

Derringer felt like the beastly cad he was. He'd not intended to make her cry. And she was trying to hide it from him. He *was* an unfeeling cad, though, and it was best she learn that early on in the marriage lest her expectations be raised. He ignored her until she regained her poise and sat like a statue beside him. Guilt pricked his conscience. He'd had no business dragging an innocent girl into his bumblebroth.

But what did he care? He really was the heartless knave Society had dubbed him. Lord Heartless, he thought with mocking contempt. How apt. And he was about to prove to himself once and for all that he had no conscience, that he didn't care, and that he was the worthless creature that his father had told him he was.

Leandra's first view of her new home was misleading. She beheld the outer wall of Derringer Crescent, a medieval-inspired castle complete with crenelated towers, rat-infested dungeons, and Gothic arches. The wall that surrounded the keep and the living areas of the estate was actually in good repair. The edifice sat on a high cliff complete with crashing waves below and phenomenal views above, like something from an Ann Radcliffe novel. Or *Northanger Abbey*, Leandra's personal favorite by Jane Austen.

Her mouth formed an O of amazement as the portcullis was raised at a shout from the duke. It creaked and shook as it went up and the carriage went under the great spikes that lined the bottom of the contraption. She gazed around her eagerly and her rapt expression faded as if it had never been.

The front gardens were a disgrace. Tangled vines and weeds ran riot. The statues that were meant to be various sprites and goddesses of Greek and Roman mythology were so decayed as to be unrecognizable. It was late autumn but it appeared that the garden wouldn't look much better in the warmer parts of the year either.

She glanced at her husband from the corner of her eye and noticed his rather pained expression. How much time did he actually spend at the Crescent? He looked as if he was as disappointed as she.

A groom scurried out from behind the castle and took charge of the horses. Leandra looked up at the high walls and released a dismayed sigh. He expected her to live here? The walls were covered with ivy and lichen to the point that the gray of the stone was nearly invisible and many of the windows were blocked, allowing no light to enter.

Derringer looked down at the diminutive female at his side. She looked up at him in that moment, hazel eyes filled with sympathy. He tried to smile but found it impossible to do so. He had to leave her here, too. He couldn't accomplish the many things he had set in motion with a wife riding his coattails.

"Come," he ordered, holding out his hand. Her fingers wrapped around his. Her lack of hesitation sent a strange, warm sensation up his arm, a sensation he couldn't name. She smiled up at him with what he assumed was encouragement. Did she realize he'd been from home for some time? She was proving to be a very observant young miss.

That could be a problem.

And she was his wife. The thought seemed to slam him in the stomach, robbing him of breath. Good God, he was married!

The Starks met them in the Great Hall. He gazed around, sharp eyes missing little. At least the interior of the castle was presentable. But why should he care when he was just going to abandon his new bride anyway?

"What do you think?" he asked in low tones that were unnecessary since his voice echoed around the vast area regardless.

"It's…interesting," Leandra offered with a grimace. Suits of armor lined the walls of the Great Hall, above which hung various weapons and instruments of torture and destruction. She shuddered at the barbarity of the décor, but at the same time, she thought it suited her husband's volatile temperament.

"I can tell you hate it," the duke mocked. "But get used to it, my dear, for this is where you stay."

Stark cleared his throat and bowed. "Welcome home, your grace," he solemnly intoned.

Mrs. Stark, the housekeeper, smiled uncertainly at Leandra and curtsied to her employer. "Your room is in readiness, your grace." She sent an inquiring look to Mr. Stark.

Derringer knew what they were thinking. He had brought home mistresses before although it hadn't been for a few years now, having spent most of the last two years in France and on another of his estates. He almost laughed to think that they would believe he would be interested in such a little colorless wren like his wife. A mocking little voice in his head informed him that he was indeed interested in his colorless little wren of a wife. He ignored it.

"Is there anything else?" he demanded, just to make them squirm. He'd known the Starks since he was in leading strings and he knew they were the only people in his employ who had no fear of dismissal. They knew the real Hartley St. Clair, third Duke of Derringer, but they still squirmed when he was upset or used the tone of voice he used in that moment.

"Will you be requiring anything in particular, your grace?" the butler asked with a pointed look at Leandra.

"Such as...?" Derringer asked, brow knitting with feigned incomprehension.

"Master Hart," Mrs. Stark said reprovingly. Derringer fancied she would stamp her foot if she were not old enough to be his grandmother.

He favored the old woman with a sweet smile. Leandra sucked in a breath, startled beyond belief that her harsh husband could appear so... so... normal, charming even.

"Oh," the duke said, dark brows raising in what could only be surprise—real or feigned, Leandra couldn't tell, "you mean her? She's my wife." Then he walked away and left Leandra to deal with the dumbfounded servants.

Leandra watched the duke skirt around the grand staircase and head toward the back of the house. Was he abandoning her already?

She smiled brightly at the servants standing mum-chance before her and held out her hand. "I am Leandra. His grace and I married just this morning."

The butler and housekeeper just stared at her and neither made any move to accept her proffered hand. Leandra pulled it back and clasped it in front of her. Frowning, she studied the two old retainers. The woman was round and motherly while the man was tall, white-haired, and very austere, just as a butler should be.

"I believe you are the ones responsible for the immaculate condition of the interior," Leandra said with a friendly smile. "I commend you. It must be very difficult to take care of so large an estate especially when the lord is off doing any number of important things."

"Important things?" the butler repeated in confusion.

"Of course," the new duchess agreed. "At least, I assume they are. I really have no idea. I just met him last night, you see. Do you know my lord at all well?" she asked ingenuously, her mind only half on what she was saying.

This confession was effective in snapping the couple out of their stupor. "You just met his grace last night?" the housekeeper said in tones of disbelief. "What is the world coming to, I ask you?" she muttered to her husband, who nodded in agreement.

"I rely on you to show me how to go on," Leandra continued, wisely ignoring the impertinent comment and inwardly amused at their lapse in proper behavior. "I have been trained in the running of a large household but nothing of this size and I have never had my own household to care for."

Mrs. Stark curtsied and replied dutifully that she would do all she could to help ease her grace into the position of mistress of the house. The butler agreed as well.

"Marvelous!" Leandra exclaimed in excitement. "And I expect you to tell me all you can about my husband. I think you know him far better than I do and I would do everything in my power to please him. I think he needs...

something. I'll determine what later," she said with a tiny shake of her head.

And so Leandra, the new Duchess of Derringer, made a friend for life in the motherly housekeeper and a champion in the aged butler. They smiled their approval and commented to each other later that they—and the duke, of course—were lucky to have such a sweet, unspoiled soul like the new duchess for a mistress.

3

DERRINGER avoided his bride until dinner that night. She sat on the other end of the long table in the state dining room and fiddled with the ring of emeralds and diamonds on her finger. He had found the family heirloom and had it delivered to her apartments. He was absurdly glad to see her wearing it, though he scoffed at his own sentimentality. It was unlike him to find pleasure in anything so mundane.

The footmen came forward with the third course and Derringer was suddenly tired of squinting down the table trying to determine what his wife was doing besides eating.

He felt the need to tell her that he would be returning to London in the morning and would probably be gone for several weeks. Instead of examining and stifling this strange need to be honest, he acted on it.

He gestured to the footman nearest him, James or John or Philip, he cared not which, ordering, "Fetch her grace's meal here." He pointed at the spot to his immediate right.

The footman rushed to the other end of the long table and informed her grace of his grace's instructions. Derringer saw her throw a considering look in his direction, then smile sweetly up at the footman and nod her head in a most regal manner. She seemed to be growing accustomed to this duchess business quickly, he thought without a trace of cynicism. He ignored the strange twinge he felt when she bestowed such a charming smile on a mere servant.

Within moments, the switch was completed. The duchess smiled complacently at her husband and continued to eat just as if she had not been moved from one end of a thirty-foot table to the other in the middle of her meal.

Derringer caught Stark's eye and dismissed the servants with a wave of his hand. The butler gathered his footmen and withdrew.

The duchess faced her husband with her dark brows raised in question. He decided to get the matter of his leaving out of the way as soon as possible. "My dear," he began.

"Do you even remember my name?" she asked with the most innocent of expressions.

Derringer opened his mouth to tell her that of course he did. Then he realized that he actually couldn't remember her name, odd for a man who remembered some truly unimportant things from as far back as childhood. He gave her a rueful look and shook his head. A lock of black hair fell across his brow.

His wife chuckled and set her fork and knife down beside her plate. "My name is Leandra, your grace. You may call me that if you desire but I actually prefer Merri," she added with a teasing grin.

"Merri?"

"My second name is Merrily, like happy. I think that's why I prefer it," she said, a thoughtful smile curving her unfashionably full lips.

"I see," the duke murmured. "I think I prefer Leandra. Who named you?"

"Papa did. His name was Leander, you see."

"You are named after your father? How extraordinary," Derringer murmured. It wasn't often that a peer named his bastard after himself.

"Because I am baseborn? I admit it is unusual but I think extraordinary is a bit extreme, don't you?"

"Perhaps," Derringer reluctantly allowed. He studied his little wife. "Leandra or Merri," he mused.

"I think you might be more comfortable calling me Leandra, your grace," she offered with an understanding smile. "I would find it difficult to call you by anything that would imply an intimate standing between us."

"Such as Hart?" He picked up his wineglass and swirled the liquid around as he watched her over the rim.

"That is your name, your true name, I mean?"

"My name is Hartley Giles St. Clair. My intimates call me Hart, my acquaintances call me St. Clair or Derringer, nodding acquaintances call me Lord Derringer, and when my back is turned everyone calls me Lord Heartless."

Leandra's expression darkened. "Who would call you such a hateful thing?"

The duke snorted. "I said everyone, did I not? I have only been called that to my face once," he admitted with a reminiscent grin. "And she was no bigger than you and equally as meek except when crossed. I crossed her and she called me Lord Heartless." He neglected to mention a certain group of unsavory individuals who knew him only as Heartless.

"Who is she?" the duchess asked, her round features devoid of expression. Instinct told him to trust that look not at all.

Derringer drained the contents of his glass and set it down. His wife's gaze never wavered from his face. "Her name is Aurora," he finally said, not liking the feeling his wife's stare was giving him. It was unnerving. "She is now happily married to a very close friend."

Leandra's expression never changed and her voice was pleasant as a summer breeze. "I would call her out if I could," she told him with deadly intent.

"Whatever for?" Did she think she needed to defend him?

She shrugged, regarding him a moment in careful thought. "Evidently nothing," she replied dryly. She looked away and applied herself to her food with a single minded intensity that made him wonder if perhaps he had gone suddenly invisible.

"Leandra," he said, "I have to return to Town in the morning."

"Why?" she asked without looking up.

He frowned. He wasn't used to being questioned about anything. "I have to show our marriage lines to my solicitor."

Now she looked up. "Why?"

"Is that any concern of yours?" His tone was sharper than he'd intended.

"No," she answered honestly. "I had hoped you would stay for a few days to introduce me to some of the locals perhaps or let me know how you prefer the castle to be run. I am like a fish out of water here, your grace. I have never undertaken a project of this magnitude before."

"I have to show him the lines before my birthday on Friday," Derringer grudgingly revealed to his petite bride. "If I fail to prove that I married, Grimsby is going to give my inheritance to my uncle's family." He wished suddenly that the words were unsaid. He was unsure what had even prompted him to reveal so much.

Leandra's fingers clenched around her fork. "You married me to save your money?" she asked through white lips. She told herself it was nothing like an heiress being married for her money instead of herself. She told herself that her feelings were not hurt. She did honestly admit that she had no business having hurt feelings when she willingly entered into this marriage of convenience. "You married a perfect stranger, a girl you happened to meet stranded at an inn, all for *money*?"

The duke's black brows drew down into a V. "Why the devil else would I marry?" he snapped.

"At least you picked one unable to say no. What would you have done had I refused?"

One black brow rose. "Found another girl," he told her bluntly.

"I see. Well, then." She shook her head slightly. "What's done is done and there is no going back."

"Just what the devil is that supposed to mean?"

Leandra shrugged and forced her fingers to ease, thus allowing the blood to flow again, causing prickles in each appendage. "How early will you be gone?" she demanded, meeting his eyes.

His frown deepened. Lines appeared around his lips— his sinfully tempting lips—at her blunt query. Leandra might have wanted to throttle him, infuriating man that he was, but in that moment she thought she might want to kiss him more.

"I am unsure. Why?"

"I just wondered when I would be free of you and your megrims," she replied sweetly.

The duke stared at her for a few moments as if trying to determine if she was serious. Then he surprised himself by saying gently, "I didn't mean to hurt your feelings, Merri. I had to wed someone and I had a sennight in which to do it. You were the first woman I came across who"—he almost said who didn't turn his stomach at the thought of bedding her—"seemed to be the best candidate to be a duchess."

Leandra barely heard anything beyond his use of her father's pet name for her. It slipped from his lips like the caress of a lover and wrapped her in a warm cocoon of contentment and hope. Her desire to kiss him increased. What it would be like to experience the feel of his lips against hers again? Mr. Hubbard had never done anything so shocking as trying to kiss her since they were not officially betrothed.

"Leandra?"

The duke's voice intruded on her thoughts and she blushed in mortification. She chided herself for this unlikely behavior. It was not as if the man could read her mind. "Yes?" she inquired pleasantly.

Derringer shook his head in a rare moment of actual amusement. "I asked if you would be all right. I would feel much better to have this business with the solicitor over and done with." He reached over and refilled her wine glass then refilled his own, fingering the stem of the glass absently as he watched her.

"All will be well," she assured him. "I have the reliable Starks to help me over any rough spots and my own sense of adventure to get me through the rest. You go and get your money situation squared away, your grace."

"Didn't we decide that you were going to call me something else?" Derringer asked.

"No," his wife replied laconically.

"I am tired of being 'your graced' at every turn, Leandra. Your birth may require such formality but becoming my wife raised your social status. 'Your grace' is no longer the proper way for you to address any duke, especially your husband." He paused, waiting for some sort of acknowledgment, some indication that she was aware of the significant change their marriage had wrought in her life. When she said nothing, he added, "By the time I return, I hope you have decided how you will address me."

"As you wish, your grace," she murmured with an impish light in her hazel eyes.

Green and brown with flecks of gold, he corrected. She had pretty eyes, made more so when she smiled, her round cheeks giving her the adorable look of a precocious sprite. When she smiled it was like watching the sun rise over the sea on a foggy morning, shedding its light on all those close enough to be blessed by the occurrence. He liked her smile.

It was a strange feeling for him which made him uncomfortable. He just met this girl the day before and knew nothing about her. She knew nothing about him and yet she seemed to be quite content being married to him.

Of course she is, he reminded himself cynically. *She's a duchess now. What girl wouldn't be in alt over such a coup?*

He rose to his feet. "I will bid you goodbye now, Leandra. And do something about your nauseating wardrobe while I'm gone," he said stiffly. He walked out before he could see the hurt he knew would be visible on her overly expressive face.

4

THE Duke of Derringer entered the building above which the sign *Grimsby, Lehman, and Bimm, Solicitors* swung in the slight autumn breeze. He walked to the back of the building, past the whiny solicitor's equally whiny assistant, and into the main office in the back. He looked from Grimsby to the man who currently sat on Derringer's side of the wide desk and smiled most unpleasantly.

"I say, Grimsby, what is all this? I had an appointment," blustered the client, a peer from what Derringer could tell from the man's dress and attitude, though he could not recall ever having met this particular gentleman before.

The duke turned a bland look on the man who shrank back into his chair as the solicitor rose to his feet. To prevent bloodshed?

"Your grace, may I make known to you the Earl of Harwood?" Grimsby asked desperately in an attempt to ease the tension.

The little man really ought to have known better, but the duke surprised him. "By all means," Derringer drawled without removing his gaze from the earl. Merri's brother, he thought darkly without even realizing that he had come to think of her as Merri.

"Lord Harwood, the Duke of Derringer."

Derringer held out his hand as the other man stood. "Pleasure," he said with an unreadable look.

Harwood bowed and shook the duke's outstretched hand. "Harwood, my lord, at your service," he murmured politely.

Derringer studied his new brother-in-law and decided he did not like what he saw. The man had a truly unremarkable appearance. His hair and eyes were plain brown. His face was that of a cherub, innocent and guileless. Derringer distrusted him immediately. No one was as innocent as this man's face implied.

And Derringer had found Merri alone at night at an inn having been turned out of her father's home. Even in the very short amount of time the duke had known his bride, he realized that her sweetness of character was not something that was learned. It was an innate quality. It had somehow survived the stain of her illegitimacy and the probably many petty little indignities she'd had to endure at the hands of her half-siblings and stepmama.

Derringer smiled at his wife's brother. "Hartley St. Clair, Harwood. Please call me Hart," he invited with what appeared to be sincerity. "I believe we are bound to become much better acquainted fairly soon."

The earl gave Derringer a look of pleased surprise. "Certainly, Hart. Please call me Lee."

The duke turned a malignant eye on the lawyer. He wanted this scoundrel gone before he gave in to his urge to draw his cork.

The lawyer interpreted the look correctly and turned again to the earl. "Lord Harwood, perhaps we can continue this later. Lord Derringer has some urgent business I think."

"But I had an appointment," the earl said in confusion.

The duke quirked one black brow at the man's obtuseness and said in a soft voice that held a menacing hint of steel, "Goodbye, Lee. We will meet again."

Grimsby shivered.

The earl stared up at the duke with a confused frown. Suddenly his brow cleared and he was out of the office before the realization of exactly whom he was dealing with had fully formed in his mind. A disturbing laugh followed him as he left.

Derringer kicked the door shut and reached into the pocket of his black waistcoat. He tossed a folded sheet of foolscap onto the lawyer's desk and leaned back against the closed door with his arms crossed over his chest.

Mr. Grimsby eyed the hotheaded young lord suspiciously. "What is that?" he asked.

"Open it and look, half-wit," the duke commanded with a smug grin.

The solicitor opened the paper and gasped. His reaction was all Derringer could have hoped for. It could only get better when he told the man that his bride was baseborn.

"You did it?" Grimsby said breathlessly. "You are wed?" He sat down with a thump, astonishment writ plain across his thin face.

"You doubted me?"

"No, your grace, not at all," the little man was quick to assure him. "It's just that the chances of your succeeding were not well to your favor."

"Were they not?" Derringer's voice was deceptively polite. "I have to disagree with you for the following reasons. One," he said as he ticked them off on the fingers of one long hand, "I am attractive to the point of pain or so I am told. Two, I am wealthy beyond anyone's wildest dreams. Three, I have the power of royalty without actually being related to that blighted family. And four, I'm a bloody duke. How were the odds not in my favor of acquiring a bride?" His voice ended on a cynical note. He waited patiently for the solicitor to speak.

"Well?" he finally asked after several moments of uncomfortable silence on Grimsby's part.

"Ah, yes, your grace, quite right, I'm sure," the man muttered expectedly. He was staring at the paper in his hand with an expression of dawning realization mixed with confusion and some horror.

"She's a Harcourt," he said finally.

"So?"

Grimsby looked up at Derringer suspiciously. "I know *Debrett's Peerage* by heart, your grace. There is no Leandra Harcourt."

Of course there wasn't. Bastards were not recorded in the peerage. "She is real, I assure you. And she is a Harcourt. Harwood is her brother."

"But, that means she's a…her parents…"

"Her parents were not married. She's a bastard, Grimsby," the duke growled. He was irritated that the solicitor's shock didn't give him quite the pleasurable feeling he had anticipated.

"Quite," Grimsby mouthed nervously.

"Do I get my fortune or not?"

"Everything appears in order, your grace," was the solicitor's reassuring reply. He flushed uneasily. "That is, I mean, provided you have, ah…"

"Spit it out, man. I have other places to be," the duke snapped.

"The marriage has been consummated," the unfortunate man blurted out.

Derringer had no words. He just stared at Grimsby, once again deciding the man had no sense of humor, thus he could not be attempting a joke at Derringer's expense

"Explain."

"Your father's instructions specified that there be no legal way for you to dissolve the marriage after you receive access to the money," the lawyer explained hastily. He sighed in relief when Derringer sank into the chair before the desk.

The duke stared at the man without really seeing him. There was nothing he could do about it at the moment. A part of him had actually considered seeking an annulment and settling a yearly stipend on the girl for her trouble. Clearly, that wasn't an option now.

"Do you not think that was something to mention before?" he inquired, voice deceptively calm.

"In all the excitement, your grace, I am very much afraid I simply forgot to tell you." He gulped and scooted further back in his chair when Derringer's black eyes narrowed. "And I assumed it would not be an issue."

The duke fixed a minatory glare on the spindly-shanked little man across the desk from him. "What kind of proof do you require?" he asked silkily. "Do you want to see the bloody sheets or is my word enough?" His tone was dangerously mocking.

"I will accept your word, of course, your grace," Mr. Grimsby was quick to reassure him. "When would you like me to send the announcement to the papers?"

"Announcement? Why the hell does anyone have to know about it?"

"If everyone knows, your grace, it will make it impossible for you to dissolve the marriage without the most shocking of scandals," the lawyer explained reasonably. "Of course, once it is announced there will be the most shocking of scandals anyway since everyone will know that…" he muttered to himself. "Shall I send it?" he asked louder.

Derringer glared at him for a full five seconds until the solicitor began to squirm again. "No," he answered finally. "I will take care of it myself."

He stood up and snatched the marriage lines from the desk, restoring them to his pocket. Then he turned on his heel and walked out.

He had, of course, heard every word the solicitor had mumbled. He had not even thought about what it would do to his bride when everyone discovered who and what she was.

And he was uncertain as to why he said he would take care of the announcement. The words had slipped out before they had actually formed in his mind. If he had just let Grimsby take care of it, he wouldn't now be on his way to the office of the *London Gazette*. He could be on his way to Nicolette's instead.

Bloody hell.

Nicolette was a beautiful woman of low birth and lower morals. She made her living in trade to the wealthy gentlemen of the *ton*. Her trade, of course, being that of a courtesan. She was the current mistress of the Duke of Derringer. He was supposed to be her sole protector.

Too greedy to be satisfied with the generosity of the duke, however, she enjoyed the protection of five different men. The danger of discovery was erotic to her and she reveled in the thought that at any moment, one of her lovers might burst through the door and demand satisfaction from the man in her arms. It was her secret desire to have a duel fought over her honor and she hoped the duke would be one of those gentlemen.

Nicolette would have been shocked to know that the duke knew every one of her lovers; who they were, what they were worth, where they lived, and any number of other things that a normal man would not have found the least bit useful to know and not even interesting to learn. The duke, however, owed his life several times over to knowing many little facts that one would have thought completely useless. Derringer rarely missed things.

After dropping the notice at the newspaper office and enduring the stares of shock and amazement, Derringer entered the outskirts of London and headed for the his house in Kensington. It was a charming little domicile of red brick with trellises that were covered with morning glories and roses in the warmer months. He pulled to a stop before the door and handed the reins to a footman who had come running from the house.

Derringer climbed down and stared at the painfully nervous footman. He almost smiled. "How is your mistress, Jem?" he asked casually, removing his black driving gloves one finger at a time.

The footman stuttered and stammered and the duke could tell he wished to be anywhere but where he was. "Never mind," the duke replied. "Wait here for my return. I won't be long." He moved toward the house. "Your position is safe," he called over his shoulder. He heard the young man sigh in relief and smiled to himself at Jem's transparency.

Sheffield, the butler, was almost as transparent. He took the duke's gloves and coat and informed his grace that Miss Nicolette was busy at the moment and would his grace care to wait in the morning room?

"No, Sheffield, his grace would not," Derringer retorted. The butler bowed and waited for Derringer's further instructions. He knew they were coming. "Bar all the doors, Sheffield. Lock the windows and set armed footmen outside the balcony of Nicki's chamber. Tell them to stop anyone attempting to leave in any way necessary. But be sure they know not to kill anyone. I have not the inclination to save anyone from a hanging today."

"Very good, your grace." Sheffield deposited the duke's things on a chair in the hall and departed to do the tall lord's will.

Derringer glanced toward the stairs. He would give Sheffield a few minutes to get his instructions well underway before he went up to catch her. He was finally going to catch her. The thought gave him a thrill that threatened to have him running up the stairs and in his haste giving his unknown nemesis a chance to escape out her window.

The duke heard the unmistakable murmurings of men surrounding the house. He could hear the little maids running through the rooms, locking the windows and securing the back door. He smiled grimly.

Determining enough time had indeed passed, Derringer mounted the stairs. He moved silently like a wraith and listened for any strange sounds. He heard some as soon as he stood outside his mistress's bedchamber. A door shut. The armoire, unless he missed his guess.

He turned the handle and walked in. "Good afternoon, Nicki," he greeted softly, seductively.

He had trouble keeping the smile from his face. The blond-haired, blue-eyed goddess had the look of a woman just tumbled. She held the bedsheets against her chest in a semblance of modesty, false modesty, as he knew all too well.

Derringer approached the bed and stood staring down at the beauty. She smiled up at him and darted one nervous look in the direction of the armoire.

Deciding her lover was safe, Nicolette smiled, revealing startlingly even white teeth, and held out her hand. "Darling, I have been waiting for you," she said in a husky whisper. She allowed the sheet to slip, revealing the rosy peaks of two very excellent breasts.

Derringer did smile then. Leave it to a whore to try to use her body to cajole her way out of a deserved punishment. "Have you indeed?" he murmured, not completely unaffected by her little ploy. He was only a man, after all. He nodded, reaching up to undo his neckcloth. "I see you are exactly how I like you, love. Naked." His reply came out with just the right amount of sensual promise, his actions fanning the flames he hoped to ignite.

"Hart, darling, join me," she implored with a tiny moan, apparently forgetting her guest in the armoire.

The duke sat down on the bed and reached out to touch her breast. She arched into his hand and he wondered if she realized that despite any sexual attraction he might feel for her, even now, he could wring her neck without the least compunction.

Derringer leaned closer, gliding his fingers up and over her shoulder, pretending a fascination with her silken skin that he did not feel. He leaned in until his lips almost touched hers, murmuring softly, "You have been very, very naughty, my pretty little whore."

The words did not penetrate the sensual fog in Nicolette's brain. Taking advantage, as was his wont, he placed one hand behind her head and held her immobile, his fingers gently caressing the nape of her neck.

"Where is he?" he asked just to give her a chance to tell him the truth; never let it be said he wasn't a fair man.

Derringer's voice was low, seductive...and very dangerous.

"Who?" Nicolette asked, a tiny thread of confusion coloring her tone. Her eyes flew open as the words and their implication sunk in.

"The man who was in this room, enjoying your favors, just before I entered," he reminded her in that same low tone. He shook her gently.

She swallowed hard. "There was no man, Hart," she assured him, the slight quiver in her voice giving the lie to her words. "There has only been you."

His hand tightened painfully on her neck. "One more chance, Nicki," he said with deadly quiet. "You know how I feel about lies."

She gasped at the pain that shot into her head. She had thought it would be titillating to have the duke discover one of her other lovers and challenge the man to meet him at dawn. She realized her mistake now. If he didn't know that Gerald was still here, she might be able to save both their lives.

"He left, Hart, I swear," she said desperately.

His grip tightened some more and she grasped his arm in an attempt to relieve some of the pressure that was threatening to send her into unconsciousness.

"Wrong answer," the duke whispered savagely. He threw her from him, sending her reeling into the pillows behind her. She rubbed at the back of her neck to ease the ache and pulled the sheet back over herself.

Derringer sat back and stared at her through half lowered lids. "Who is he, I wonder," he murmured almost to himself. He watched her. He wanted to know which man he was dealing with before he murdered him.

Derringer did not tolerate unfaithfulness in his mistress. He'd never been married before now but he was sure he wouldn't tolerate it in his wife either. He saw red at the mere thought of Leandra taking a lover. Rather than wonder at the whys of such a feeling, he ignored it.

"Perhaps it is Lord Sotherby." Her expression didn't change. She was controlling her reaction, he thought with some amusement. Very well.

"Maybe Viscount Meiers," he suggested calmly. He crossed his arms over his chest and continued to study her lovely face. "Archie Haverford?" Still no reaction. That was three. The last he knew she had only four other lovers beside himself.

"Hmm," he said thoughtfully, rubbing his chin. "That only leaves Gerald Greaves, the young Earl of Cheshire."

Ah-ha, he thought in satisfaction. Her hand clutched the sheet tighter and she held her breath. Cheshire it is.

Derringer stood and took a turn about the room. "So, young Cheshire is in this room somewhere. I wonder where. He couldn't be such a coward as to hide from a thrashing he deserves, would he?" He again faced the woman on the bed, assuming an inquiring expression as if he might actually care about her opinion.

Nicolette remained silent. She knew that if she said anything he might actually kill her along with Gerald. Lord Derringer was a monster. He was... heartless.

Derringer grew tired of the game. He crossed the room in three long strides and threw open the door of the armoire. Huddled inside was the very young Earl of Cheshire. How the lad had managed to catch Nicolette's eye was a mystery to Derringer. The boy was under twenty with dull sandy hair and a skinny body. He stood taller than Derringer, though, which was unusual.

"Get out," the duke commanded harshly.

The boy swiftly complied with Derringer's orders. He stood before him in nothing but his pantaloons and an expression of terror on his long face.

"I must have been misinformed. How much are you worth?" Derringer asked more out of curiosity than any real reason to have that particular piece of information.

Cheshire's eyes widened at the question. He opened his mouth and stuttered something but Derringer waved him to silence. "Never mind," he said. "You do realize I have to hit you now? My reputation and all that rot?"

The earl closed his eyes briefly then opened them again and nodded. Nicolette got up from the bed with the sheet wrapped around her naked body. "Hart, he didn't know I was with you," she tried to explain.

"I did," the young man answered. "I knew about the others, too." He seemed quite calm now, Derringer mused.

"You all knew?" the woman demanded in outrage.

Derringer laughed. "You are a terrible liar, my dear."

A second later, the earl lay on the floor with blood pouring from his nose and mouth and the duke was on his way out the door. He paused next to Sheffield where he waited like a statue in the foyer and told him to call off the guard.

"Have Nicki's maid pack all her belongings. I want her out of this house by tomorrow morning."

The butler bowed. "Very good, your grace."

5

GOLDEN sunlight poured through the east facing windows, streaming over the thick Aubusson carpet and Leandra's still fingers. She sat in a little used morning room, situated on the castle's east side to allow the most from the early morning sun. Staring out into the bare gardens, her eyes focused on nothing, her fingers not nimble enough to embroider without looking.

This room was Leandra's haven, her sanctuary. She'd instructed the new indoor servants to remove the heavy, dark furnishings and replace them with light and airy Hepplewhite. With Stark's help, she'd replaced the barbaric hunt scenes with bright tapestries of nymphs and sprites. The room that was once dark with red and brown was now bright with blue and gold, earthy browns and greens, with warm golden threads woven into the tapestries and the carpet.

This was the room she retreated to when the odds of her circumstances threatened to overwhelm her. This was where she went when she needed to think, or not think at all. And this was where she went when thoughts of her husband threatened to overwhelm her.

She'd tried to immerse herself into Folkestone Society but Folkestone Society refused to accept her. She assumed they'd somehow heard of her illegitimacy. She had no way of knowing that her husband had managed to alienate local Society the same way he'd alienated high Society. They didn't believe she was really his wife. But there was no way she could know that.

Instead of trying to gain that which she'd never had—a place in Society—she instead focused on establishing relationships with each and every one of her husband's servants, old and new. Her first conquest was Liza.

Liza had always wanted to be a lady's maid, she confided to her mistress. After a brief discussion with Mrs. Stark, Leandra promoted her to the post, confident the girl would prove her worth. It was through Liza that the new duchess learned of the other servants and of others who needed work. Leandra felt no compunctions about hiring additional help and saw no reason to inform her husband of any changes she made. It was due to her that he had his inheritance so it was only fair she decide how to spend that money. She had no idea how to contact him, so seeking his permission was moot.

Righteous indignation wore off rather quickly, especially when the object of one's wrath was not present to witness it. Leandra settled into a routine, thoughts of Lord Derringer little more than an uncomfortable reminder of her lack of style.

Liza replaced her mistress's wardrobe with all the frills and stylish garments Leandra could ever wish for. Or her husband could wish for, rather. For Leandra, despite having been raised in a home where the latest London fashions were regularly bestowed upon the daughters of the house, fashion had never been an interest for her. She was content to wear clothes that covered her, allowed her to move, and didn't require much forethought.

Returning her gaze to the bluebird previously forming beneath her fingers, Leandra smiled at the memory. Liza's excitement had known no bounds.

Leandra was sure the local gossips were positively agog with all the castle activity. Besides the summoning of the local seamstress, milliner, and staymaker, outdoor servants were hired in droves, any man, woman, or child who desired employment. Within the few weeks of her husband's absence, Leandra transformed the castle grounds. She turned no one away, finding something for each person to do, even those whose physical limitations made labor difficult. It was no surprise to her when those from further off began arriving, all pitiful, all desperate, and all seeking help. Leandra remembered her own brief moment of desperation, those hours after her brother and stepmother threw her into the streets, and was unable to turn any of them away.

Adding to the indoor staff meant she could fix all the misnamed salons that dominated her new home. Whoever heard of making the Blue Salon gold and orange or the Green Salon crimson? The resultant confusion probably entertained the duke to no end. As Leandra inspected every room in the vast castle, she made notes of what to change and what could stay. Upon entering the Egyptian Salon, she immediately turned around and never entered it again. How she despised that particular affectation!

Leandra soon found herself at loose ends but that didn't last long. She'd given up on winning over the townspeople, settling for the good opinion of the estate farmers instead. When several learned a master of sorts was in residence, they swooped in on her with complaints, demands, and requests ranging from new farm equipment to new houses.

One man even requested a wife. The little scullery maid shyly volunteered for that particular post and Leandra was satisfied to note that the man was only too delighted with the pretty girl. That was the easiest problem she had come up against to date.

Leandra tried to handle every tenant's problem to the best of her ability and limited experience but she felt at a distinct disadvantage and wished that her husband were there to relieve her of some of the responsibility. At times, when things were particularly hectic, she felt a surge of anger at the man who had given her his name and then so insensitively abandoned her to fend for herself in a social station of which she knew nothing, among complete strangers who made their distrust and antipathy apparent.

Hence, her relief was immense when Derringer's secretary arrived to lend support and knowledge where necessary. She was so grateful for his timely arrival that she failed to realize that her husband had sent the man specifically to help her. Had she thought about it, she would have been touched by the duke's unusual show of concern.

Now, nearly two weeks after her husband's departure, Leandra sat in the morning room and stared through the window. She wore one of her new gowns, a charming creation of white sprigged muslin with cherry red ribbons at the high waist and along the hem and tiny puffed sleeves. A matching cherry ribbon was threaded through her curls, which were arranged into a loose chignon, a few wayward tendrils escaping to frame her face. She wore no jewelry since she had none, but Liza had taken a length of the leftover ribbon and tied it around Leandra's slender throat. Her feet were shod in delicate slippers of white silk embroidered with tiny red roses. She wondered if her appearance would be pleasing to her husband.

His birthday had passed, the All Hallows Eve celebration had passed, and still she received no word from him. She hoped he was well.

She'd spent the past three days with Mrs. Stark learning all she could about her husband and trying to understand why he was... well, the way he was. Every new piece of information was surprising, shocking, depressing, or so completely unbelievable that Leandra wondered if she had fallen into a Gothic novel. She listened in awe to the housekeeper's stories as the woman went about her duties.

"Master Hart was only six when his mama died, God rest her soul," Mrs. Stark began. "The poor lad had no sooner stopped mourning his mother than his father passed on as well. He was a duke then and his uncle moved right in and tried to be the duke himself. No, Alice, not there. Here. Where was I? Oh, yes, Master Hart's uncle. He wasn't so bad as his wife, let me tell you. She was a greedy shrew. She made the young master's life miserable."

Mrs. Stark paused to show little Mary, the new scullery maid, what she was doing wrong. Leandra was pleased to note that the housekeeper was more of a mother to her underlings than a stern taskmaster. In the new duchess's opinion, a happy and well-contented worker was a more efficient worker.

"So his grace was forced into the role early in life," Leandra murmured. "How terrible for him. How did his mother die?"

The housekeeper's lips pinched in at the corners, her eyes darting away from Leandra's. "I reckon that would be for the master to tell, your grace."

Leandra let it drop but placed it in the back of her mind to ask her husband when he returned. "How did his father die?" she asked instead.

"That was a strange thing, if you ask me," the older woman replied, head shaking as her brows drew down into a V. She handed a bucket and brush to Hannah, one of the upstairs maids, then stood there and silently stared at her feet for a few moments before finally raising her eyes to meet Leandra's hazel gaze. "He died in a boating accident, they do say, but I have my doubts."

"Are you saying it wasn't an accident, Mrs. Stark?"

The housekeeper glanced around uneasily. "Perhaps we should continue this in private, your grace. I wouldn't want to frighten any of the maids with my opinions."

"Very well," Leandra acquiesced. "Will you take tea with me?"

"Oh, I couldn't do that, your grace!" the woman exclaimed, one hand flying to her ample bosom in melodramatic shock.

"Whyever not?"

"Well, it just ain't done, your grace."

Leandra gave her a sympathetic look. "Have you noticed any of my actions these past two weeks as things that are 'done' by duchesses, Mrs. Stark?"

The housekeeper smiled reluctantly at that. "No, your grace. I would be honored if you would take tea with me in my sitting room," she offered. "There is less chance of interruption there."

"So be it," the duchess smiled.

6

WHAT she had so recently learned about her husband left Leandra feeling distressed, helpless. She hated that feeling.

She had finally, somehow, gotten Mrs. Stark to divulge the huge secret about Hart's mama's death—Leandra had begun to think of him as Hart without even realizing it. The late duchess had been found on the second floor landing, her neck broken. It was the night footman who found her, according to Mrs. Stark, but Hart had been an odd little boy ever since then. He refused to speak and when his father had favored him with any sort of attention, Hart did everything in his power to hide until his papa lost interest.

Mrs. Stark told her the little duke uttered not a word until his father's body was brought in to lie in state in one of the spare family bedchambers. Then he was suddenly a happy child who asked all sorts of questions and demanded attention from the Starks and several of the other servants.

Until his uncle showed up with his wife and children in tow. Hart's uncle took over Derringer Crescent as if he were the duke and not the seven-year-old boy with the sad dark eyes. His aunt was a shrew with pretensions above her station. She believed her husband should be the duke and took every opportunity to let the little duke know it, too.

The staff had taken to protecting the tiny peer after one of the grooms reported to Stark that the lad's saddle cinch had been cut and it was only a coincidence that a stablehand had caught it before saddling Hart's pony.

The older of Hart's cousins, Martin, now acted as his secretary. It was this man that Stark announced at that moment, jolting Leandra from her reverie.

She looked up with a wary smile and studied the handsome man. With his waves of golden hair and great blue eyes, he was the exact opposite of her husband. His pale skin and the meek expression on his pleasing countenance furthered the contrast. He smiled hesitantly and bowed.

"You are my husband's cousin?" she murmured, a slight disbelief coloring her words.

"Yes, your grace." His voice was as pleasing as his appearance, soft and gentle with a slight huskiness.

Leandra set aside her needlework. She stood and moved across the room, holding out her hand when she neared. "I am Leandra. Please call me Merri since we are related now," she offered with a charming smile.

The man smiled back and took her hand. "I am Martin, Hart's secretary, at your service. Merri." He studied her for a moment and then flushed when he realized that he still held her hand. "I apologize," he murmured in embarrassment. "I was wondering…may I ask you something that may be considered impertinent?"

"Certainly." The duchess clasped her hands in front of her and waited.

"Why do you ask me to call you Merri?"

The question was so different from what she had been expecting that she laughed. "Is that all? Well, my second name, Cousin Martin, is Merrily, like happy. I prefer to be called Merri. It was what my father called me."

"Who was your father?"

This was the line of questioning she had been expecting. Leandra gestured to the seat across from her own and then sat down. Martin followed suit and waited for her answer with slightly raised brows.

"My papa was the late Earl of Harwood," she said softly.

His brows lifted ever so slightly higher. "I was unaware that Hart was acquainted with your family," he told her. "Apparently I was wrong," he continued before she could correct his assumption. "Are you expecting a visit from your family soon?"

"Merciful Lord, I hope not!" Leandra exclaimed gently. "They did never like me much, you know. I would not know what to do with them were they to suddenly arrive."

"Excuse me?" the secretary sputtered in confusion. "Surely your mama will wish to visit now that you are the wife of a duke?"

"I'm sure my mama would, and she would be more than welcome, I'm sure, were she still alive."

"The Dowager Countess of Harwood has died as well?"

The duchess laughed softly. For some inexplicable reason, she always enjoyed this part of meeting someone new. Perhaps she possessed a cruel streak, an odd desire to torture others with discomfort, the same discomfort she often felt, or was made to feel, when in the company of others.

Confusion mixed with chagrin and a little disbelief on Martin's mobile features.

Leandra refused to feel shame for her parentage. Why should she? It was not her fault that her father had fallen in love with her mother after he was already married. He could have restrained his affection, not made love to a woman who was not his wife, thus fathering an illegitimate child, but it was hardly something Leandra could have prevented. Why should she herself be blamed?

It was one reason the duke's staff now boasted three maids heavy with child. Their lovers had fled, leaving them to fend for themselves. Mrs. Stark had always fired the girls when they fell from grace because it was the duke's instructions to do so. It was the first thing in which Leandra had outright defied her husband. The girls' troubles had hit a little too close to home for Leandra to be content with their immediate dismissal.

Not that she had neglected to make it painfully clear that their conduct was unacceptable. They were warned that dismissal was the punishment for any servant indulging in loose conduct. But then, Leandra, unlike the majority of the aristocracy, encouraged marriage among her servants.

Now she sat staring at Mr. St. Clair as he waited for an explanation that she knew he was not in the least suspecting. Or maybe he was. How was she to know?

"No, the dowager Lady Harwood is still alive, sir. But she is not my mama."

Her eyes fairly bubbled with laughter when Martin's pale brows all but disappeared into his hair. He goggled at her for all of thirty seconds before he recalled his manners. "Have you had any problems since your arrival?" he asked in a sudden change of subject.

"It is all right, you know," she told him gently. "I know that I am baseborn. Hart knows as well. It is nothing I can help and there is no reason to be embarrassed about it."

He nodded once, his face flaming.

"I am sorry, Cousin Martin," Leandra said sincerely, all traces of her smile disappearing. "I am a beast to tease you so."

"You mean you are not...?" he trailed off.

"Oh, no, I am indeed Harwood's by-blow, sir." Leandra cocked her head to one side. "As to any problems I've had, they have been many and some quite serious, I'm afraid."

"In what way?" His relief was palpable but oddly mixed with concern for her troubles.

"Well, Mr. Jackson told me that the lower fields are flooded and I honestly know not the first thing to do to solve such a problem. Mr. Owens claims that Mr. Spellman had been stealing his sheep and would not relent until I promised to purchase more for him. Poor Mr. Jeffries lost his wife and child recently in childbed because there is no doctor in Folkestone at the moment. I hired him to work on the gardens since the lonely man was beside himself with grief and he shows a particular talent for landscaping." She paused, gathering her thoughts. "Hmm, Lily, the scullery made was replaced by Mary since Lily married Mr. Wilson. He wanted a wife, you see, and Lily was more than willing to take the position. Old Mr. Huber requested a new roof for his cottage and I granted the request. He really is too old to be working. Is there something we can do for him, do you think?"

Martin just stared at her, his mouth hanging open. She shrugged and continued.

"Mrs. Miller complained that her oldest boy was being worked to death in the factories outside Folkestone. Does Hart own them?" She shook her head. "No matter. So I transferred Billy here to be a groom. He earns more money that way and he is in less danger of getting hurt. He has to take care of his family, you know. His papa died leaving his mama with eight mouths to feed. I also hired the two oldest girls to train to be maids. That's who Mary is, actually. The other is Martha. She works in the kitchens, too. And then there's—"

"Lady Derringer!"

"Yes?" she asked innocently.

Martin smiled. "Perhaps later we can go over the details. I have been instructed to find out if anyone has been giving you any trouble personally."

"Instructed? By whom?"

His brows rose again. "By your husband, of course."

"Of course," she murmured. Did her husband actually care about her, after all?

Over the course of the next week, Leandra spent most of her time with Martin St. Clair. She found the man charming and not the least disturbing. It was a relief to not have to constantly look for hidden meanings in his expressions or comments. He made her feel like a lady.

She was amazed to realize that it was something she had always wanted. Despite her own personal conviction that she was not to blame for her parentage, she couldn't help but wish that others would treat her with the same respect and courtesy that her papa and now Martin showed her. She had always desired to be treated as the lady she was raised to be.

He took care of many of the things that she had no experience with but he was careful never to overstep his authority. He bowed to her wishes and was very tactful when letting her know that she was wrong about something.

The Starks remained mum about the entire situation. Personally, they thought the master should come home and be a husband to the sweet girl he married instead of gallivanting off to God only knew where stirring up trouble and ignoring his responsibilities.

7

A<small>T</small> that precise moment, the Duke of Derringer was not stirring up trouble, nor was he ignoring his responsibilities. He was sitting at a corner table in a seedy little hedge tavern in Dunkirk near the French coast. He watched the door closely while appearing to be captivated by the noxious brew in his mug. He waited for the arrival of a man named Gaston who, it was said, had word of Derringer's cousin Gabriel St. Clair.

Gabriel, who was supposed to be dead.

Derringer was determined to find his cousin, who'd disappeared at Waterloo. Gabriel was the only family member Derringer would trust with his life. He trusted Martin, Gabriel's older brother, but Gabriel and Derringer were the same age and had shared much more in the way of adventures and such when they were young. Martin's serious demeanor and overblown sense of propriety annoyed Derringer, though the man's managerial skills were a godsend.

A slight disruption at the tavern door caused several myopic eyes to glance up. Derringer caught sight of a man clothed in a raggedy old French military uniform, no doubt something that earned him many a drink out of pity. That had to be Gaston.

The man turned in Derringer's direction and approached. "Be you the one they call Sans cœur?" he asked in a guttural French accent.

"I am Heartless," Derringer confirmed in his own perfect French, revealing his aristocratic background. He motioned to the landlord, who brought fresh ale, leaving without a word.

Gaston sat down across from the duke and threw him a grateful smile before draining his tankard. After swiping his dirty sleeve across his mouth, he spoke in his native tongue. "The man you seek is in Maubeuge. Do you know it?"

Derringer nodded. "About eighty miles or so southeast of here." He frowned, shaking his head. Maubeuge was so close to Waterloo. Was it possible Gabriel hadn't ventured far from the scene of his injury?

"Aye. Take care, Heartless. There are some French still wanting to overthrow the English and would look on the corpse of one such as you with great delight," he warned right before he stood to leave.

A sudden cry of rage rent the air and Derringer's head jerked in the direction of the door. Gaston looked as well, blanched linen-white and muttered something about French devils and their English friends. Derringer straightened his slumped shoulders and stared at the brawl that seemed to be taking over the taproom. The circle parted briefly, allowing

Derringer to see who stood at the edge of the melee, faces lit with savage delight as the combatants darkened each other's daylights.

Cursing in a low tone, Derringer stood and, keeping his back to the contretemps, pressed several coins into Gaston's hand. He knew he had to get out before he was discovered. There were too many uncertainties in this situation. He was at a disadvantage. The Duke of Derringer never entered a battle without an edge over his opponent.

With a nod for Gaston, Derringer quickly traversed the room, blending easily into the shadows along the wall. He slipped out a side door and into a dark alley before anyone even realized he had been there and gone.

It would be the height of stupidity to return home now, the duke thought. He was so close to finding Gabriel, a search that had lasted five long years. But why was the Earl of Harwood in France? As Derringer's new brother-in-law, shouldn't he be making a nuisance of himself at Derringer Crescent? And what the devil was the man doing with a loose screw like Fraser D'Arcy?

Derringer had once had a run-in with D'Arcy that nearly ended both their lives. Unfortunately, the crazy Frenchman survived.

Harwood's relationship with D'Arcy was a mystery and Derringer felt he was not best equipped to solve it at the moment. He needed information, and the only place he could get that was at home. Home, where his bride waited, a bride he'd thought of far more often than he'd wanted to.

Derringer kicked Satan into a run, racing toward the cliff's edge. It appeared that he would run the animal right off the crag and into the sea but he turned Satan's head right at the last possible moment and steered him onto a hidden cliff path that led down to a little cove below. To the casual observer, he vanished over the edge of the bluff.

He slowed the great black beast and let Satan pick his own path along the rocky path. They were soon at the bottom and standing near a small yacht anchored just off shore.

Within moments they had set sail for Folkestone. Derringer was suspicious of Harwood's presence in France. He wanted to make sure Merri was safe. And perhaps she would know something of her brother's activities.

Gabriel would have to wait. For now.

"Here? Now? But why?" The dismay in Leandra's voice was very much at odds with the smile that stretched across her face.

"I hate to speak ill of the Quality and all, your grace, but I would venture to say it's because our a duchess now," Mrs. Stark told her in a rare bout of cynicism.

"Oh, why did they have to come now? If Hart were here he'd know what to do to get rid of them," she murmured to herself. "But I can't bear the thought of being rude to them. I can't."

The housekeeper's eyebrows rose at this evidence of Leandra's unwarranted faith in her absent spouse but she said nothing.

"There is nothing for it but to welcome them, I suppose. Show them in, Mrs. Stark."

"In here, madam?" the woman asked, surprised that the duchess would want her family in her little sanctuary.

Leandra looked around the morning room and sighed. "Have they all come?"

"As to that, I wouldn't know. So far there are four ladies and three children."

"The earl didn't come?"

Mrs. Stark shook her head.

"Very well. Have the children taken up to the nursery —we do have a nursery, do we not?—and appoint Bessie to watch over them if they have not brought their own maids. Have the blue, rose, and violet chambers prepared on the second floor. Be sure to place Lady Michaella in the yellow chamber on the third floor. Escort the ladies into the drawing room until their chambers are ready and I will join them shortly."

The duchess withdrew to the door, then paused. Without turning around she said, "He will not be pleased about this, will he?"

"No, madam, he will not," the old woman replied. She didn't even pretend to misunderstand.

Leandra took her time about changing her gown and freshening up her appearance, delaying the inevitably distressing confrontation. Liza arranged her dark brown hair in curls and waves with a pretty gold ribbon and helped her into her emerald green silk gown with the gold velvet piping. She wore little gold slippers and a gold locket around her neck that had been loaned to her by Mrs. Stark. The dress was a trifle fancy for afternoon wear and lower at the neck than she was used to but the ensemble gave her a confidence that she was very much afraid she would need.

What she didn't realize was that the gown made her look quite pretty. The green of the dress made her eyes stand out behind her spectacles like emeralds of the finest quality. The flecks of gold were still there and perhaps even more prominent because of the gold trim on her gown.

Leandra walked with a natural grace that most other women envied. The ladies from her old home were no different. When she entered the drawing room, Leandra noticed the barely veiled anger and hatred in the stares of her family. She ignored it and welcomed them to her home, hiding well her disinclination to do so.

The maid and footman standing at attention in the room were astonished at the lack of warmth in their mistress's soft voice. She held her head at a haughty angle that was unusual and her smile did not reach the emerald of her eyes. In fact, they thought proudly, she looked every inch a duchess.

As was often the case, the servants had uncovered the circumstances of Leandra's birth, something not very astonishing since Leandra herself was rather outspoken about it. Though at first they were inclined to condemn her, it didn't take long for them to, for the most part, accept that she was a person worthy of their devotion and respect. Hence, they answered to no one but her or those directed by her.

"My dear," the Dowager Lady Harwood—Leandra's stepmother—gushed with every appearance of enthusiasm. "How are you, child?"

Something flickered in Leandra's green eyes. They suddenly dimmed in color and appeared to change to a gold color very much like that of the dowager's. Anyone who knew her well would notice the change. Her servants noticed.

She smiled though everything in her resisted. "My lady. I hope your journey was uneventful."

Miss Michaella Harcourt, Leandra's unwed stepsister, stood and curtsied properly, as befitted her half-sister's new station. Rising gracefully, she then approached Leandra. "Are you well, Merri?" she asked, sincere concern quivering on every word.

Leandra gave her sister a genuine smile. "Oh yes, dearest Michaella. I am quite well. You look tired, though. Would you like to retire to your room for a rest?" She sensed it would be best for her gentle sister to be absent from the room when the other ladies' spiteful tongues were given permission to let loose their venom.

Michaella released the breath she'd been holding. She'd sensed it, too. "That would be lovely, thank you."

"Alice, please show Lady Michaella to her chamber. Mrs. Stark will tell you which one, if she hasn't already done so," she told the maid, favoring the servant with the same bright smile she'd given her sister.

"We will have a comfortable coze later, hmm?" she told Michaella. The young lady nodded and excused herself to her mother who reluctantly let her go.

"And now," Leandra said coldly, turning back to her unwelcome guests, "why are you here?"

The remaining ladies gasped. Who would have thought the little viper would get so above herself just because she married a duke? Her husband's station did not change her parentage one whit.

"We are here to help you adapt, of course, my dear," the dowager said with a hard edge to her well-modulated tones.

"Adapt?"

"Yes, of course," Lady Schuster, Leandra's half-sister, agreed. "How could you possibly know how to go on in a household such as this? Why, we have been here all of an hour already and you have not even offered tea."

"And you have not curtsied as befits my station above you, so let us not quibble over the definition of proper behavior."

They gasped again.

"You little slut!" screeched the younger Lady Harwood, wife of the current earl. She strode up to Leandra, blond curls bobbing, and stood looking down at her with a malevolent gaze. "Are you increasing, you little whore? Is that why he married you? Does he know you're a bastard?"

"It was his primary reason for asking me, I think," she replied calmly. "And no, I am not increasing." Her tone was exceedingly dry.

Young Lady Harwood's expression revealed her shock at Leandra's denial. "You're lying! Why would anyone willingly marry a bastard unless she's with child?"

"Why would I lie?"

"Maybe you told your husband that you're increasing and he doesn't know that you are not and you want us to keep the secret."

"Just so," murmured Leandra. She caught the look of horrified amusement in the footman's eyes. She winked at him surreptitiously. "Would you like tea?" she asked with a mocking curtsy directed at her stepmother.

Alas, she'd underestimated the hawklike gaze of her stepmother.

"How dare you mock me!" The dowager turned to the footman. "You, leave this room immediately. And if you show such disrespect again, you will be dismissed."

Everyone froze. The footman glanced nervously at his mistress. Leandra looked her stepmother in the eye and said in the iciest voice she had ever used, "You will not order my servants about nor threaten them with dismissal. If I hear that you have tried during your stay here, you will be tossed out. Do I make myself clear, my lady?"

A moment of extremely tense silence passed.

"Very well," the dowager said grudgingly. "It will be as you wish, Merri, but do not come crying to me when the lazy creatures have turned the duke's home into a circus."

"Please address me properly, my lady," was all Leandra said to this comment before she swept from the room as regal as a queen.

Dinner that evening was a nightmare.

Leandra dressed in a gown of gold velvet trimmed with Brussels lace at the neckline and the wrists of the long sleeves and an overskirt of matching lace. She wore Mrs. Stark's gold locket again since she still had nothing of her own in the way of jewelry. Her dark hair was gathered up on the side of her head and cascaded in a riot of curls over her left shoulder.

She felt terrible. Drums hammered in her head, making her tetchy. She wanted nothing more than the departure of her family. Except for Michaella, of course.

The dinner conversation was nonexistent, thank the Lord. Leandra had dinner served in the State dining room for just that reason. There were yards of table between each of the guests.

The duchess invited Martin to join them. Amusement danced through her eyes as looks of horror passed between the dowager and her daughters. How galling they must find it to have to sit down with a servant!

Leandra sighed and wished the duke was there. For some reason, she'd been unable to stop thinking about him. She barely knew him and yet she found herself constantly doing things that she hoped would please him. And praying the things she did that would not please him were never discovered.

The duchess rose to withdraw to the drawing room. Martin stood as she did and she gave him a sympathetic look. She would not ask him to join them. She whispered to Stark to give Martin whatever he wanted to drink. He'd more than earned it.

As soon as the doors of the drawing room closed, the ladies started in on her.

"You are far too lenient with your servants, Merri. Why, I saw a fat housemaid. I do believe she is stealing food," the dowager informed her haughtily while seating herself regally in a chair by the glowing fire.

"You have not the least knowledge of how to conduct yourself, Merri. You should let me help. Schuster's home was at sixes and sevens when I arrived and I managed to fix everything," Lady Schuster told her with a smirk as she went to the piano in the corner and sat down to play.

"You have no sense of fashion, Merri. You should dismiss your abigail and hire one that knows what she is about," young Lady Harwood complained as she adjusted the skirts of her charming lemon yellow satin evening gown.

These comments were all said at the same time.

Michaella stared at them all as if they were sideshow freaks at Bartholomew Fair. "What are you all talking about? Merri has done a lovely job with her new social status."

"It's quite all right, Michaella," smiled Leandra. "They are only concerned for my well-being."

She turned her attention back to the other three ladies. "The housemaid you saw is not fat, she is expecting. I conduct myself very well, from all I have heard and observed. And Liza is an excellent abigail." With that, Leandra sat down on the settee next to Michaella and took up her needlework, ignoring her spiteful female relatives.

Thankfully, everyone was more than willing to avoid any type of socially correct conversation and so avoided any type of talk at all. Lady Schuster played the piano with skill and soon the dowager was dozing in her chair by the fire. Lady Harwood had found a book that seemed to hold her interest and Michaella watched Leandra ply her needle, asking questions once in a while about a certain type of stitch that she herself had had particular trouble over. Considering her own lack of skill in that department, Leandra knew her sister's questions for the distraction they were, and she loved her all the more for it.

Fifteen minutes later, shouts could be heard coming from the Great Hall. Leandra looked up and the color drained from her face. Such a gamut of emotions swept through her that she didn't know quite what she felt. Surprise, relief, and unease each took their turn on her mobile features.

Servants could be heard rushing here and there, while commands from the Starks rose above all the furor.

"I told you that you are far too lenient," said the dowager, thin lips stretched into a smug grin.

But Leandra wasn't listening. She tossed her sewing aside and flew to the door, flinging it open and darting down the corridor. She didn't stop until she was in the Great Hall.

The Duke of Derringer stood before the main stairs with his arms crossed over his broad chest, staring in Leandra's direction. His black eyes were hooded and his expression grim.

"Oh, Hart, you're home. Thank God!" And Leandra threw herself at him without so much as a by-your-leave.

Quick wits and quicker reflexes served Derringer well. He opened his arms at just the right moment and caught her, his arms enfolding her close to his chest. He stood holding her for a long moment before the impulsiveness of her actions struck him. His eyes widened to their fullest and he grinned. She'd called him Hart.

He stared down into her eyes, dark green and gold, and was suddenly very, very glad he had decided to come home before going after Gabriel. Her mouth opened and he watched her tongue dart out to wet her lips. The sudden desire he felt for her took him completely by surprise.

And so he kissed her. In full view of the servants and her family who had come out to see what all the ruckus was about. He kissed her the way he'd wanted to since that first time at the Maidstone Inn. His tongue swept the inside of her mouth and she moaned deep in her throat. And she kissed him back.

He would have taken her up to his bed right then had not the dowager gasped and said in her strident tones, "Of all the disgraceful behavior! And what, Merri, do you suppose your husband will say if he walks in to see you kissing one of the outdoor help?"

Derringer leaned his head back and smiled at his bride. "So, my Merri, did you miss me?" he asked unnecessarily. He looked down at her with something akin to tenderness, a soft smile on his lips.

Leandra realized suddenly what a spectacle she had made of herself and him. She struggled out of his embrace and stepped back, smoothing her hands over her gown in an attempt to return some order to her appearance. It was then that her stepmother's words finally sank in and she looked up at her husband.

Then she laughed. Uncontrollably.

8

THE duke, in the glory of his tattered and stained tavern attire with his long black hair in windblown disarray, stared at Leandra while she laughed. She laughed so hard that tears sprang to her eyes and ran down her cheeks. One hand covered her mouth in a desperate attempt to stifle her own merriment while the other clutched her middle.

Her laughter rang like music in Derringer's ears.

Then he noticed the ladies standing a few feet behind his wife and the unnatural silence of his servants. He studied the ladies for a full minute, an unpleasant smile finally settling on his lips.

Leandra stopped laughing, her eyes fixing on the duke in trepidation.

He recognized the older woman with the graying hair. Her son took after her quite a lot. The next oldest lady appeared to be Harwood's sister. The blond had to be his wife since she resembled the rest not at all. And the young one that so resembled Leandra must be…

"You are Harwood's clan, are you not?" he asked.

The dowager stiffened. "Who are you, sir, to address us so disrespectfully? I'll have the duke toss you out on your ear for your impertinence."

Derringer turned his black eyes on Leandra. "Do you think he will, Merri?"

Leandra shook her head as a hysterical laugh bubbled up and came out her nose in an unladylike snort—which only made her laugh harder.

"How dare you address a duchess so, sir. You are dismissed immediately," declared the Dowager Lady Harwood roundly. The other ladies just goggled at the way the situation was progressing.

"Aw, Merri, now she's gone and fired me," complained Derringer. He was enjoying himself immensely.

"And you, young lady," said the dowager to Leandra, "ought not encourage him in this behavior. It really does not become you."

Derringer studied his wife until she blushed most becomingly. "I would have to disagree with you, ma'am. She is enchanting when she laughs."

The sincerity in his voice took Derringer and Leandra both by surprise. Her giggles ceased as she stared at him and he stared back with an expression of dawning realization on his face. He truly found her enchanting. How was that possible having only spent a handful of hours with her in the weeks since they'd married? She was an irritation, a necessity to secure his money, nothing more.

And yet, he thought about her more often than he cared to. He found her unwillingness to quake in the face of his temper oddly intriguing. It was no reason to think he loved the witch, but it was curious. And that made him want to know her better.

Leandra forced her eyes to turn to her stepmother and said, "I told you upon your arrival this afternoon, Dowager, that you are not to try to dismiss my servants. If you do, you will leave." She turned glowing eyes up to her husband and winked in the most audacious manner before she took him into her arms and murmured huskily, "And I like this servant too well to see him go."

"You are a whore, I knew it!" declared the triumphant voice of the young, infinitely stupid Lady Harwood.

Leandra tightened her hold on the duke.

"Let me go, Merri," he growled.

"No," she whispered back. "I'll not let you kill my brother's wife."

He gave Leandra a hard glare, one of his worst, but just as he suspected, she didn't back down. She stared right back, determined to prevent the massacre of her unwelcome family.

"Stark!" he bellowed over his wife's head. The butler appeared before him with a wooden expression. "Throw them out, now!" he commanded.

The butler bowed.

"You cannot toss us out. You are a servant." The current earl's wife was none-too-quick, Derringer noted. "And she is no better than she should be, you know. She used to live under my husband's roof and she was caught in the footman's bed."

Derringer's sudden stillness gave Leandra a pang of disappointment. He believed the little cat. She had never been discovered in any man's bed let alone the footman's. She'd never even been in someone else's bed. She released him with a sad little sigh and stepped back.

Derringer crossed the hall in a flash. Leandra blinked, unable to believe her eyes. He was right beside her one second and the next he was gone.

He glared down at Harwood's wife until she shrank away from him in fear. It was all he could do to keep his hands off her. They itched to curl around her slender white throat.

"Aye, you should fear me, my lady. If you say one more thing against Merri, I'll have you horsewhipped," he threatened in a tone of voice that made believers of them all.

"You will do no such thing, young man."

Derringer rolled his eyes and looked at the dowager. "Won't I?" he asked insolently.

"No, you will not. The duke would not allow his guests to be treated so shabbily."

Another dull-witted one. Wonderful. Glancing at his bride, he asked, "How is it, beautiful Merri, that you are so perceptive while the rest of your family seems to play a few cards shy of a full deck?" She shrugged in answer, her eyes wary.

The duke crossed his arms over his chest and cocked his head curiously at the dowager. "And you know Derringer so well, my lady?"

She appeared nonplussed. "Well, of course I do. He is my son-in-law."

"Is he? So Merri is your daughter. How lucky for you if not for her," he retorted caustically.

"She did lie!" exclaimed young Lady Harwood, clapping her hands in glee. "Everyone believes she is legitimate."

"You mean she is not related to her ladyship?" the duke asked in apparent shock. He glanced at Leandra. "Is this true?"

"I am afraid it is," the duchess murmured contritely, her earlier wariness replaced with silent laughter.

Derringer grinned. "Thank God. Were you related to a harpy like her ladyship here, I'd pity the duke, Merri."

"Would you?"

"Truly. To have to endure such family would be the death of him. I hear he's a trifle crazy, you know," he added confidingly to the dowager and her children. Derringer saw the youngest female pale and felt an unusual qualm about frightening her unnecessarily.

"Nonsense!" stated the dowager in accents of annoyance.

"Do you know Derringer, then, my lady?" inquired the duke with every appearance of interest.

"No, actually. But he is a duke. And dukes are above reproach."

"You being the expert on dukes," he retorted.

Leandra's stepmama lifted her chin haughtily. "It is none of your concern, young man, but I do happen to be acquainted with several."

"Gammon!"

"I beg your pardon?"

"And well you should," he replied smugly. Leandra giggled.

"Just who are you, young man?" the Dowager Lady Harwood demanded imperiously.

He straightened and addressed everyone. "I am Derringer," he said with a mocking half-bow. "Welcome to Derringer Crescent and all that rot. Have a lovely stay. If I see any of you even once during your short visit, you will regret it." Michaella squeaked and he swung around to look at her. His left brow cocked in inquiry. "Except you. Who are you?"

"Michaella," she whispered.

He bowed. "Lady Michaella, welcome. If you have need of anything, do not hesitate to ask any one of my servants. They will be pleased to serve you." His tone implied there would be dire repercussions if they were not.

The man was very charming when he tried, Leandra thought wonderingly.

"And now," he continued in the best good humor, "I must go and make myself presentable. Merri, come with me. I need to speak with you."

"I will in a moment, Hart," said Leandra softly.

Derringer, who had started toward the back of the house, stopped and turned slowly around. He ignored everyone and focused his attention on his wife. "Excuse me?" His voice was deceptively soft.

"I must see to my guests and then I will wait upon you, Hart," she said with determination, trying to still the sudden trembling in her limbs.

Derringer marched up to his wife in three determined strides. "They are not your guests, Leandra," he bit out in an undertone. "They are uninvited, unwelcome, unwanted. You are not to cater to them." He paused and looked at that unwelcome group. "Except her," he added with a nod in Michaella's direction causing that young lady to blush.

"Then I am taking care of Michaella's needs, *your grace*," Leandra returned stubbornly.

Derringer's face darkened and he pushed a hand through his loose hair in frustration. "Woman, you try my patience." He turned abruptly on his heel and continued to the back of the house.

"Where is he going?" she whispered to herself.

"That man is no gentleman," announced the dowager.

Leandra turned on her stepmother. "Then I suggest you avoid him for the duration of your visit, my lady." She turned a bright smile on Michaella but addressed all four ladies. "If you will excuse me, I really should see what it is my lord requires. Ask Mrs. Stark if you need anything. Good night."

Leandra had no intention of seeing what it was her husband wanted. She went instead directly to her room and allowed Liza to remove the gold velvet and slip a white cotton nightrail over her head. She knotted her white silk dressing gown around her waist and sat down at her dressing table to allow the maid to brush out her hair.

Besides, she was unsure where he was. He had walked to the back of the house. She assumed he was in his study or the library perhaps and she was not going to wander around the house searching for her husband.

He was infuriating. How dare he order her around as if she were one of his servants! She was not; she was his wife and it was high time he realized it.

She slammed her hairbrush on her dressing table and squeaked in dismay as a bottle of scent tumbled to the floor. Honeysuckle soon took over. She coughed and gazed ruefully at the mess, part of her feeling an urge to clean it up while the other part wanted to walk away and leave it to Liza. With a sigh, she retreated to her bedchamber.

She stopped short on the threshold. "What are you doing here?"

Her husband lounged with apparent comfort against the pillows on her bed, his hands behind his head and his eyes closed. Through the deep V of his loosened shirt she could see a gold chain, a thin, bright line against his sun-darkened skin. His black breeches were tucked into black Hessians, feet crossed at the ankles.

Derringer opened his eyes and gave her a benign look, one dark brow cocked in unspoken irony. "Waiting for you."

"But why?"

He slid from the high bed with the grace and ease of a well-kept cat, crossing the room in a few easy strides. "Do you recall me requesting your presence?"

Request was hardly the word she'd use. Ordered, perhaps, in the autocratic manner he was used to using with those around him. She doubted he was often defied in his "requests."

Derringer reached out, his face revealing nothing of his thoughts. Leandra watched as one long finger stroked the frothy lace on the bodice of her dressing gown. "Yes," she managed to whisper.

"Then I wonder why you did not come," he said almost to himself.

He followed the lace with his finger, never looking at her face. Starting at her neck, he moved down to the point where the fabric met between her breasts. In that moment, his eyes met hers and all the breath left her lungs. Heat pooled in the obsidian depths, a heat that she couldn't identify.

Derringer leaned closer until his lips hovered a mere hairsbreadth away from hers. "Why did you not come, Merri?" he whispered, the soft query encased in steel.

Before she could even think of the way her name on his lips made her feel, the duke slipped his hand down over her gown and cupped her breast. She gasped and tried to pull away.

He dropped his hand and pulled her up against him so that they were at eye-level. For lack of a better place to put them, Leandra wound her arms around his neck.

"Why did you not come?" he repeated. He put his hand on the back of her neck, under her thick hair and said, "You should have at least inquired as to my comfort. Is that not the duty of a good wife? To ensure her husband's ... *comfort*?"

Leandra stared at him, brow furrowed. "Is everything not to your satisfaction?" she asked breathlessly.

He smiled. If everything had been to his satisfaction, he thought in surprise, she would have been waiting naked in his bed.

"No, not exactly," admitted the duke. "But I didn't expect it, either."

His wife released an exasperated sigh, the movement brushing her sensitive breasts against his hard chest. It took a considerable amount of will to calmly inquire, "What is this all about then?"

Derringer removed his hand from her neck and set her back on her feet, very little of his natural grace apparent in the abrupt movement. Then he turned and strode into the sitting room that was situated between their bedchambers.

She stared after him, clutching her robe close over her breasts. His recent caresses still burned her flesh, sending a white hot shiver down her spine. The calculated intimacy of his touch incited her longing for even greater intimacy, as was no doubt his intention. But his own reaction, the way his breath hitched just before he let her go, incited her curiosity. What thoughts occupied his mind when he held her as close as any lover? Surely, he didn't desire her?

She took a deep, steadying breath and with cautious steps, followed him.

The duke had already settled into a chair near the fire when she entered the room. He looked up at her, his eyes sweeping over her, a frown growing with each passing second. Those black, black eyes lingered over her chest.

Leandra took an involuntary step back when that frowning countenance returned to her face.

"Don't do that," muttered Derringer. The way she clutched at her robe only outlined her breasts, emphasizing their perfection. He groaned when her hand clenched even tighter. Eyes closing, he allowed his head to fall back.

"What did I do?"

Derringer's head shot up. "You sound distressed," he remarked. His lips twisted into a pleasantly surprised smile. "You are not quite the calm young woman you pretend to be."

His experiment of a few moments ago as well as her kiss in the Great Hall confirmed his discovery. He clenched his teeth, a thrill coursing through him that was part excitement and part malicious glee. She was definitely not as calm and collected as she let on. How exhilarating would it be to destroy that peace, to render her unable to think, unable to object, unable to do anything other than respond only to instinct?

Her chest rose and fell with three deep breaths, and right before his eyes, Leandra Derringer regained her calm, the peace settling over her like a protective, impenetrable shroud.

Upon this transformation's completion, Leandra's hands ceased twisting the front of her dressing gown—thank the Lord above!—and clasped before her. Her eyes gazed back at him, calmly, from behind her thick spectacles. The whole look of her reminded him of a pious nun. Derringer's mind shied away from that particular idea. What use did he have for a nun?

Still, he watched this transformation with a small amount of envy. He'd never before met anyone who exercised so much control of their emotions. Not even Aurora was so, so... passionless. Of course, Derringer had only been in the company of his bride for a grand total of two days, if that. And if one were to add up the actual hours of their association, it wouldn't even amount to a day. He had no idea the kind of woman he had married. He thought he might actually enjoy finding out what went on behind those glorious eyes of hers.

He still hated the spectacles, however.

"Do you sleep in those?" the duke inquired with a careless gesture in her direction.

"In what, your grace?"

Derringer sighed. "It appears we must have this discussion again. I refuse to be called 'your grace.' Choose something else. Even if it's Lord Heartless, I don't care. And I was referring to those things on your face."

"Lord Derringer, you seem to be in an odd temper this evening. I will bid you goodnight and we will talk in the morning." She turned to leave.

"Just who the devil is the master in this house?"

Leandra turned around and smiled sweetly. "From your tone of voice, I assume the correct answer would be you, my Lord Derringer." She offered a mocking curtsy as she uttered his name. "But since I am the one who has managed everything in your absence, I would have to honestly reply that I am."

With a triumphant grin, she darted into her room and slammed the door, turning the key in the lock.

9

THE duke searched for Leandra all the next morning. He started with every likely room only to come up empty-handed. He searched through rooms he hadn't set foot in since he was in short coats and rooms he had never entered his entire life.

He avoided the second floor stairs. He was unsure why he did this; it was just something he had always done. He never gave it much thought before but now he stopped on the third floor landing and stared down. A feeling of foreboding slithered up his spine and swirled through his mind until he stepped back, the movement jerky and involuntary. The feeling so unnerved him that Derringer turned around and headed for the servants' stairs at the back of the house.

After looking throughout the entire castle and still finding no sign of his wife, the duke thought she might have taken a horse for a ride about the estate. If she rode. Did she ride?

This question followed him into the Great Hall where he found Stark showing a young footman the particulars on polishing silver. The duke did not recognize the young man and his brow furrowed as he approached.

"Stark, a moment," he called.

The butler relinquished his rag and polish to the footman and traversed the distance between him and his master. "Yes, your grace?"

"Who the devil is that?" asked Derringer with a nod toward the other servant.

"His name is Thomas, your grace. Her grace hired him during your absence."

The duke at that moment got a better look at the boy and noticed a patch over his right eye. "What happened to his eye?"

"An accident at one of the factories, your grace."

"One of mine?"

"No, your grace. One of Lord Harwood's, I believe."

"Harwood? Why the devil must that man plague me so?" muttered Derringer with feeling. He shook his head slightly and said, "So her grace hired a man with one eye because…"

"I imagine she felt sorry for him, your grace. As she did with the other twenty or so that she hired."

Derringer looked at Stark as if he'd lost his head. "Twenty or so— She hired more than just the boy?"

"Yes, your grace."

Derringer studied his butler for the space of ten seconds. The old man wore his proper wooden expression but there was a stiffness in his bearing that had never been there before. The duke wondered about it.

A pregnant housemaid crossed the hall within the duke's view. He eyed her in shock and she released a frightened yelp before darting into the relative safety of an antechamber.

"Where is the duchess?" he asked.

Stark looked him in the eye and replied, "I believe her grace is with Mr. St. Clair, your grace."

"She's with Martin? What the devil is she doing with Martin?"

"I'm sure I don't know, your grace."

"Where are my wife's guests?"

"The Dowager Lady Harwood and Lady Harwood have not yet risen; Lady Schuster is in her sitting room and Lady Michaella is with her grace and Mr. St. Clair."

The duke's stance eased just a fraction. Why did the idea of his wife closeted with his cousin cause him such disquiet? The inordinate amount of relief he felt at the knowledge that Lady Michaella was with them caused him unease of a different sort. He shouldn't care. It shouldn't matter. And yet, it did.

As to the other ladies, he was pleased that they had taken his warning in earnest. He really didn't think he could be civil to them and he very much preferred not to have to try. He decided not to ponder why he thought he'd have to try.

All that aside, he still hadn't found his wife. And it appeared that Stark, for whatever reason, was unwilling to divulge her exact whereabouts. It had never occurred to Derringer that his staff would switch their loyalties, but it appeared they had. His bride seemed to have won them over and even added to their ranks those who would have more than one reason to feel grateful to the new Duchess of Derringer.

"Where might I find my wife, Stark?" inquired the duke, his swift loss of patience evident in his silky tone.

"In your study, your grace," replied the butler with what looked suspiciously like a smirk.

Derringer turned to leave but before he walked away, said, "I want to meet every new servant, Stark. Have them assembled here in one hour."

"But I don't understand," insisted Leandra calmly. "If the workers are properly taken care of, they will work more efficiently, will they not?"

"In theory, Merri, in theory," replied Martin. "But it could also incite rebellion if the workers feel others are being treated better than themselves. Even if the others are not your tenants or employees and simply the workers on the neighboring estate. And with all due respect," he added evenly, "we really should confer with Hart since he is here. It would be unconscionable to make these decisions without the permission of the landowner."

"You are right, of course, Martin, but I cannot believe Hart would not want to treat his workers with the kindness and respect they deserve. Mr. Harper needs a new roof. I rode out to see it myself before you arrived and I would have set the workers to it immediately but then you came and many of my plans were halted." She scowled ever so slightly. "It is most vexing to have to answer to someone when you truly believe you are in the right and your... master, for lack of a better word, may not agree."

Martin smiled indulgently at her. "Do you ever think of anything that does not pertain to your husband's tenants or land?"

For some reason, annoyance flared to life at his innocent question. Did he think she shouldn't worry her pretty little head over matters that were better left to the gentlemen? Did he think she should fret more about her wardrobe, local gossip, and her own consequence?

Probably not, she told herself. Martin had never suggested that she should be an empty-headed widgeon like her brother's wife. He'd never been anything other than polite, encouraging, and the proper gentleman. Exactly the type of gentleman Leandra had dreamed about in the brief moments she'd allowed herself to dream of marriage and a family.

But even with all the estate problems Leandra had seemed to automatically acquire with her marriage, she still worried over her dress. It had always been in the back of her mind that the duke could return home at any moment and she wanted to prove to him that she had some sense of style even if it was with the help of her maid.

And now he was home and although she wouldn't admit it even to herself, Leandra was hiding from him. After last night, she was unsure how to act around him and, worse, she was unsure how she felt about him. He was an uncouth lout, to be sure, one who found unusual pleasure in the discomfort of others, but she'd seen evidence of his goodness in the way his servants spoke of him in his absence, the overheard word here and there when the speaker was unaware of her presence. The people who served him admired him, loved him even, though not all of them understood him. Leandra could hardly blame them. She found herself oddly attracted to him even when his unkindness lashed her like a whip. Perhaps it was a weakness in her. Or perhaps she simply believed there was a better person inside him, a better man who made an occasional appearance.

Michaella walked over to the large desk where Leandra sat with Martin on one side. She smiled sweetly. "There will be quite a lovely view from that window"—she pointed in the direction of the window where she had been standing—"in the spring, I think. Which garden is that?"

"That would be the South Gardens, dear," Leandra told her.

Michaella nodded and turned toward the door. "I think I will go for a walk on the grounds and…" Her voice trailed off as she passed out of their hearing.

Leandra shook her head fondly at her somewhat featherbrained sister. "She is such a sweet young lady, though," she murmured to herself.

"What was that, Merri?" asked Martin.

She smiled. "It was of little import, Martin. I was merely thinking aloud."

The blond gentleman studied Leandra for a long moment. She grew a trifle uncomfortable under his intense scrutiny. It seemed to be a St. Clair family trait to stare a person out of countenance.

"I wonder, Merri, if you would care to go for a stroll through the gardens as well. We can follow Lady Michaella and all the proprieties would be observed," he suggested, much of the intensity fading from his gaze.

"That sounds lovely, Martin. I must run and get my pelisse and then I will join you…?"

"In the Great Hall after I've determined exactly where your sister has gone."

"Very well," Leandra replied serenely as she rose to her feet. Martin rose as well and waited until she walked out before he slumped back in his chair with a strange frown on his face.

Leandra grabbed the first pelisse she touched which thankfully was a lovely rose pink that matched her gown of pink sprigged muslin to perfection. She threw it on and buttoned the row of tiny buttons down the front and shoved her feet into some sensible half-boots instead of her soft kid slippers.

She was leaving her dressing room when Liza rushed in out of breath. "Oh, your grace, the duke is looking for you," gasped the maid. "Mr. Stark said as how his grace has searched all of the morning and he was headed to the study when I saw you running up the stairs and thought to warn you."

"I was not running, Liza. A lady never runs," replied Leandra in her best duchess tones.

The little maid grinned. "Of course not, your grace."

"Thank you for letting me know that his grace is looking for me. I'll be sure to seek him out…as soon as I return from my walk with Mr. St. Clair."

The maid gave her mistress a knowing look. "And what shall I tell his grace when he asks me where you have got to?"

Leandra paused in the act of drawing on her gloves and stared at the girl. "Tell him the truth, Liza. I am out walking." She threw the maid a smile and walked out the door.

Derringer entered the study mere seconds after Martin had left. He stood in the center of the rather small chamber and stared around him with an annoyed frown on his harsh features. He had the feeling that he was being avoided.

Oh, well, he thought in resignation. If his wife wished to avoid him, he'd oblige her. He'd grown weary of the chase. Besides, she couldn't hide forever, even in a mausoleum like Derringer Crescent.

The study used to be his father's domain. He remembered coming here once as a very small boy. The old duke had been discussing something with Mr. Comfrey, the man who used to serve as steward. Little Hart had stood patiently waiting for his father to acknowledge him and was disappointed when his father had told him to leave instead and not to enter the study again until he was asked.

Derringer could still remember the feeling he got every time he had been around his father. And for some reason, this room only emphasized the fact that his father had not loved him. Perhaps it was because it still felt and looked so much like the late Duke of Derringer. Except...

Derringer approached the desk and looked down. The top was scattered with sheets of vellum and parchment covered in a delicate feminine hand. His wife's. He studied the handwriting minutely. He noticed she had a tendency to underline some of her words with the tail of the last letter. Oddly flighty for such a common-sense sort of girl.

Then he realized what he was looking at. Plans to renovate the dower house that was located on the grounds outside the castle wall. Why the devil did she want to do that?

The suspicion crossed his mind that she might be considering living there herself. He was surprised that he didn't want her to. But why should he care? He didn't love her. She was nothing more than a poor abandoned girl he had felt sorry for and married. She was nothing to him. That he got a fortune in the bargain was just a bonus for his act of selflessness.

Selflessness, hah! Even Derringer had to admit that it was his own sense of injustice that he should be denied his rightful inheritance by a father who had more than proven that he had not a speck of regard for his son that had prompted his proposal to Leandra Harcourt. The fact that he actually desired his bride was the bonus, he thought with a wicked smile.

And she desired him, he knew from her reaction last night. Well, part of her reaction anyway. She had definitely responded to his teasing as he had hoped. But the way she so quickly recovered her poise was enough to make him wonder.

Derringer strode from the study in more of a temper than when he had gone in. He wasn't even planning to quiz her about her behavior of the night before. He only wanted to ask his wife if she knew why her brother would be in France and if she knew Fraser D'Arcy. She probably knew nothing but he had to ask.

Then he had to set sail again and retrieve his cousin before the trail grew cold.

10

"Forgive me for saying this, Merri, but you do not appear to hold Hart in very much affection," pointed out Martin as they strolled companionably in Michaella's wake.

The rear gardens were bare of vegetation since it was November and the air was crisp but Leandra found it lovely to walk about outside anyway.

She pondered Martin's observation and wondered if perhaps she ought to tell him of her odd relationship with her husband. But did Martin have any right to know? If the duke had not seen fit to inform him, why should she?

She was strangely ashamed of herself for leaping at the chance to be married to a duke anyway. She had, of course, actually agreed before she had learned he was a duke, but it had only enhanced the appeal to be rescued by such an attractive man possessed of both title and consequence. Leandra had always known what a plain young woman she was and had never imagined that a handsome man would fall in love with her and insist that she marry him. Derringer had not professed love but how could he when he had only just met her?

She'd not had any romantic notions in regard to the duke because of their unique circumstances, but she was not about to cavil at fate for her marriage. She had taken the leap and she would deal with the consequences even if they were not particularly palatable at the moment. Perhaps things would change and her husband would fall in love with her.

But could *she* fall in love with *him*?

"Do I not?" she asked her handsome companion, returning to their conversation. She gave a little shrug. "I am sorry I seem so, but I truly do have a great regard for your cousin," she told him truthfully. "I am annoyed that he insists on spending so much time away when we are so newly married, but…" She shrugged.

Martin seemed to take this with a grain of salt but he said nothing to that effect. "How soon did he leave after you were married?" He swiped at an overgrown rosebush with his walking stick and turned to gaze at her steadily.

"The day after we married," she replied. She was definitely not going to tell him that the marriage had yet to be consummated.

"I have to admit I was shocked when Hart told me. I would never have thought he would marry. He had always said he never would."

"Oh, and he may not have, had circumstances been different," Leandra said without thought.

Martin seized upon her statement. "Circumstances?" he inquired idly.

"Oh, you know, meeting me and falling in love," she answered blithely. She cringed inside at her slip and consequent fib. She hoped her husband never heard what she had said.

"Yes, Martin, so I am sure you won't mind me stealing my bride for a moment," said a smooth voice behind them.

"Oh, Lord," the duchess muttered before she turned with a bright smile on her lips and a pleading expression in her eyes.

That was when Derringer realized he could never deny her when she had that particular look in her eyes. He would slay dragons for her just to see that look disappear. He wanted her to truly smile again. Damn, but that was not a feeling with which he was comfortable.

"Hello, Hart," said Martin, offering his hand.

The duke shook it warmly. "How do you do, Martin? It's been a while, has it not?"

"Indeed it has," Martin smiled. "And now I will leave you with your bride. We can catch up later."

The secretary walked away and Leandra watched him go with something akin to regret. She really did not want to be alone with her husband.

"Leandra." The duke held out his arm and waited for her to take it.

He was being everything that was polite—a circumstance that made his wife very uneasy. Leandra placed her hand gingerly on his arm and smiled up at him. "How was your morning?" she asked brightly.

They walked for a bit before the duke responded to her question and then in a way she had not expected.

"Doing it a bit too brown, my love," he murmured with a sharp look at her face.

Her heart skipped a beat at the mocking endearment. He was not being polite then but merely toying with her like a cat toys with a mouse before killing it. She glanced behind her back, saw they were not being observed by Martin or any of the outdoor staff, and dropped her hand from his arm. The duke said nothing and linked his hands behind his back.

"I do not know what you mean," she said stiffly.

"And I thought your one redeeming quality was honesty."

She inhaled sharply. "Why don't you just say what you mean instead of playing games," she snapped.

He looked at her in amusement. "And I have succeeded in driving away your serenity once again," he remarked. "And with so little effort on my part."

She strove for calm. "Nonsense, your grace. I am ever calm."

"I recall another time in which you were less than serene, my dear. You were in fact quite...bothered," finished the duke with a wicked smile.

Her heartbeats picked up and color rose to her cheeks. Whether it was from anger or embarrassment or something entirely different was anybody's guess. "That was a unique situation, your grace. And you are no gentleman to bring it up," she retorted.

"I never claimed *that* title, Merri. I only ever claimed to be a duke. And I am that."

They were silent for several minutes. They had wandered toward the stables without either one of them noticing. Derringer led the way into the stables and to two stalls near the end. Leandra knew that Satan's Son and Lucifer's Lady were stabled there. She herself had grown quite fond of Lady.

Derringer was oddly silent as he approached the stallion. He said something low to the animal that made Satan whinny in answer. The duke smiled and reached into his pocket. He held his hand palm-up and gave him a small apple. Satan nodded and whinnied his approval. Then Derringer did the same for Lady. He received much the same reaction he had gotten from Satan.

Leandra stood a little distance away and watched this. She was amazed at how very gentle he was with the animals. He even reached down to pet the huge black dog that trotted up to sit at his feet.

She approached the man and his pets. "Why do you name them so?" she asked with a gesture toward the horses. She had been wondering since she had first come to live at the Crescent.

Derringer smiled. "An affinity with the Dark Prince?" he quipped. "It was an act of rebellion. It helped that they are so black, too." He pointed at the dog that now lay at his feet and the black cat that had just joined them. "Have you met Cerberus and Beelzebub?"

"Not properly," she replied with a twinkle. She stooped down to pet the dog and cat who were more than happy to let her. After a few moments of this, she looked up to find the duke's black eyes trained on her. She couldn't read the emotion there but it set her heart to beating erratically.

"They don't like anyone," he commented. "That's why I like them. Do you ride?"

"I have enjoyed a few good gallops on Lady. I hope you don't mind."

"She didn't throw you?"

Leandra gave her husband a puzzled frown. "No, why should she? I do know how to ride."

"She—"

"Doesn't like anyone," finished Leandra dryly. "Are all your animals like their master, your grace?"

"No," he said harshly. "They all seem to like you."

Leandra didn't give him the hurt look he had expected. The look she gave him was blank, completely and totally devoid of any expression or emotion. He even searched her eyes but they were equally blank behind her spectacles. She gave him this steady look for a full ten seconds before turning on her heel and walking away with her head held high.

She was twenty feet away before he realized that her eyes had been brown and the gold flecks had disappeared. What that meant, he was unsure. But he was sure that he didn't want to see it again.

"Tell his grace that I am indisposed and will be unable to join him for dinner," Leandra instructed Stark as she entered the house and headed in the direction of her room. "If my family goes in to dinner, apologize to them as well."

The butler bowed and watched her walk away with a concerned frown marring his normally expressionless face.

Leandra dismissed Liza as soon as she entered her dressing room. She slowly unbuttoned her pelisse and carefully removed it, laying it across a chair back for Liza to take care of later. Then she removed her gloves and shoes, laying them neatly by the chair as well. She unwound the ribbon from her hair and shook her head slightly causing the dark brown tresses to bounce around her head and over her shoulders. Her head hurt and she needed no extra stress upon it.

The duchess sat down before the mirror at her dressing table and stared at her reflection. She refused to think. She couldn't think. If she thought about it now, she would cry and that she refused to do. She would not shed any tears over a man who was so... so...

She tried to understand. He was a very disturbed man. He had been a duke since he was seven years old. He was placed in a position of responsibility at a very young age and further imposed upon by his family who sought to rule through him. He was unsure how to act around someone who showed that they cared. He was untrained in proper behavior. He felt unloved and unimportant. He had no reason to be polite. He was a duke.

He was rude and unfeeling and without a shred of sensibility!

Of all the things he had ever said to her, his words of moments ago had been the most hurtful. Leandra had been able to brush off all his other disparaging comments about her appearance, her actions, and her serenity, but he actually admitted that he did not like her.

Choking back the tears stinging her eyes, she tried to swallow around the growing lump in her throat. But even the strongest woman will cry at some point in her life. And Leandra was not the strongest woman. She was just as sensitive as any other member of her sex even if she was sometimes better able to hide it.

The girl in the mirror stared back at her with an expression of such sadness in her golden brown eyes that Leandra clapped a hand over her mouth to hold back a sob that refused to be stifled. Tears bubbled up in her eyes and spilled over, under the wire rims of her spectacles, down her cheeks, across her hand to land with a quiet plop on the dressing table. Several more followed the first and soon she was sobbing with her eyes tightly closed and her fists pressed against her lips.

She didn't realize Michaella had entered the room until that young lady knelt beside her chair and wrapped her arms around her murmuring nonsense in her ear. Leandra hugged her sister tightly and cried her heart out into her shoulder.

When the sobs finally ceased, Michaella stood and after patting Leandra gently on the shoulder, said, "I will ring for Liza, dearest, and have her bring a pot of tea."

Leandra silently nodded, wiping her face with the lavender dampened square of muslin that her sister had handed her. She realized her hair was a mess and patted at it ineffectually for a moment before giving it up as a lost cause. Liza would have to brush it and re-style it. The door opened and she heard Michaella say something to Liza. The door closed again and Leandra sat still waiting for her sister to return to her.

But it wasn't Michaella who came to stand beside her chair. She looked down at glossy black boots connected to black pantaloons connected to a black waistcoat and an equally black jacket. She knew the shirt and cravat would be black along with the eyes and hair.

"What do you want?" she whispered. "I would have thought you would be happy enough to avoid the company of one you so dislike." Her voice sounded petulant, childish, and she bitterly cursed herself for revealing how his words had hurt her.

Dragging another chair forward, the duke sat down and gave her a steady look. "Don't whine, Merri, it ill becomes you."

"Get out."

"I will not. This is my house. I admit I should not have said what I did. But that does not mean I will tolerate being ordered around in my own house by my wife."

"Get out," she repeated stubbornly.

Derringer leaned forward and placed one finger beneath her chin, forcing her to look at him. She glared through her spectacles like an avenging fury.

"We have gotten off to a bad start, I think," sighed the duke. He released her chin and leaned back, crossing his arms over his chest. "And what I have to tell you will not help matters, I am afraid."

Leandra stared at him. She blinked once, twice, and a third time before a tear appeared on her lashes and another slipped down her cheek. She dashed it away furiously and continued to glare at him.

Her tears had a strange affect on the duke. He stared at her helplessly and hoped that she would stop before he gave in to his desire to hold her.

"Merri, please don't cry," he finally begged when two more tears fell from her glorious eyes. He reached out to her but she backed away as if he had the plague. The hurt he felt at her reaction knifed through him, stunning him. Why should he care what this plain little girl thought of him?

Derringer stood and took two steps away from his wife. "I only came here to ask you something. Well, a few things, in all honesty."

He paused and rubbed his chin thoughtfully as he looked at his silently weeping wife. He couldn't talk to her when she was in this state. A sudden idea lit in his brain and he only cringed slightly at the ruthlessness of it. That feeling alone alarmed him enough to make his words sound sincere.

"If you would kindly stop blubbering like an infant, I will reveal what I came here to tell you and then leave you be," he snapped.

11

His cruelty had the desired effect. Her head snapped up, tears drying and eyes blazing. She pursed her lips and crossed her arms, and waited for him to continue.

Derringer grimaced. "That's better, I think." He resumed his seat. "First, how well are you acquainted with your brother's activities?"

Leandra started, her anger dissolving into confusion. "Harwood? Why?"

"I wondered if you could tell me what he might be doing in France. Has he business interests, or personal interests there? Perhaps a family member resides there? A mistress? Something equally innocuous?"

He watched the changing expressions on her face. He knew by the confusion and unease that she knew something but not everything. So he waited.

Leandra stared at him in some consternation. She knew Harwood had the habit of jaunting off to France at odd times, usually in the company of his friend Mr. D'Arcy. She had never cared for the Frenchman and so had avoided him whenever he came to visit. Her father had distrusted him as well but believed that his son would not get involved in anything untoward and so allowed them to come and go as they pleased.

And now Derringer wanted to know about Harwood's activities in France?

When she gave him a suspicious look, he told her sharply, "It is important that I know, Leandra. His association with a certain Frenchman is not in any way innocent and I have to know why the devil they were on the continent the same time I was."

"Fraser D'Arcy," she said.

"You do know something about it, then," he said with a mixture of satisfaction and disappointment.

"I know my brother and Mr. D'Arcy were often in each other's company but I am unsure where they chose to go. It could have been any number of places but I suppose France is a logical assumption."

Derringer stood and paced about the small chamber. "But how did D'Arcy get into England in the first place?" he wondered aloud. "That frog should not have been able to get anywhere near these shores. Did you ever have words with D'Arcy?"

"Only once or twice," she replied. "I never cared for the man and so avoided him."

"Good girl," the duke murmured almost to himself. Leandra wondered at his sudden preoccupation.

"Were you in France, your grace?"

Derringer stopped pacing and looked down at Leandra. "Are you still vexed with me then?" he asked with more curiosity than anything.

"I can't answer that with a simple yes or no," she remarked.

Her serenity has been restored at least, he thought. "Must you insist on 'your gracing' me?"

Leandra smiled. Was that what had him suddenly perturbed? "Yes, I think I must, your grace." Her smile disappeared. "Considering how you feel about me, I have not the right to address you with less formality and certainly not without the propriety our respective ranks require."

The duke slumped back in the chair next to his wife. "Are you going to resurrect that every time we speak now?" he asked, annoyed and disturbed by his own feelings of guilt.

"No, your grace, only until I find a situation for myself," she told him in a flash decision. "Then we shall cease to speak altogether."

The duke became as still as one of the statues that stood sentinel in every garden at the Crescent. "What?" His voice had that dangerous silkiness to it and Leandra shivered despite herself.

"I see no reason for us to reside together as a married couple if we do not even like each other, your grace. It would be best if I were to live somewhere else and find work of some sort."

"And how long have you been planning this, Lady Derringer?"

"Since early this afternoon."

"What of the plans for the Dower house?"

"What of them?"

"Is that where you are planning to reside?"

"No, your grace. Where I reside will not be found anywhere on your estate."

Derringer stared at her for a long moment. If she left and Grimsby found out about it, he'd take the money away. Worse, the duke thought morosely, he'd miss her.

"You're not leaving," he snapped.

"But don't you see?" Leandra begged. "If I were to stay here, it would become nearly impossible for us to dissolve this mockery of a marriage. Since we have not c-consummated the marriage, an annulment is still possible."

Derringer laughed. "An annulment is not as easy to acquire as you may think. A divorce would be easier."

"Then we shall divorce. The scandal will die down eventually, allowing each of us to remarry."

"You know nothing of the law, my dear girl. We could only remarry if the courts allowed, and even then only one of us can, the one who is not found guilty of adultery."

Her brow furrowed. "We shall find a way. You should have your freedom, as you never wanted me in the first place. If admitting to adultery is what it will take, then I will do it."

Derringer stood, rage burning through him at the thought of her admitting to such a thing. "This marriage will not be dissolved!" he roared at her. He leaned down over her chair, one hand braced on each side of her. "You have to stay with me."

"Why?" she asked defiantly.

"Because you're my wife, dammit! You need no other reason."

He stepped back before he gave in to his urge to throttle her... or kiss her. Damn, but he wanted to kiss her.

"I'm afraid I do, your grace," Leandra informed him, crossing her arms in stubborn imitation of her husband.

Derringer placed his hands on his hips and stared, truly amazed at her tenacity. "You would defy me in this?"

Leandra took in his rigid posture, his stubborn countenance, and the lurking emotion behind his eyes. She lifted her chin. "I would."

Derringer stared at her in stunned disbelief for several seconds. Then he suddenly dropped down to his knees in front of her and took both her hands in his own. "You can't go, Merri," he said. "I lied when I said I didn't like you. I do. Really. And it frightens me to death," he admitted with a bit of her candor. "I don't like people. I try not to but truthfully there are a few that somehow get around my defenses. It's dangerous to get close to me."

Leandra looked into pain-filled black eyes and knew in that moment that it would be very easy to fall in love with this man. He had a heart in spite of what everyone said. He was just afraid of being hurt.

Oh, how she could relate to such sentiments!

She gently disengaged one of her hands and cupped his cheek. "I forgive you for the comment, Hart," she told him softly. "And I would like to stay and be your wife."

The duke grinned at her. "Truly?"

She took a deep breath. She knew what he was asking. It wasn't very hard to determine the way his eyes suddenly glinted. "Truly."

Derringer kissed her gently, the merest touching of lips, and leaned back with a bemused expression on his face. But chagrin replaced bemusement when he remembered the other reason he had sought her out. Perhaps it should wait until after dinner. He had to tell her at least part of it now.

"There is another reason I had to talk to you, Merri."

Leandra studied his face and felt her heart sink to her toes. "You are leaving again, aren't you?"

"How did...?" Derringer shook his head slightly. "Yes, I am. I have to leave tonight, as a matter of fact."

"Tonight?"

"Yes. After dinner if you can arrange for it to be served an hour or so earlier. I will tell you the whole story before I set sail."

"You are going to France again."

"I am," nodded the duke. "I will be back as soon as possible, I promise."

"But…" her voice trailed off uncertainly and a blush climbed her cheeks. Raising her chin a notch, she persevered in her inquiry. "What about…?" her hand fluttered helplessly between them.

The duke regarded her blankly for a moment. Then, understanding dawned and he smiled genuinely.

Leaning forward until his forehead touched hers, he whispered, "As much as I long to make you my wife in truth, a hurried joining is not how I envisioned our first time together."

He lifted his head and slid his arms around her waist, pulling her up from the chair as he rose to his feet. Holding her gently against him, the duke kissed her again, a little less reverently than before and with far more passion.

Leandra returned his embrace tenfold. All of her reservations were temporarily silenced so she held nothing back. And was pleased to hear her husband groan and tighten his arms around her.

Setting her firmly from him, he breathed, "A hurried coupling does not sound so bad right now."

Leandra blushed at the coarseness of his words but couldn't help agreeing with his assessment. She almost told him as much but decided she was not *that* bold yet.

He laughed lowly, touching one long finger to her pink cheek. "I can guess the course of your thoughts, my darling wife, but I have to decline such a winsome invitation." He gazed down at her with more fondness than he had hitherto displayed toward her and Leandra felt her heart expand.

Daringly, she extended one small hand to lightly brush his black-clad chest. Not meeting his eyes—her boldness was not that... well, bold... yet—she murmured, "I am sure... something could be managed."

His reply was a muffled snort. Leandra's eyes shot up to his, shocked and questioning.

Derringer shook his head, trying very hard not to burst into outright laughter. Her eyes narrowed suspiciously at him and he was sure he wasn't quite succeeding.

He drew her back into his arms. "Ah, Merri, my girl, you have no idea what kind of... managing I require."

It was her turn to snort. "I have a very good idea, Hart," she returned dryly.

His black brows rose. "Indeed? A very good idea, you say? Meaning, you still have some doubts?" He grinned wickedly, positioning her in his arms just enough to let her know exactly what he required.

Her eyes widened and she surprised him by pressing closer, her lips parting in curiosity. Her hands moved around his back, fingers splayed.

Dear Lord, leaving her this time was not going to be easy, Derringer thought. He was tempted to consign Gabriel to the devil and instead take his wife… well, anywhere and everywhere that happened to be convenient.

He kissed her again, just a light brushing of the lips. Hugging her tight, he told her impudently, "Merri, were you anything but the innocent I know you are, I'd take you here and now without a thought for niceties." He sighed in apparent frustration and firmly detached her from his person.

Leandra considered lying to him, telling him she wasn't a stranger to what went on between a man and a woman but she had a feeling he'd see right through such claims. So she settled for her own frustrated sigh, not a little perplexed by the strange flutterings and yearnings the press of his body had caused in her own.

The duke chuckled, knowing her thoughts, transparent as she was. "As soon as I return, my love, I promise." His gaze swept her flushed face. "And it will be worth the wait, Merri."

Michaella and Martin joined them for dinner. Leandra had it served in the family dining room, which was a good deal smaller and had a much cozier feel to it with the colorful tapestries on the walls and the intricately carved sideboard that sported numerous dings and nicks of past generations. Dinner conversation was lively and informed with the duke heading most of the topics and Martin adding his opinion without reserve. Even shy Michaella was encouraged to say her piece.

Overall, Leandra was pleased with the way things were progressing. But she worried about what Derringer would tell her later. What was so important that he had to go back to France so soon after his return?

She swallowed her fears for the time being and smiled at the group gathered around the table. She was glad that Harwood had not accompanied his wife. But she was uneasy about his reasons for being in France. Perhaps he was just there to visit, she told herself hopefully.

Without his wife and children? Her gaze settled on her sister. Would Michaella know anything of their brother's doings? Perhaps she would query her later.

Later? What later? Later she would be discussing with her husband his imminent plans for departure and then she would be going to bed. Alone. Again.

Had it really only been two days she had spent in his company? It seemed like forever although she still did not know the man behind the cynical black eyes and harsh features. Was she making the right decision to allow him to come to her bed? He wouldn't, of course, until he returned from this latest jaunt to the continent. But when he returned, she would not know him any better than she did now.

She knew that her decision was not the wisest but she wasn't going to change it, either. She had seen a side of Hartley St. Clair that made her want to uncover all his secrets and know the man he attempted to hide from the world.

Heartless. He had told her himself that he knew of the epithet and thought it appropriate. A friend of his had even called him that once. What had he done to make her think such a thing?

Leandra suddenly wanted to meet the woman. Derringer had said her name was... Amanda? Autumn? Aurora? Aurora, that was it. And she married Lord... Garwood? No, Greville. Lord Greville. They resided in Warwickshire. She would simply write to them and invite them for a visit. They may not even know of Derringer's nuptials.

Leandra smiled brilliantly at her husband whose glass halted midway to his mouth as he threw her a wide-eyed look. What had given her the cat-in-the-cream look all of a sudden? She had been a trifle withdrawn throughout the meal and now she looked as if the sun would rise expressly for her. Derringer thought that perhaps it would with a smile like that.

She had agreed to be his wife. Truly and finally his wife. It was amazing to think that when he had met this girl, he had actually planned never to touch her. He had thought he would never have to. He had never dreamed that he would, in fact, *want* to. She was not the kind of woman who usually caught his eye.

But although he had not actually come right out and told the lawyer that the marriage had been consummated, he had led the man to believe that it had. Derringer felt guilty for what amounted to a lie. His confusion over this strange feeling of contrition was enough to make him fall silent and glare at his now empty glass as if it had somehow caused all his troubles.

And tonight he'd be leaving again, this time to retrieve his cousin and, hopefully, bring him home.

He and Gabriel had much more in common than simply growing up together. Gabriel could have been his twin. He had the same black hair and tall, muscular frame. His eyes were not quite so dark. They were more of a midnight blue than the pitch black that Derringer's appeared to be.

They very nearly shared a birthday. Gabriel was born only a few days after Derringer had been. The boys had been inseparable since the day they met. Derringer now wanted to restore his cousin to his side.

That he was to blame for his cousin's absence and consequent disappearance was something that never left the duke's mind. He blamed himself completely and always tried to prove to himself that he was quite as heartless as society claimed him to be. If he believed it himself, perhaps his blasted conscience would take the hint and leave him alone.

But he still had to find Gabriel and restore him to his family if it was possible. Then he would try to make amends for his sins.

Derringer leaned back in his chair and sighed, drawing the attention of his dinner companions. He had allowed his mind to wander over things that he had no control over at the moment and now everyone glanced at him with interest.

As the normal wave of discomfort washed over him, Derringer fought the urge to lash out. He would have succeeded, too, had not Martin chosen that moment to mention his brother to the ladies.

"He was a bit of a here-and-therein, you know, and had a disreputable reputation. But one doesn't like to speak ill of the dead, especially when he was one's own brother."

Derringer smashed his delicate crystal glass on the table, surging to his feet. "Gabe is not dead! And I'll thank you to never refer to him as such within my hearing, sir!"

Michaella squeaked, Leandra gasped, and Martin shrank back in this chair in sudden consternation. He nodded once and Derringer strode from the chamber.

"I wonder if he will still tell me," the duchess murmured to herself. Then, "I have the headache."

Michaella and Martin shared a confused look. Michaella rose to her feet and gently but firmly took her sister's arm. "Come, Merri. I will help you to bed. Please excuse us, Mr. St. Clair."

Martin had risen to his feet when Michaella did and now bowed to both ladies and said, "I hope you will feel more the thing tomorrow, Lady Derringer. Goodnight, Lady Michaella."

12

DERRINGER entered his wife's room right before he was set to depart. She sat up in bed against a mound of pillows, her hair loose and a lavender compress on her forehead.

"Are you well?" he asked with a frown.

Leandra opened her eyes and lifted her lips in a pained smile. "Just a touch of the headache," she murmured.

"Oh." He came further into the room and stood beside the old-fashioned four-poster bed. He glanced around for a chair, then shrugged and perched on the edge of the bed, facing his wife. "Do you feel well enough to hear my story?" he asked with an even deeper frown than before.

Leandra reached out and patted his hand. "Yes, only don't speak too loudly. Do you mind if I keep my eyes closed?"

He shook his head in quite a childlike gesture. Leandra smiled at the thought then closed her eyes after even that tiny movement sent a dull hammer blow through her brain.

Derringer realized for the first time that her spectacles were lying on the table beside the bed. He almost grinned when he recalled asking her if she slept in them.

Then he hesitated. Where should he start? Should he tell her the reason for his going to France or tell her why he felt the need to go in the first place?

The silence lengthened. Leandra opened her eyes, fixing them on his with deep sympathy darkening them to an emerald green. "Tell me about your cousin Gabriel, Hart."

"How did you know?"

She gave an infinitesimal shrug of her delicate shoulders, a tiny smile curving her lips. "Your comment at dinner combined with the excursions to France and Martin's information about Gabriel's supposed death."

"Oh."

"Tell me, Hart," she implored him. Her eyes slid shut again after he nodded briefly.

The duke took a deep breath, leaned back against the bedpost and began. "Gabriel St. Clair is Martin's younger brother but he looks just like me. We almost share a birthday. As children we were more than just cousins; we were best friends. We should have been brothers, how close we knew each other's minds.

"It was with Gabe that I learned to ride, hunt, fence, box, and shoot. It was our spy games that gave us the ability to read in a look or gesture far more than a person is willing to convey. When Gabe decided he wanted to fight Boney, I bought him a commission since his father refused.

"I have spent the past five years searching for Gabriel. He went to fight Napoleon in 1812 and disappeared in Waterloo three years later. Everyone believes he is dead but I have received word that he is alive and in France. I was there recently to get him but then I saw Harwood and D'Arcy and thought it would be best to come home and see if you were all right."

Leandra's eyes fluttered open. "Where did you see them?" she asked with a slight frown.

"In a hedge tavern in Dunkirk. Why?"

Her eyes widened ever so slightly. "A hedge tavern? Why on earth would Lee be in a hedge tavern? He avoids taverns and bars like the plague. In fact, he claims drink is the devil's brew."

"Indeed," murmured the duke thoughtfully. "Now I have even more reason to suspect his activities in France."

"You said you came back to make sure I was all right," she reminded him softly. "Why?"

The duke shifted, uncomfortable with his own concern. "It struck me as odd that your brother was in France. It made me feel guilty for leaving you right after we married," he admitted.

"You felt guilty for leaving me? You have no reason to feel that way, Hart," she told him gently. "We married under odd circumstances; our hearts were not involved. I never expected anything more from you than your name and a place to live. Your magnanimity in allowing me free reign in your home and a veritable blank cheque for refurbishing the castle and myself truly touched me."

"It was the least I could do considering that without you there'd be no money," he commented unwisely. He realized too late that it was probably a subject best laid to rest.

She was unable to mask the hurt in her eyes quickly enough to avoid his sharp gaze. He blinked, offering no apology.

"It was still generous of you," she insisted in spite of the hurt. "And I am well taken care of here. Martin is ever helpful and now that Michaella is here I am quite content. If I could only convince my stepmother to depart and leave Michaella here, all will be as it should be."

He did not like the mention of Martin at all. It annoyed him so much, in fact, that her impolite jab at her family— an action under normal circumstances he'd have found terribly funny—amused him not at all. There had always been something faintly suspicious in the way Martin was quick to ingratiate himself with everyone who possessed a title or money. And Derringer was ever suspicious of those who felt the need to curry the favor of those in a higher station. Perhaps that was the reason he had always gone out of his way to make his disgust with Society known.

He refused to admit even to himself that he was jealous of his cousin. Just because Martin was the opposite of himself and probably very lovable did not mean Leandra might fall in love with him. But could she actually fall in love with himself? Did he care? If she fell in love with anyone Martin would be the obvious choice. Why did he care?

"Why did your father require your marriage?"

Derringer started, completely shocked by her query and unsure how to answer. Why did his father feel the need for such a codicil, especially since the son involved was a mere child at the time?

"I don't know," Derringer admitted to his wife, his fingers curling into a fist in his lap. "I knew he hated me, suspected it always, even as a child. But to limit my control over my inheritance, I—I don't know."

Leandra shook her head. "It is unbelievable. My father loved me, raised me as one of his legitimate children. But your father— His own son and heir— It is simply too Gothic for words."

Her eyes sparkled with tears, a reaction Derringer hadn't expected. He wasn't naïve enough to believe she loved him. Could she care for him after so little acquaintance?

"Where is Gabe now?" Leandra asked, breaking into his thoughts. She pressed her hand to her head and winced, her eyes sliding shut once more.

Derringer leaned toward her, all his internal ponderings of just moments before fleeing in the face of her discomfort. "Are you quite certain you wish to talk now? You seem to be in some considerable pain."

"It will pass, I assure you."

He sat back again, frowning despite her reassurance. "If you say so."

Her lips twitched. "I say so."

"Very well." He took a moment to gather his thoughts, calm his emotions, stifle his sudden urge to flee the room and this woman. "I met a man who was able to tell me that Gabe resides in a town about one hundred miles southeast of Dunkirk. I will probably be gone for several days possibly more than a sennight depending upon the weather and Gabe's health."

"And so you will leave tonight."

"Yes. And I am taking your new footman, Thomas, with me."

Her eyes popped open. "Whatever for?"

The duke shrugged one black-clad shoulder. "He wants to learn to sail."

"But he has only one eye!"

"As any proper sailor should," snorted Derringer.

A giggle escaped Leandra. "Yes, I suppose you are correct. How silly of me to think he would be at a disadvantage."

"Not silly," Derringer told her gruffly. "Caring. You seem to care about everyone and everything you meet. I don't know how you do it."

"Yes you do, Hart. You care, too, or you would not even consider taking a boy with you on such an important journey. If you did not care about his dreams you would order him to stay home." Her eyes flashed. "If you did not care, Hartley St. Clair, you would have dismissed every lame servant I hired in your absence." Her body tensed, shoulders straightening as she leaned closer. "If you didn't care, you would never have looked at me twice in Maidstone. You would have left me to fend for myself. So do not try to tell me that you do not care, sir."

"Calm yourself, Merri," the duke murmured. "Do not distress yourself over something you cannot control. I am heartless like they say. Everything I do has some benefit to me. I do nothing from altruistic motives."

The duchess closed her eyes again and whispered, "Say what you will, your grace. I will never believe you are heartless."

"He did what?" Martin exploded.

Leandra took a cautious step back. "He sailed to France to get your brother." She stared at him in consternation. "I thought you would be pleased."

"Oh, I am," he quickly assured her. "I was just surprised, is all."

Leandra cocked her head to one side, not entirely convinced of his claim but finding it very difficult to believe anything untoward of Martin St. Clair.

Dismissing her suspicions with a flick of her hand, she added, "He should return with him in a week or so. Meanwhile, I wished to speak to you because I have decided to hold a small house party."

"You have?"

Leandra crossed her arms over her chest at his disbelieving tone. "Yes, I have. I want to invite Lord and Lady Greville to stay for a few weeks. My family is already here and have made no imminent plans for departure. I may as well invite someone I can actually like." She looked away from her husband's cousin. "I hope," she added under her breath.

The look Martin gave her then made her want to step back again but she held her ground and lifted her chin a fraction. Her wide eyes glittered gold behind her spectacles. She wasn't about to bow before the duke's secretary. He was there to help her, not rule her.

"Is there something you wish to say to me, Mr. St. Clair?"

"No, your grace," he replied with the slightest emphasis on her title. His blue eyes glinted like chips of ice for the barest moment before they became the usual soft blue. His face eased into his normal placid expression.

Leandra wondered what he was thinking but decided she'd rather not know. The unnerving look in his eyes vanished so quickly she was unsure of its existence. So she brushed it aside as her overactive imagination. When had Martin—kind, gentle, sweet tempered Martin—ever given her cause for worry?

"When would you like this invitation to go out?" he asked.

"Immediately, please, Martin."

Leandra knew that the invitation went out that very afternoon. Liza informed her that Billy, one of the new grooms in the stable, was sent personal to deliver it to Warwickshire. Leandra was pleased and settled herself to wait for her guests to arrive.

Her time was divided between her duties as hostess to her still present family and her duties as mistress of Derringer Crescent. The former was a strain on her emotions and her patience and the latter was just time-consuming. But she threw herself into them just as if she relished every second of it.

Two days after the duke's departure, three more guests arrived in the form of Martin's mother, sister, and brother-in-law, along with three nephews. The boys were sent to the nursery to play with Leandra's nieces and nephews and the ladies were shown into the drawing room where Lady Harwood and Lady Schuster were chatting and the gentleman went off with Martin. Leandra joined the ladies in the drawing room the same time as the Dowager Lady Harwood and Lady Michaella.

"Oh, Merri, have you met Lady St. Clair? She is quite as frightening as mama," whispered Michaella.

"No, is she?" Leandra asked with a twinkle. "I have had much experience dealing with your mama, my dear. I have little doubt how to handle Hart's aunt." *I hope the Grevilles arrive soon,* she thought as she led the way into the room.

"What has happened to the paintings that were in here?" demanded Lady St. Clair haughtily.

"I had them removed," Leandra murmured as she sat on a striped sofa with Michaella.

She studied her new family members. Derringer's aunt was nearly as wide as she was short with fat gray curls all over her head in a style much more suited to a young girl. Her white muslin gown sported a gold key pattern, high-waisted but thankfully high-necked as well. She sat up straight in her chair and glared about her with the air of a... well, duchess, casting disapproving looks at all those around her.

Her daughter, Lady Kathryn, was the opposite of her mother. She had masses of dark hair with a shy, barely expressive countenance. Her height was closer to that of her brother and Leandra decided that the late Lord St. Clair must have been quite as tall as Derringer. She sat beside her mother, hands clenched tightly in her lap. Leandra realized the young lady was nervous and uncomfortable.

"*Why* did you remove them?" Lady St. Clair demanded with a pointed look at Leandra as if to imply that she had no business removing anything from the castle walls.

"I didn't like them," Leandra replied evenly. "They were crude and barbaric and I found I had not the stomach for them."

"A real duchess would never think so," sniffed the lady.

"A real lady would never make such a rude comment," retorted Lady Michaella, in a rare show of spirit.

Leandra patted her sister on the arm and barely shook her head. "It is all right, my dear," she soothed. "Lady St. Clair is entitled to her opinion. This was her home, after all, until Hart was old enough to say otherwise."

"You are a fortune-hunting upstart, young lady," declared Lady St. Clair. Lady Kathryn gasped slightly and muttered something that no one could understand.

Leandra stared at her husband's aunt for a full ten seconds, trying very hard to stifle her rising laughter. But she failed. She couldn't help it. The idea that she was a fortune hunter when it was Derringer who'd had to marry to get his fortune was just too ironic for words. And she had not even known until the deed was done!

Everyone stared at her as if she'd lost her mind. Perhaps she had. She was married to a man that she'd not seen more than a few days at best and was forced to entertain his family along with hers and none of them liked her much at all. What was the world coming to?

"What is this world coming to when a duke marries a little nobody and then welcomes her upstart family to visit as well?"

"Mama, please," protested Lady Kathryn.

The fat old lady turned a glare on her daughter. "Please, what, Kathryn? I will not oblige this bunch of mushrooms by pretending that they are welcome. They are not."

"Well, I never!" declared Leandra's stepmother. "You, madam, are the mushroom. I am the Dowager Countess of Harwood."

"And I am the Countess of Harwood," that young lady told them all proudly.

"I don't care who you are," retorted Lady St. Clair. "I am Derringer's beloved aunt and that has more power than any twenty titles."

"Ladies, if we could have some calm, it would be much appreciated," inserted Leandra quickly before her stepmother could say another word.

There came a scratch on the door that silenced the ladies more effectively than anything Leandra could have said. "Enter."

Stark opened the door with such a pained expression on his old face that Leandra stood to ask if he was well. He nodded and swallowed hard. "Your grace, there is a... person... here, requesting entrance."

"Who is this person, Stark?" Lady St. Clair demanded imperiously, just as if she were still the mistress of the house.

"It is not your place to ask," snapped the dowager. "It is Merri's."

So nonplussed by this about-face on the part of her stepmother, Leandra did not ask the butler who the visitor was. She stared at the dowager until that lady demanded imperiously, "What ails you, child?"

"Who is this person, Stark?" asked Michaella in her soothing tones.

The butler bowed to Lady Michaella but his words were directed at Leandra. "Her name is Nicolette and she says that his grace is expecting her, your grace."

"Nicolette? My lord has never mentioned her."

Stark grew noticeably red while his mouth opened and closed several times. Dawning light flashed through Leandra's brain and she fought the sudden anger and dismay that welled up within her.

She stalked over to the embarrassed old man and whispered. "She is his mistress, is she not?"

"That is what I am given to understand, your grace."

What was the world coming to? Family converged on her, her husband's mistress dropped in for all the world like she was welcome, and no one seemed able to find their manners.

Leandra smiled brightly though her eyes glittered dangerously behind her spectacles. "Have her shown into the Egyptian Saloon, Stark. I shall be with her presently."

13

It should have been much easier to locate him, Derringer fumed as he exited yet another tavern as yet empty-handed. His cousin had proven impossible to run to ground and Derringer was sure the man was not trying to avoid him. Why the devil would he want to?

The duke swung up onto his horse's back—Lord, how he hated rented nags!—and turned the dark beast to the next tavern he'd been told to search. It proved to be even more rundown than the last. Derringer cursed. Of all the devilish luck. How good were the chances he'd locate his quarry here?

Very good, unbeknownst to Derringer. He entered the tavern, strode to the bar, and casually inquired after a man known as the Dark Devil. When he had first heard that Gabe had been given an appellation that better applied to himself, Derringer had laughed. Whoever would have thought his cousin would bear such a name?

The very large man wiped holes in the bar before him, angry lines marring his wide forehead. He grabbed up a dirty glass, polishing it with the rag, eyeing the duke with no little amount of distrust. "Who be askin'?" he growled in guttural French.

"Heartless," replied Derringer with nary a blink to betray the very real nervousness the barkeep instilled in him.

The man's eyes narrowed. Not much; most observers wouldn't have noticed, but Derringer did. His mind went on the alert. He leaned against the bar with apparent negligence although his every muscle was tensing for a brawl. His eyes scanned the taproom while never fully leaving the man behind the bar.

"'Eartless, ye say? I'll be seein' if 'is lor'ship be willin' te see ye." The man stalked around the bar and disappeared into a dark corridor to his left.

His Lordship?

Derringer passed a casual glance over the few men spread around the tables, relieved they appeared to be paying him not the least attention. He moved as casually as possible in the direction the barkeep had taken but stopped short when the little hairs at the back of his neck prickled alarmingly. Someone watched him.

Derringer leaned against the bar again and wondered aloud if he should have ordered a drink before requesting to see the man. A short man of indeterminate years and foul breath answered his question.

"Ooo do ye be to think 'is lor'ship'll see ye?" he demanded.

Derringer smiled at the man. His smile contained no mirth, no hilarity, just dark intent. The scraggly little man beside him sidled a bit to the right until he was just out of Derringer's reach.

"Well, who be ye?" the man repeated.

Derringer wondered exactly how well known he was in this country. The barkeep had seemed to know him. He was sure D'Arcy had had something to say after their little tussle. But how many of these men were friends of the demented little Frenchman and how many were foes?

"Heartless," he told the man. He watched as yet another man's eyes widened and fear took the place of dumb insolence. He stuttered something incomprehensible. Though Derringer possessed an extensive knowledge of French, even to the point of understanding the guttural dialects without actually being able to speak them quite so well, he could not decipher the man's ramblings. The sound of the man's voice aroused the rest of the men in the pub and they rose as one and left the building with many furtive glances over their shoulders.

Derringer scratched his head. What had been said about him to cause such unparalleled fear in a roomful of grown men? Much of his reputation was of his own making and quite disturbing, true, but the fear shown this day made no sense.

Perhaps he stood out as a man of wealth and title? No, he couldn't possibly. He glanced down at his worn and tattered black clothing and decided that he very well looked like a dangerous man. Who would want to tangle with a man who dressed completely in black, as if he were in constant mourning?

Very few, the duke knew from experience. D'Arcy had been one. He suspected Harwood might be another.

The thought of Harwood recalled expressive hazel eyes to his mind's eye. He wondered how his Merri was handling her family all by herself again. Probably much better than he would, he thought ruefully. He didn't know what had come over him, but the need to play with those women's minds had been too tempting to resist. And he had gotten much out of it, he thought, remembering his wife's response to his later question. Now he just wanted to fetch Gabriel, return home, and take Leandra to bed.

"This way," the barkeep muttered hoarsely, returning to the taproom about fifteen minutes after having departed it.

Derringer lifted a black brow at the man. He sounded as if he'd been in a chokehold for several minutes. Fifteen, perhaps?

Shoving his hands nonchalantly into his trouser pockets, Derringer sauntered in after the huge man. If the man got it into his head to turn around and thrash him, Derringer would barely stand a chance. Barely.

With a mental shrug, the duke contemplated how long it would take to actually subdue a man who was nearly of a size with Tiny Boy, his giant of a friend who sometimes acted as his bodyguard. He'd managed the feat a time or two in scuffles with Tiny. A few well-placed hits to his neck and temple would do the trick.

He followed the man down a dimly lit corridor until it ended at a door. He had not noticed any doors along the way and he wondered why. The door opened to reveal a room of startling cleanliness and bright colors. He almost squinted in the glare of several oil lamps and gaslights. Was the room a separate building he'd failed to notice?

"Sit down, Heartless," commanded a voice from the one shadowed corner of the room. "I have been waiting for you."

Nerves jumping at the threat he heard in the voice, Derringer moved cautiously into the room. He was pointed to a chair that sat a few feet away from the shadowed speaker. He felt at a distinct disadvantage and his every instinct was telling him to flee. Despite the urge, he knew any attempt would be swiftly quashed by the barkeep who lingered behind him.

So he sat instead, after flipping the hard wooden chair around and straddling it. He leaned his arms across the back, his gaze insolent.

"Leave, John," the shadow voice ordered.

John? The barkeep grunted and left the room. Derringer was sure the man was French. Why John?

"Goodbye, Helene," the voice said next. A willowy redhead rose from her place next to the man in the shadows and made her way out of the room. Derringer watched her leave, watched as she passed him, avarice and cunning shining from her dark green eyes. As quickly as she disappeared into the corridor beyond, Derringer's thoughts moved from her back to the man in the shadows.

The only ones left in the chamber, besides the shadow man himself, were two men of average height and what appeared to be average intelligence. Derringer was too smart to underestimate them, however, since he could see quite clearly—or discern through practice and firsthand knowledge of low types—that each man had two pistols, five knives, and a pair of brass knuckles on him. He remained cautiously silent and waited for their master to make his next move.

"What did you have to say to me?" he asked in a voice that Derringer now recognized was disguised somehow. And the man was English although he spoke fluent French. The duke was willing to bet his life on it.

"I know who you are," Derringer replied in a voice devoid of emotion or inflection. While his instincts screamed that he knew exactly who this mysterious man was, part of him, a small part, remained unsure.

Silence stretched. Derringer listened to the rustling of the man he couldn't see and heard the mutterings of the men who were obviously guards of some sort. He caught a few words he was probably not meant to hear and his lips curled into a sardonic grin.

"I mean you no harm, as I am sure you know, my lord Saint."

There was a murmur from the shadows, a grunt from the guards, who then left the room, surprising Derringer to no small degree.

"Just who do you think me to be?"

Derringer chuckled low in his throat, leaning back slightly, any doubt as to this man's identity fading. "Like myself, you are probably whoever you need to be when the moment calls for it. Ragpicker. Servant. Shopkeep. Villain. Aristocrat." The duke paused, a smile tugging at his lips. "Although, I am quite sure those last two may be one and the same."

A short laugh came from the other man. "You are as heartless as they say, your grace."

Derringer slowly stood, setting the chair from him. "At times, cousin, I am the Black Prince himself."

14

THE woman was everything that Leandra was not: tall, blond, voluptuous, confident, and absolutely beautiful. But she was also boorish, uncouth, and gowned in scarlet satin like the whore she was. This was the kind of woman he preferred? Then why would he want to bed his drab little wife? Leandra didn't know what to think.

"What do you want?" Leandra asked in her best duchess tones.

Nicolette was momentarily taken aback, shock flashing in her arresting blue eyes. But she rallied quickly, drawing herself up to her full height, so as to look down her nose at Leandra. "Hart is expecting me."

"No, he is not," Leandra insisted mildly, though she couldn't be positive of her own claim. She did not offer her unwanted guest a seat or refreshment. She wanted this woman gone. Then she would murder her husband as soon as he returned.

"Who are you?" Nicolette asked with a slight narrowing of her baby blue eyes.

"I am the Duchess of Derringer."

Those baby blue orbs widened at this statement and Leandra almost laughed. "Who did you expect me to be?" she asked in genuine curiosity.

"When did Hart marry?" the woman asked instead. "He never told me."

"I expect he didn't," Leandra replied evenly. "Would a gentleman tell his mistress such a thing, do you think? I have little knowledge of such matters."

"He should have told me," the beauty insisted.

Leandra wearied of the game. "Please leave," she told her guest coldly. "I need no more unwelcome guests."

"I can't leave. My carriage has broken an axle and I can't go anywhere."

"Hart is a dead man," Leandra muttered to herself. "Very well, Miss... Nicolette. You may stay until your carriage is repaired. But you will not be able to join my guests, I am sorry to say. You must understand that their sensibilities must be taken into consideration."

"Well, I never," blustered the woman.

"Well, maybe you should," retorted Leandra irritably as she exited the room.

She met Stark on the stairs, rage simmering just beneath the surface. "Show that woman to a room and have her carriage repaired as speedily as possible. I do not want her here when my lord returns."

"Very good, your grace."

She felt threatened. For the first time in her life, Leandra Harcourt-Derringer felt threatened. And she was mad as hornets at the man she'd married. She didn't know why his mistress was in the house and she didn't know why she felt so threatened by the woman. Surely, her husband could not prefer that uncouth woman to herself?

But he could. He very well could. With a mistress, he knew exactly where he stood. She existed for his pleasure and nothing more. With a wife he met stranded at an inn and married a few hours later, he was on shaky ground. Even though she'd agreed to be his wife in truth, she couldn't know if that would satisfy him. And after meeting a woman of his own choosing, she was sure he would be displeased with his bride. Leandra didn't know what to do. All she knew was that she didn't want to care about any of it.

Her family was no help, of course. Derringer's family even less so. When Leandra told Martin of Nicolette's presence in the castle, he had gotten such a strange look on his face that Leandra had begun to fear for his health. Then he was once again the cool, reserved Martin with nary a suggestion to help rid the Crescent of the harpy's presence. Leandra was at *point non plus*.

As if her day could possibly get any worse, the Earl of Harwood arrived. He gave her that look that she had always mistrusted, the one that made her shiver because it was almost predatory, almost…lecherous. She invited him into the drawing room and offered him tea, both of which he accepted with the charm for which he was known. She hated it. She hated him. And she hated that she felt that way about another human being.

His wife seemed pleased to see him, making Leandra smile. Everyone knew that the couple hated each other and a few were well aware that Lady Harwood had threatened her husband's life if he ever came near her bed again.

Leandra sought comfort with her sister Michaella. She reveled in their pointless conversation and endless reminisces about their father. Michaella was her anchor during turbulent times.

And Christmas was approaching. Leandra knew that these people would try to extend their stay until the holidays. She had no idea if this would please her husband or not. All she could do was await his return so she could lay the problem at his feet.

Then she would murder him.

Leandra offered a tight smile in reply to one of Harwood's offhand compliments. Then she concentrated all of her energy on not killing Lady St. Clair. That woman still criticized her as though Leandra had no right to make any of the changes she had made to the castle. Indeed, she acted as though Leandra had no right to be the duchess.

And she was probably right, Leandra sighed.

"Is there something wrong, Merri?" Michaella asked, her fingers curling over Leandra's arm.

Leandra forced her stiff lips into something resembling a smile. "No, dearest, I was thinking is all."

"About how much you'd like to see the backs of us," Michaella joked, releasing her grip on her arm.

That made Leandra laugh. "Some of you, perhaps, but never you, my dearest sister."

Michaella embraced her warmly. How interesting, Leandra mused, that she could be surrounded by people, family no less, and yet feel so alone. Thank God for sweet Michaella!

Relief shot through Leandra when the clock on the mantle struck the hour of five. It was time to dress for dinner and though she longed to tell Mrs. Stark that she would dine in her room, she knew she could not. It would be most impolite of her to do so.

The guests reluctantly withdrew from the drawing room to ascend to their individual chambers. Leandra parted company with Michaella on the third floor after giving her a hug and assuring her that she would always be welcome at the Crescent.

Another day of endless family bickering and another day of endless annoyance. Leandra was sure she'd lose her mind soon if she hadn't already. Perhaps she could already lay claim to the title of lunatic, believing all this time that she was perfectly sane. Or she truly was sane, living in an insane situation. It was a conundrum on which she tried not to dwell.

She managed to escape for an hour or so in the afternoon to sit in her little morning room and read or sew or just stare out at the bare garden beyond the window and think. She tried not to think but it was inevitably what she did. And her thoughts always led to her absent husband.

At least they had managed to get Nicolette to leave. She had been a particular thorn in Leandra's side. After the servants had pleaded with the woman for the better part of an hour, the duke's mistress had finally been ejected by two of the footmen. Leandra cringed to remember that scene and hated to know what her husband would think when he returned, but it could not be helped now.

The wind outside blew and Leandra watched a bit of dead grass breeze by the window. She stared at it for a moment and then switched her attention to the new statue that had been erected in the center of the garden. It was Aphrodite, the Greek goddess of love.

She was surrounded by beauty, Leandra mused, a touch of dismal self-pity swirling through her mind. Her sisters and her husband's cousins all boasted the trait, a trait Leandra had never envied until that moment.

Leandra shook her head fiercely. *Stop it! It doesn't matter. You will never be beautiful and you have lived nearly twenty-one years without it, why do you need it now?*

Giving her head a little nod of agreement, Leandra ceased staring out the window and tried to concentrate on her book. Normally, Miss Austen could hold her attention through anything. But *Persuasion* was not going to do it today, she realized after she'd read the same sentence four times without the least idea of what she'd read.

Giving up on Miss Austen's work, Leandra reached for another book. *Ivanhoe*. Perhaps this story would capture her interest and stop her thinking such unworthy thoughts. Why did Walter Scott not just step forward and claim the work as his own? Everyone knew it was he who wrote the novel.

A knock sounded on the door. Leandra called for the person to enter, thinking it was Michaella, who sometimes sought her out in her sanctuary to chat and, most likely, to avoid the family as well.

It was not Michaella, however. Stark opened the door with something approaching a smile on his lined countenance.

"What is it?" she asked.

With a bow, Stark announced, "The Earl and Countess of Greville have arrived, your grace."

Her delicately arched eyebrows rose. "You did not put them in the drawing room?" she asked the butler, a slight tremor of fear coloring her tone.

"I did not, your grace. Would you like me to show them in here?"

"Yes, Stark, please do."

Leandra rose to her feet and waited for her invited guests to put in their appearance. It would be the first time, other than Michaella, that she would allow anyone in her sanctuary. And this was on blind faith.

She had no idea what these people were like. She only knew her husband called them friends. And when he mentioned Lady Greville, admiration was clear in his voice.

The lady entered first, not dressed in the latest fashion but fashionably dressed nonetheless. Blond curls were swept up into a becoming style, giving her the look of a sprite, beautiful, ethereal, and as small in stature as Leandra. She carried a little boy with dark hair and blue eyes, while nudging a little girl ahead of her into the room. The little girl was the very image of her mother with glorious blond curls and great big blue eyes. Except her mother's eyes were the most extraordinary shade of turquoise.

Lord Greville, quite simply, was huge. He wasn't as tall as Derringer, Leandra could tell that right away, but his arms and legs were as big as tree trunks. Her eyes widened as he turned ever so slightly to fit through the door.

"Who is she?" whispered the little girl. She glanced at her father and reached up. The earl swung her up into his arms.

He smiled at Leandra and extended his free hand. "I am Greville. My wife, Aurora. You, I assume, are Hart's new, unannounced, bride?"

Leandra shook her head slightly to break herself from the stupor their appearance had caused and approached her guests, accepting the hand he held out. "I am sorry Hart did not inform you of our marriage. It was... unexpected," she admitted, not entirely sure why she did so. "It is a pleasure to meet you. Please call me Leandra. I know Hart would prefer it, as would I."

Greville smiled a boyishly charming smile and nodded. "Then I am Levi. This mischievous little cherub is Rhiannon." The child in his arms giggled and bestowed a smacking kiss on his cheek.

Aurora smiled at them and introduced their small son.

A pang of longing struck Leandra near her heart. "You have such beautiful children."

The look shared between the married couple caused an embarrassed tremor to course through Leandra's slight frame. It was apparent they'd heard the catch in her voice and wondered at it.

"Spend more than a few minutes with them and you just might change your mind," the earl replied dryly.

"I am sure these two are wonderful for hours at a time," Leandra said with some feeling. She was able to tell just by looking at them that they were not like the spoiled miscreants she called niece or nephew.

Aurora grinned, her maternal pride very apparent. "You must call me Rory. I have a feeling we are to be very good friends."

Leandra studied the young woman. Her eyes narrowed. She wanted to question her about calling the duke *Lord Heartless*, but Aurora asked if there was somewhere that they could put the children.

"Oh, yes, forgive me." She walked to the door, pulled it open, and smiled at Jem, the first footman. He was an oddity with his missing arm, but had proven vastly efficient in his duties. "Jem, can you escort the children to the nursery, please? Tell Martha and Meg to keep an eye on the others to be sure no one is mistreated. And have Mrs. Stark bring the tea tray."

"Others?" inquired Aurora as she relinquished her hold of the children to the footman and a young maid who arrived to lend him aid with the baby.

Leandra turned and favored her with a bright smile. "Yes. My family is here with my nieces and nephews and Hart's aunt and cousin arrived with his three little cousins. We have quite a full house at the moment."

Aurora's remarkable eyes widened. "Is Hart here?"

"He is not. He is in France at the moment."

Greville's eyes almost popped from his head at this, but he said nothing.

"Please sit," Leandra offered with a gesture toward the sofa. "I have ordered a tea tray but if you would rather rest before dinner, that can be arranged."

"Tea sounds lovely," Lady Greville smiled.

The duchess sat in a chair opposite the little sofa where the Grevilles perched. She eyed Aurora Greville for a moment, her hands twisting in her lap. Aurora threw a confused look at her husband, who shrugged and returned his dark brown eyes to their hostess.

Leandra opened her mouth, then closed it again. She sighed and then blurted, "I don't quite know how else to ask you this, Lady Greville, but I have to know. And I have found that it is usually easiest, if not always best, to come right out and say it, though that's hardly polite." Leandra took a deep breath. "Why did you call my husband *Lord Heartless*?"

Aurora laughed. She couldn't help it. It was the last thing she expected to hear. She saw the look of anger start in her hostess's face and quickly apologized. "I am sorry, Leandra, but you have to understand that I had very nearly forgotten that incident. It was over two years ago, you see, and I am so used to being asked other, more... personal questions that I had not even anticipated that it would not be the same here. And I had not thought that Hart even remembered that. Why he would tell you of it, I can't begin to guess."

"He didn't exactly volunteer the information. We were discussing what I was to call him and he suggested I call him *Lord Heartless* since that was what everybody called him. He told me that you were the only one who ever called him that to his face."

"And so I did," nodded Aurora. "I regret that I did, although at the time, I believed it."

"But what did he do to make you think that? I know Hart very little and I want to understand why he is so accepting of such an appellation."

She knew him very little? Aurora looked at her husband and he gazed back with the same confused expression. As one, their eyes returned to Leandra.

Aurora leaned close, squeezing Leandra's hand. "I will explain the situation and then I think, my dear, that you should tell us your story. Perhaps we can help."

15

D ERRINGER returned to his yacht's cabin where he had placed his insensate relative and sat down on a hard chair to think. Gabriel had changed drastically. He was missing an arm, for one thing, but even worse, he seemed to be in some sort of trouble. Derringer had not the least idea what that trouble might be but Gabriel had muttered something about D'Arcy right before he lost consciousness.

Why he fainted was yet another mystery. Gabriel did look a good bit thinner than he had when he had first departed England to fight Napoleon. What had happened in the eight years since Gabriel had left? And a better question, what had happened in the five years since he had disappeared?

"Hart."

The duke shot out of his seat at the whispered word and crouched next to his bunk. "I'm here, Gabe. What is it?"

Gabriel St. Clair grimaced slightly. "Where the devil are we?" he asked hoarsely. "And why does my head hurt?"

"I imagine your head hurts because you struck it when you fainted. As to where we are, we are aboard *The Merry*

Belle. We will be home soon. Don't try to speak." He gently lifted his cousin and held a glass of water to his lips.

Gabriel swallowed the clear liquid, sputtered a bit, then complained, "Haven't you anything stronger, Hart?"

Chuckling softly, Derringer rose to fetch a brandy decanter from a locked cupboard on one wall. He removed two glasses and filled them both, then returned to the bed, unaffected by the slight rise and fall of the floor beneath his feet.

"Here," he said as he handed Gabriel one glass and, pulling the chair closer to the bunk, sat down with the other.

"Much better," Gabriel sighed as he sipped at the brandy. He gazed up at his cousin. "How did you find me?"

Derringer shrugged. "Never stopped looking. Everyone thought me mad, I know, but something told me you were not dead. Something here," he told him as he dramatically struck his breast. A self-deprecating smile fluttered on his lips. "A trifle melodramatic, I admit, but true nonetheless."

"I know what you mean, Hart," Gabriel admitted. He shifted on the bed, a faint groan rising to his throat. "Though I wondered time and time again if each day would be my last, I knew you would appear eventually."

"And when you learned it was me, you behaved as though I were your enemy. Why?"

Gabriel shrugged. "I trust no one since Waterloo."

It was said with such finality that Derringer wondered at it. "What happened at Waterloo?" He settled back in his hard chair, expecting quite a tale of derring-do. He was more than surprised by his cousin's response.

"Someone tried to kill me."

Derringer snorted a laugh. He couldn't help it. "You were in a war, Gabe. Many men were trying to kill you."

"No, someone was trying to kill me and it wasn't a Frog."

That made Derringer pause. Someone was trying to kill him? It was something Derringer knew all to well.

"Explain."

"It wasn't just the French, Hart. One of my own men attacked me. Had I been a more disagreeable fellow—like you—I'd have not thought much of it. But me? Who would want to kill me?"

Derringer had nothing to say. His cousin may have sounded a mite conceited but it was nothing but truth. No one would want him dead... unless they were French.

"I didn't know who to trust."

"Thus, you distrusted me?"

"I'm sorry."

Derringer chuckled, waving a hand at Gabriel. "Don't be. I wouldn't trust anyone either."

Silence fell. Derringer watched his cousin, saw him wince when he moved his missing arm, and wondered at his fidgety movements. It all became clear when Gabriel continued.

"How is Martin? And Mama?"

The duke leaned back in his chair. "Martin is well and working as my secretary. Your mother is well as far as I know. I haven't seen her since you disappeared. Kathryn is lovely, married, and has three boys. I wrote to you about the oldest. She's had two more since then."

"And you, Hart? How are you?"

"I am married," Derringer told him reluctantly.

Gabriel tried to sit up and get a better look at his cousin. "You...you are married?"

"I had to according to the old duke's will. I was told seven days before my birthday that I had to marry before I was thirty. I saw Merri at an inn in Maidstone and asked her to marry me. She really had no choice. She was on her own because her father died and she had no money and no prospects."

"You married a girl you happened to meet just to get your inheritance?"

"I... uh, yes. I suppose I did."

Gabriel regarded him from wide blue eyes that revealed nothing of his thoughts. "How could you?" he finally stated after what seemed like an eternity.

Derringer stood and paced the confines of the tiny cabin. He shoved one hand through his loose hair, a sigh dragging from his chest. He stopped, placed his hands on his hips, swung around, and sighed again.

"How couldn't I?" he finally retorted. "How could I just walk away and leave her there to fend for herself? How could I look into those glorious eyes of hers, see the laughter bubbling there, and just turn around and leave her? I couldn't do it. I denied any altruistic motives at the time but I did it more for her than for me."

"Dear God, Hart, you're in love with this girl," Gabriel accused with an awestruck expression.

"In love with her? No, I'm not, Gabe. I married her because I felt sorry for her. I do not love her."

"Would it be so wrong to love her?" Gabriel asked softly.

Derringer stared at him a moment. "Yes, Gabe, it would. You have not been there enough to notice, but everyone I care about, everyone that cares for me has been cursed with misfortunes of some kind." He held up his hand, ticking off his woes. "Mama died. Uncle David died. Old Sam lost his leg. You disappeared. Rhiannon was kidnapped. Rory was shot. Levi was plagued by worry over his family. Then, Rory almost died in childbirth."

"Unless you caused her pregnancy, I fail to see how that last has anything to do with you at all, Hart."

The duke grunted. "Perhaps not."

"Your mama's death was not your fault. Uncle David was a traitor to England no matter how much he cared about us. Old Sam was a drunk and bound to fall into trouble whether he knew you or not. I don't know who Rhiannon, Rory, and Levi are, but I'm sure you cannot be blamed for their woes. And you most certainly did not cause my disappearance."

A shake of his dark head revealed Derringer's disbelief of this claim. "I couldn't bear to think that Merri should suffer just because I care."

Gabriel wisely held his tongue. He just watched his cousin move around in obvious agitation and pondered the oddity of his childhood playmate falling in love with... his own wife. It was ludicrous.

"Tell me why you muttered D'Arcy's name when you realized it was me," commanded Derringer suddenly. He stopped pacing and stared down at Gabriel.

"Did I? I don't remember."

He was hiding something, Derringer was sure of it. "Come, Gabe, you've never been able to hide things from me. Tell me what's amiss."

Gabriel turned stubborn blue eyes on the duke. "It doesn't concern you, Hart. It is my problem."

"The devil it is! I have searched for you for five years. I think I have some right to get you out of whatever mess you've landed in."

"No, you don't. You're not my keeper, Hart. You're my cousin."

"Yes," snapped the duke, "I am your cousin. The same cousin who pulled you out of the briers on too many occasions to count. The same cousin who defended you more than once when your father tried to beat some sense into your thick skull. The same bloody cousin who sent you off to war and nearly got you killed in the process!"

Shock sucked the air from Gabriel's lungs. "You blame yourself, Hart? Because I enlisted?" The duke's self-conscious shrug was his only answer. "I was army-mad, Hart. I would have gone if I'd had to take the King's shilling to do it. You know that. There was never anyone closer to me than you. You know, Hart."

Derringer stood and went to the one porthole in the cabin. He stared out into the night at the myriad stars hanging in the heavens. He didn't want to talk about this. He didn't want to be free of the blame. Deep down, he knew he was responsible. He was responsible and no one else.

"You are not my keeper," Gabriel repeated emphatically. "I made my choice and now I must live with the consequences."

Derringer didn't turn around. "How did you lose your arm, Gabe?"

Gabriel glanced down at the missing appendage, then laid his head back and closed his eyes. "Waterloo," he said. "Shrapnel lodged in too many places to be easily removed.

Infection." He threw his remaining hand up with a flourish, intoning dramatically, "Goodbye, arm."

The hand he waved was, naturally, the one that held the thick brandy glass. Thankfully, it was empty. It did, however, fly from his hand to land with a thwack against the door of the cabin. Derringer jumped at the sound and swung around to see his cousin doubled over. He rushed over, fearing the worst, and was astonished to realize Gabriel was laughing.

"What the devil!" he exploded.

"I am s-sorry, H-Hart," sputtered Gabriel, holding his side with his one arm. "It w-was just s-so f-f-funny!" And he succumbed to another round of hearty laughter.

Derringer slumped into his chair and watched his cousin in amazement. How could he find the loss of his arm amusing?

Then Derringer felt his own lips twitch upward. He tried not to, but his own long-dormant sense of humor rose to the fore and he found himself giving in to his cousin's infectious laughter.

16

THE breakfast room at Derringer Crescent sat on the east side of the castle so as to catch the early morning rays of sunlight all year. That would have been the case, too, had not this particular autumn day started out overcast and blustery. But a cheery fire blazed in the hearth and thanks to the new mistress, none of the fireplaces smoked like they used to.

Leandra entered the room late that morning, a warm wool gown of dark green making her eyes sparkle like gems behind her spectacles. She surveyed the gathered company and pasted a determined smile on her face. She felt pretty, she felt confident, and she was determined not to let these people take that away from her.

Lord and Lady Greville had yet to make an appearance but Lord Harwood was present with his—for the benefit of the guests—adoring wife at his side. Lady Harwood sent a frosty smile Leandra's way. Leandra returned it with the poise that had on several occasions been her safeguard. Lady Kathryn and her husband extolled the virtues of their three boys to Lady St. Clair, who agreed with every word spoken, paying Leandra not the least attention.

The Dowager Lady Harwood greeted her stepdaughter with a regal nod designed to nettle that young woman but this tactic failed. Leandra crossed the room and smiled pleasantly at her, unflustered by her late father's wife. Her sister, Lady Schuster, ignored her completely much as she had done the entirety of Leandra's life—which bothered Leandra not at all.

Toast and a single egg made up Leandra's breakfast that morning. She returned to the table and seated herself beside Michaella.

"Good morning, Merri," her sister bubbled. "What are you planning to do today?"

Leandra absentmindedly smeared marmalade on her toast and considered the question. "I think I may spend some time in the nursery," she replied thoughtfully. She bit into her toast and grimaced. "I hate marmalade. Why ever did I put marmalade on my toast?"

"I wondered," Michaella admitted. "I was sure you had never liked the stuff but you seemed so intent when you prepared your toast that I thought perhaps you'd developed a fondness for it."

"No, I have not. Jem, will you take this and replace it with fresh, please? And fetch me a jar of strawberry jam." The one-armed footman bowed and departed to do his mistress's bidding.

Michaella watched him go with round amber eyes. "Do you not think it difficult for him, Merri, to be always running about, fetching and carrying? Why, earlier this morning I saw him polishing silver. He had to sit in a chair and hold the tea service with his knees. I was so amazed he had to ask me if I needed anything before I realized I was staring. I do hope I didn't make him uncomfortable."

Leandra shrugged indifferently but her hazel eyes glowed with anything but indifference. "He feels useful, Michaella. I did inquire as to whether he preferred a different position but he has always dreamed of being first footman. We try to treat him as if he has two hands."

"Oh, I see. It is a matter of pride, then."

Leandra smiled. "Precisely."

Michaella took a bite of her own toast, thoughtful wrinkles marring the perfect alabaster of her forehead. "This may seem insensitive, but would it not be easier to hire servants who are better able to perform their duties?"

"Of course it would, dearest. But that does not help those who are injured, those in need. Many of my outside servants were hurt in the war with Napoleon years ago and have been looking for work ever since. These men have families to care for and deserve the chance to do so. I cannot abide the sight of starving children just because Parliament is too busy deciding whether or not trousers are acceptable attire for gentlemen instead of trying to help all these poor men who fought bravely and were unfortunate enough to be injured. Thank you, Jem."

Jem bowed with a tiny smile on his face, having heard part of Lady Derringer's calmly uttered words. Although quite young, Jem was one of those injured at Waterloo and had four children and an ailing wife to care for.

"What were we discussing? Oh, yes, plans for today. What are you going to do?" queried Leandra as she spread the preferred strawberry jam on her fresh toast and took a hearty bite.

"I am not visiting the nursery, to be sure," Michaella decided. "I have not the least desire to be attacked by those savage nieces and nephews of ours and I don't think Mr. St. Clair's nephews are any better behaved."

"You are probably correct," sighed Leandra. "I want to make sure they are not mistreating the Greville children, however. The baby is only one year old, you know, and can hardly protect himself from the older children and little Rhiannon is so very mild and sweet I fear she will be overcome by their enthusiasm if not their outright villainy."

As if conjured by thoughts of their children, the earl and his wife entered the room and greeted the company at large. Greville had his arm around his wife's waist and murmured something in her ear that made her giggle and blush. She moved away from him and sat on Leandra's other side while he went to fetch them breakfast.

"Good morning, Merri," she said brightly. "Lady Michaella."

Michaella greeted the countess with a shy smile, then returned her attention to her breakfast.

"So when do you suppose Hart will return?" Aurora smiled up at her husband and accepted the plate he set in front of her. She buttered her toast as she waited for Leandra's response.

"He said a week, perhaps longer."

"And you are missing him dreadfully, I think," murmured Aurora for Leandra's ears only. It wasn't a question.

"In a way," she admitted. She caught a look of commiseration on Greville's face and smiled. "The truth is," she went on as her lips threatened to curve ever further upward, "I am anxious to murder him."

Silence greeted her words. It dawned on Leandra that her listeners did not share her joke. Greville's dark eyes studied her, brow furrowed, while his wife's expression revealed her shock and alarm.

"It was a sort of jest," she assured them hurriedly. "I don't actually want to murder him, it's just that…that…"

Aurora patted her hand. "Just what, dear?"

"I would very much like to ring a peal over his head if I can't actually strangle the man. His mistress arrived claiming he asked her to come here."

Aurora slapped a hand over her mouth to hold back a laugh and Greville chuckled before he turned his complete attention to his heaping plate.

"Oh, dear. That wasn't very well done of him, was it, my love?" Aurora asked her husband. She looked at Leandra. "Hart was ever one to follow his own path. It was very bad of him to invite her here, to be sure, but do not take it to heart."

"She didn't even know he had married," Leandra informed her. "And John Coachman thinks her carriage was tampered with. I thought it was odd at the time." She paused, frowning as she contemplated recent events. "She claimed that Hart invited her and yet she was surprised that he wasn't here. Then she claimed that her carriage axle was broken."

Greville's eyes twinkled merrily. "The little cat was lying. What was her name?"

"Nicolette," Michaella offered shyly into the conversation. "Stark said her name was Nicolette and she was demanding entrance. He seemed so very embarrassed by the whole situation and I determined that she was a... well, you know." She blushed at her own temerity, glanced at her mother to make sure she hadn't been overheard, then addressed herself to the remains of her toast.

Greville grinned. "Just so. Nicki has been a harpy for years. I wonder that Hart was able to put up with her unfaithfulness for so long."

"Is a mistress required to be faithful?" She knew it was not a proper subject, but at the moment, she didn't care.

"If she is the Duke of Derringer's mistress, yes," Greville told her simply.

Leandra made her way to the nursery having decided that she would at least peek in to make sure all was as it should be. The nursery lay tucked away on the fourth floor, occupying nearly the whole of the south wing. With several bedchambers, a schoolroom, and the actual nursery, it had seen the raising and education of at least two of the dukes of Derringer, as well as the rest of the St. Clair family.

Somehow Leandra had overlooked the entire fourth floor under the mistaken impression that the servants were housed there. She inquired of Stark whether or not the servants' quarters were satisfactory and having received an affirmative reply, she'd forgotten it.

Now, she was absurdly glad she'd done nothing to the nursery floor. Enchantment flooded her senses as she entered the schoolroom. Evidence of childish contentment lay scattered about the chamber, childish drawings and inexpert paintings on the walls, carvings in the desktops, and books stacked on the shelves of a huge oak bookcase.

Perusing the gold-inked titles on the spines revealed more than just children's tales. The more recent Miss Austen and Mr. Scott claimed space—an indication that someone was adding to this room even while no children occupied it—as well as common improving works like Mr. Porteous's sermons and *The Book of Common Prayer*. This room was clearly the preferred spot for the older children as well as the younger.

She continued to peruse the shelves, smiling at such titles as *Sir Jason and the Dragon*, *Lady Marigold's Wish*, and *Turning Frogs into Princes and Other Great Spells*.

This last made her laugh aloud. She removed it from the shelf and flipped through it. The contents made her laugh even more. To think someone had actually thought to entertain children with pretend spells and incantations. And she knew they were pretend because some of the spells called for ingredients such as the "tooth of a red fire-breathing dragon of immense size and considerable ferocity" and "seven hairs from a swallow-tailed man-eating carrot." A carrot?

Turning the page revealed a spell for changing little brothers into lizards. Written next to it in a childish scrawl were the words *must surely work for sisters and cousins too*. Which of the St. Clair boys had desired to turn one of his family members into a lizard?

Tucked in the back of the book was a folded sheet of vellum. Leandra set the book aside, foreboding sliding over her skin as she opened the sheet.

A little boy with coal-black hair stood over the body of a woman whose beauty was apparent even in such an amateur painting. The boy's face displayed his shock as he stared down at the pool of crimson beneath the woman's head. They were on a landing and Leandra, in dawning horror, recognized the landing, the second floor landing in the very castle she now called home. She recalled taxing the servants about a stain there. Blood. Could it be?

The drawing was dated 1796.

She felt prickles on the back of her neck as she stared at the picture. The previous duchess died that year. Only a few weeks in the castle had provided that bit of information to the new duchess, though the staff remained mum about how she died.

The child looked amazingly like Derringer.

It couldn't be true. Could it? Leandra stared at the vellum in her hand, studied the image minutely, searched her mind for every tiny thread of gossip she'd overheard, and shuddered at her own Gothic conclusions.

It wasn't possible, she told herself.

Leandra replaced the book on the shelf but held onto the drawing. Her own conclusions terrified her, casting her husband into a whole new light. She needed to keep the image with her, at least until she could shed some light on the mystery she'd fallen into.

The title of another book caught her eye. Or, rather, the lack of title caught her eye. A small, leather bound book peeked from between two larger books, all but hidden from view. Leandra herself would have missed it had she not been perusing the shelves so carefully. She removed it gently and turned it over in her hand. It appeared to be a journal of some sort. Whose, she wasn't sure. It was of medium thickness and looked to be fairly old.

Opening the front cover, the mystery of ownership was solved. The name "Penelope Marie Watts" was written in a careful copperplate and underneath the name it said "From her father on her tenth birthday, 23 December 1782." She flipped to the last entry in the journal and found it was dated 2 March 1785. The entry ended in such an abrupt manner that Leandra was convinced there was another journal somewhere. But where?

Her gaze ran over the shelves until it lit upon a spot on the third shelf from the very top. There appeared to be an empty space between two books. She scanned the room and her sparkling eyes fastened on one of the desks. With many grunts and several muttered curses, Leandra managed to drag the heavy desk over to the shelf.

"Damn," she grumbled as she stood on the desk and reached toward the space. She was about three feet too short.

"Need some help?" asked a deeply amused voice from the doorway.

Heat crept over Leandra's skin. She scrambled down from her precarious perch on the desk. "Your pardon, Lord Greville. Was there something you required?"

Greville's eyes gleamed with amusement and all for her. "If we are going to be friends, *your grace*, I suggest you get used to calling me Levi."

"It is hardly proper on such little acquaintance, as you well know."

"You are married to Hart. You will have to get used to impropriety."

Leandra couldn't help but smile at that, though a tinge of unease colored her mirth. "Very well, *Levi*, is there something you need?"

"Is there something up there you need?" he asked, pointing to the shelf she'd been reaching toward. "If you break your neck while I'm on watch, Hart will have my head on a platter. Tell me which book you require and I will fetch it for you."

She thought about it for a moment and decided that she would much rather ask this gentleman to retrieve the book for her than a servant who might gossip about her find.

Leandra pointed at the seemingly empty space between the books and said, "I think there is a much smaller book between them. Like this one." She held up the journal in her hand.

Greville nodded once, stepped up on the desk—Leandra was amazed that it supported his weight—and felt around in the space between the books above his head. He pulled his hand out with a triumphant grin and climbed down, handing her the journal with a magnificent bow.

Leandra curtsied and laughed, reaching for the book. Greville held it just out of her grasp and cocked his head to one side, brows raised.

"What is this?" he asked with apparent bad manners.

Leandra frowned. "It is none of your concern, sir," she told him haughtily.

Greville just grinned at her. She finally smiled and said, "It is nothing more than an old journal. I thought it might be interesting."

The earl considered her round, serious face for a moment, nodded, and handed over the book. He bowed. "Please forgive me for teasing you so. I had to know what it was that attracted Hart, you see. He needs more than just a pretty face."

She started at his candor, blushed at his offhand compliment, then replied, "He had need of a wife to get his inheritance. He was not attracted to me in the least."

Greville gave her an enigmatic look and offered his arm to escort her from the room. "As you get to know your husband better, Leandra, you will find that there is not a force on Earth that can make Hart do anything he does not wish. I am willing to bet that you were not the first lady he came across and considering all you told Aurora and me last night, by far not the most eligible."

17

LEANDRA decided to forgo her visit to the nursery in favor of a morning ride while the weather was still chill and blustery. She enjoyed being out of doors when there was a nip in the air and the threat of rain. It seemed to act as a sort of outlet for her calmly pent-up emotions.

She retreated to her dressing room and had Liza dress her hair more securely and fetch her a riding habit and a warm cloak. After tying a dashing shako with a curling white feather on her dark brown tresses and donning her habit of chocolate brown, Leandra stepped out into the Great Hall and took up her riding crop. Stark smiled indulgently and opened the door for her.

Lucifer's Lady was soon saddled and stomping impatiently in her desire to be off. Leandra smiled and patted Lady's nose.

"Patience, my sweet," she told the horse in a low whisper. She kissed the velvety muzzle and smiled. "You are too beautiful to send yourself into such fits and starts."

Amazingly—to every stable hand and groom, if not to Leandra—the horse quieted and stood still as a statue as a groom with a crooked nose and disfiguring squint hefted her into the saddle.

"Thank you, Jeb," she told the groom. He doffed his hat and gave her a shy smile that appeared to be closer to a leer on his ugly face. Leandra only smiled brighter and lifted her crop in salute.

"Sum'un ought to go wit 'er," she heard the head groom say just before she kicked Lady into a smooth gallop.

The huge black mare with the tiny black-cloaked figure soared over the ground as one being. She directed the animal toward the cliffs that were on the east side of the castle wall. Just when it seemed they would plunge over, Lady came to an abrupt halt.

Leandra stared out over the choppy waters. The waves were gray and green with hints of blue and frothy white caps of sea spray. They crashed on the rocky shore below. Seagulls flew about shrieking their displeasure at the approaching storm adding a strange counterpoint to the music of the surf.

This very sight had enchanted Leandra since the first time she had beheld it two weeks ago. She had been waiting for another chance to see it all over again. Lady would not fret; the horse was as much a storm-hungry being as Leandra.

Giving in to the impulse, Leandra tore her hat from her head and flung it far out over the cliff and into the sea below. She watched it fall, a small smile touching her lips as the hat was swallowed in the crashing waves. A brisk breeze ripped the feather from her hat and carried it far out over the water before it was swept into the sea.

The next things to go were the pins from her chignon. They scattered to the ground at Lady's feet and the wind whipped Leandra's hair every which way, across her face, down her back, and over her shoulders. She threw her head back and released a joyful cry.

"Isn't it the most wonderful thing, Lady?" Leandra breathlessly queried the animal beneath her.

Lady nodded her head as if in agreement, then stamped her foot.

"It would be wonderful, would it not? To ride like the wind and pretend that we have no guests and nothing to worry about ever. To revel in the power of God and admire all His magnificence and beauty."

The horse nodded her great black head again and snorted.

"'Tis heaven up here, so high above the rest of the world." She released the reins and threw her hands up in the air. "I feel so free!" she shouted joyously. "I feel like I could fly!"

Both of Lady's front feet left the ground briefly and Leandra grabbed up the reins to keep from tumbling off, laughing. "Careful, my pet, or you will lose me. And I have no desire to take a tumble off this cliff."

Lady shook her head and twisted around to nibble at Leandra's skirts, one great black eye watching her closely. Leandra marveled that the creature could so resemble her master with her black coat and black, expressionless eyes. She gave herself a mental shake and leaned down to pat the horse's silky neck.

As she resumed her straight-backed position, Leandra caught sight of an object far off in the distance bobbing along in the water. She squinted her eyes, trying to decipher what it was but it was still too far away.

"Come, Lady, let us investigate."

She urged the horse into a canter toward a cliff path that led down to the shore below. She let her arms fall slack on the reins and Lady picked her way down the rocky path. It was quite a distance and the object Leandra had seen from the cliff top was much closer by the time horse and rider reached the bottom. The wind was not so fierce down here and Leandra's hair fell in damp strands around her shoulders and down her back. Her cloak was thrown back over her shoulders due to the wind and all the elegance of her deep brown habit was visible.

She should have been cold. But curiosity and excitement fired her blood and she did not feel the cold bite of the wind or the stinging spray of the surf. She was too intent on what she now recognized as a ship.

She could make out the sails and saw that it was moving quickly in her direction. The little bay by which she stood was where her husband docked his boat, she knew. So thinking, she assumed it must be Derringer returning from France.

She suppressed a shiver. He was coming home.

She hoped he had his cousin with him. When Derringer had spoken of Gabriel St. Clair, pain echoed in his voice. She knew how important it was for him to restore his cousin to his family and recapture some of the innocence they had shared as boys.

As these thoughts ran through Leandra's mind, Lady stomped and snorted almost as if she knew the ship in the distance. Leandra patted her neck and murmured, "Yes, my beautiful Lady, he is returned."

After watching the ship for a few minutes, Leandra turned Lady and began the treacherous climb back up the cliff path. Lady stumbled once, setting Leandra's heart to beating wildly, but the nimble creature regained her footing and carried her mistress to safety.

Once more upon the cliff top, Leandra gazed out to sea, the wind whipping her hair in every direction. She could make out the shape of a man on deck of the ship, staring up at her. She waved once and galloped back to the castle, her cloak flying behind her like the wings of a raven.

Derringer stood with his arms folded and his feet spread on the dipping and swaying deck of his ship. He looked like a storybook pirate with his black hair whipping around his shoulders, his black shirt open at the throat, and his thigh-hugging black breeches tucked into his black boots. His black cloak flew behind him in much the same way the horsewoman's did.

He watched the woman ride away, the wind nipping at the horse's hooves. Was it Leandra? It had to be. Who else would it be? And that had to be Lucifer's Lady that she rode. As far as Derringer knew, Lady would not allow anyone but him, and now his wife, to ride her. He would recognize Lady anywhere.

So it had to have been Leandra on that cliff top watching him. Why? What possible reason could she have for anticipating his arrival?

But perhaps it was simple coincidence. She may have been out riding along the cliff and happened to see the ship. She probably decided to watch in an effort to determine whether or not it was he. Yes, that was it. It was the only logical explanation.

He was surprised to feel disappointment at this likely explanation. He would much rather believe that she had ridden out just to see if he was returning. He wanted her to anxiously await his return with bated breath. He wanted her to...

He shook his head and frowned awfully at his own sentimental thoughts. Why the devil did he care, all of a sudden? He wasn't in love with the chit no matter what Gabriel said. He couldn't be. He didn't even know her.

Besides, he swore he'd never fall in love. It was imperative that he did not. People in love tend to reveal their secrets and fears and Derringer had no desire to tell anyone anything. His secrets and fears were best left in the back of his subconscious mind where they could harm no one.

Where they could not harm him.

Leandra rushed back into the castle, eyes shining and lips smiling. She handed her cloak to Stark who gaped at the sight of his mistress without her hat and her hair loose about her shoulders. In her excitement, Leandra had completely forgotten her scandalous appearance.

Oh, well, as long as no one else saw her, no harm was done.

All her guests seemed to pour from the upper stories at one time, intent on converging in the drawing room for afternoon tea. Her face crinkled in dismay as one by one each person stopped and stared at her with varying degrees of surprise. She could feel the heat start up her neck but she fought it down and pasted on a bright smile instead. She stifled the urge to smooth out her curls and lifted her chin.

"Disgraceful!" exclaimed the Dowager Countess of Harwood and Lady St. Clair in unison. They looked at each other as if surprised that the one could ever agree with the other on anything.

Michaella stood beside Martin St. Clair, wide-eyed but silent. Contempt and disgust emanated from the younger Lady Harwood and Lady Schuster. Lady Kathryn and her husband stared at Leandra as if she had two heads. The Grevilles exchanged amused glances.

Greville leaned down to whisper in his wife's ear, she grinned and sailed forward, laughter shining in her turquoise eyes. Linking Leandra's arm with hers, she said, "My dear, you appear to have enjoyed your ride immensely."

Leandra admitted this was true and waited. What would Aurora say next?

Leaning forward so they would not be overheard, Aurora whispered, "Is he home?"

Leandra exhaled in a rush and had to restrain herself from bouncing up and down. "Yes, I saw his ship. He should be in the castle by dinner."

"Splendid," Aurora enthused, squeezing Leandra's hand. "It has been so very long since I have seen Hart and I have to admit I miss him. Even with all his megrims, he is ever amusing."

Amusing? Hart? "Are we speaking of the same person, Rory? Hartley St. Clair? The Duke of Derringer? Tall man with black hair usually tied back at the nape and piercing black eyes like a starless night? That Hart?"

Aurora giggled. "Yes, my dear, your husband. He is amusing. Levi assures me it is true and he never lies." A shadow crossed her face but it was gone almost before it ever was so Leandra thought she must have imagined it.

"Let us go up to your room and I will help you change into something very flattering. Then we will join the rest of the guests in the drawing room and dazzle them with our witty repartee."

Leandra allowed herself to be led away while Greville ushered everyone else into the drawing room. He winked outrageously as they passed and Leandra couldn't suppress a giggle.

18

Derringer stumbled into the castle, Gabriel leaning heavily on him. He had tried to tidy his and Gabriel's appearances as much as possible before leaving the ship but the wind was still blowing fiercely outside. The duke was afraid his efforts had all been for naught.

In fact, he knew they were. His hair, which he had tied back with a leather thong, hung loose about his shoulders. There was nothing he could do about it now.

"Are we home, Hart?"

"Yes, Gabe." He paused in the act of carrying his cousin up the stairs. There was no way he could get the man up the back stairs and Derringer was unsure he'd be able to face the main stairs. He could always take him to the other staircase in the other wing but it would add close to a mile on his journey.

"Stark," called the duke. "Take Gabriel up to the Green Chamber on the third floor. I don't know if the duchess has given it away but if she has, evict them."

At the butler's raised hand, a large footman stepped forward and lifted the duke's cousin, no visible strain in his massive shoulders.

"I can walk," protested Gabriel. The footman ignored him.

Derringer turned to Stark and gestured to the departing pair. "Other than his size, what's wrong with that one?"

"Deaf, your grace."

"Wonderful."

Derringer strode into his bedchamber and shrugged out of his coat as he made his way to his dressing room. He would have to dig out some clothes for Gabriel, he thought as he untied the black cloth around his throat. He sat down and removed his boots, placing them neatly side-by-side on the floor by the chair. He remembered his wife's greeting the last time he had returned home and he was alarmed at the intense disappointment he felt that she did not rush out to greet him this time.

He moved into his bedchamber and glanced at the clock on the mantle. That would explain it, he thought with a weary sigh. They were all at dinner.

Moving back into his dressing room, Derringer divested himself of the rest of his tattered and travel-stained clothing, donned a clean pair of trousers and a robe of black silk, and padded barefoot from the room. He walked down the corridor, passing three doors before he came to the

Green Chamber. He knocked once, then pushed the door open.

Gabriel was lying on the bed in a white nightshirt, buried under a mound of blankets. A fire roared in the grate and the wind howled at the floor-to-ceiling windows. The footman was doing something over on the table by the window, his back turned to the rest of the room.

Derringer cocked an eyebrow in the direction of the busy footman. Gabriel laughed. "He said he has something that will help the pain in my... well, lack of arm."

"Really," drawled Derringer, his gaze swinging once more to the footman. "Did you learn his name, by any chance?"

"You'll laugh," grinned Gabriel.

"Indeed."

"His name, or so he told me, is Hartley St. Clair Hughes."

Gabriel had the duke's full attention. "What tomfoolery is this?"

"Sure as I'm standing... no, lying here, God as my witness, s'truth."

"How did that come about, do you think?" queried Derringer as he sat down on the edge of the bed, facing his cousin.

"I asked, believe me. Apparently, his mama had a *tendre* for a daring young duke by that name. She named her firstborn after that duke, much to the chagrin of the boy's papa."

"Who is she?" He ran the name of Hughes through his vast store of useless knowledge but came up blank.

"Remember Clara Smythe? She started on here when we were off at Eton. We came home and she was the new housemaid, very pretty, and very willing. I had thought to make a go at her but she wanted no one but you."

Derringer remembered the maid. She had been quite a taking thing with strawberry blond curls and dimpled cheeks. She'd had a way of moving around a room that made a man think inappropriate thoughts.

The duke cast a sidelong look at the footman. His eyes narrowed. No, it wasn't possible. He looked at Gabriel, who was laughing at him. "Is it possible?" he finally asked his cousin.

Gabriel grinned. "No, it is not possible, Hart, you clunch."

"So what am I supposed to call him? I can't go around calling him Hart. People will think I'm mad, talking to myself and all that."

"Hughes, I suppose."

Derringer threw another suspicious look at the footman before putting the whole thing from his mind. "I suppose you'll be needing clothes."

"Naw, I think I'll go around naked," teased Gabriel. "Any ladies in the house? Other than your Merri, I mean."

"Unless they took their leave—which I very much doubt despite my threats—Merri's family is here. There is the unhappy Lady Harwood, wife of the current earl, her mother-in-law the dowager, a widowed sister-in-law by the name of Lady Schuster, and a young beauty named Michaella. And I believe the nursery is overflowing with little Harwoods and Schusters of all ages and sizes. Dear God in heaven, I hope they've left! Michaella was the only tolerable one in the bunch."

Gabriel smiled. "Bad as all that, are they? Why don't you toss them out on their collective ears? That would be like you from what I hear."

"What have you heard?"

His cousin yawned before saying, "Lord Heartless, they call you. I've known all along where you were and what you were up to, you know. I couldn't seek you out because… well, I just couldn't. Are you really as heartless as they say?"

"How did I become that well-known in France? Every pub and tavern I went in seemed to be filled with men quaking at the mere sight of me."

"You are legendary, cousin. You have no conscience, no sensibilities, no morals, no heart. I laughed when they said you were worse than Satan himself. I know you better than that. I did at one time anyway."

For some unexplainable reason, Gabriel's assessment of his character hurt Derringer. He had heard it all before so it shouldn't cause this ache in his chest.

"Do you believe all that rot?"

Hughes approached the bed and forestalled Gabriel's answer. He handed the patient a glass and Gabriel gulped it down without even asking what was in it. His face twisted into a grimace, he shook his head slightly as if trying to get rid of the taste, and then he grinned.

"Sleep now," mumbled the footman in a guttural voice that made Derringer shiver.

The duke rose to his feet, bid his cousin goodnight, and left the room after promising to look out some clothes for him.

As Derringer settled himself into his high bed, the thought did cross his mind to seek out his wife and settle a few important matters between them. But his eyes refused to stay open and he was soon deeply asleep.

He came awake a few hours later with the feeling that he was being watched. Darkness coated the chamber, the only light a sliver of moonlight coming from a crack in the drapes.

Someone—or something—watched him, but he couldn't tell exactly where it crouched in the vast chamber. Lids half-lowered, even breaths, forced calm, Derringer waited for he knew not what.

Whoever was there was not his friend. They were probably there to dispatch him to his maker. One too many incidents in the past left the duke attacked, injured, the clear goal to end his life. He wasn't about to let that happen until he at least determined who went to such trouble to see him dead.

His dark eyes shot to the window where a shadow momentarily blocked the thread of moonlight. So he could expect the attack to come from his left. Every muscle in his tall form tensed with anticipation. He would know who wanted him dead, once and for all.

The attack took him by surprise. It came from his right and he narrowly missed being skewered to his mattress. He rolled to the side, throwing the blankets off him as he did so. He heard a muffled grunt and surmised that the bedclothes had caught at least one of his assailants. There was still the man near the windows. His eyes adjusted to the dark and he could make out the man's dim outline.

Derringer headed right for him. A sharp pain sliced through his left shoulder—the same shoulder he injured two years previous in an attempt to rescue Aurora Greville —but he ignored it and slammed his fist into what he hoped was the man's face. The man retaliated with an uppercut that slammed Derringer across the room. He landed on his back, his injured shoulder protesting the impact, and fought to regain his breath.

With the agility of a cat, the duke regained his feet. Arms outstretched, his eyes searched the Stygian gloom.

A muffled sound came from his right and his eyes darted in that direction. A blade glinted in the shaft of moonlight. He twisted his body to avoid the weapon. His arm shot out, caught something very human, and he twisted until he had the man in his arms with the knife at the man's throat.

"Show yourself or your friend dies," he told the other man in that silky tone that most men knew indicated blind fury.

The other shadow detached itself from the wall and sauntered toward the duke. Just before he would have been in arm's reach, he darted around Derringer and escaped through the door and out into the winding, labyrinth-style passages of the castle.

"It seems your friend has deserted you," the duke drawled.

Much to the duke's surprise and horror, the man in his arms jerked his body convulsively. His arm, imprisoned by Derringer in a death grip, gave a sickening crack. The man groaned, Derringer relaxed his hold an infinitesimal degree, and in that split second of surprise, the man twisted and jabbed his fist into the duke's ribs. He disappeared in the same direction as his accomplice.

The duke went after them. He left his chamber, shouting for help, and ran in the direction of the stairs leading to the second floor. He stopped short of descending them and stared down for about three seconds before his eyes rolled back in his head and he slumped to the floor in a dead faint.

19

LEANDRA rushed from her room at the first bellow for help. She witnessed her husband's appearance on the landing, clothed in nothing but his breeches, blood running from his shoulder, over his chest and down his arm. He stopped short, wavered, and collapsed in a heap. Was he dead?

She stopped next to Derringer's inert form, but her head whipped around at a sound behind her. Eyes widening, she beheld the sudden appearance of another man, one who possessed an uncanny resemblance to her husband. Same dark hair, tall, muscular form and angular features, but this man lacked one arm, the sleeve of his nightshirt rolled up and pinned at the shoulder.

Then he was beside her and looking down at the duke. He cursed.

Leandra ignored him, dropping to her knees beside her husband. She gently smoothed the hair from his face. He was breathing, she was relieved to note, but the blood didn't seem to be stopping. Rather, it flowed faster. With no thought for modesty, she ripped a large strip from her generous nightclothes. Pressing the cloth firmly to

Derringer's shoulder, she threw an anxious glance at the man standing above them.

"You must be Merri," he said in a voice much like the duke's. He knelt down and ran his one hand over Derringer's ribcage. "Cracked," he muttered to himself. He pressed his hand hard against the wound in the duke's shoulder, cursing under his breath the whole time. He glanced into Leandra's worried face and said soothingly, "He'll survive. He's lived through worse, you know. And he's merely fainted."

The pounding of feet heralded the arrival of Lord Greville, Lady Greville not far behind.

"What happened?" inquired that lady as she, too, knelt down. Her fingers traced a line over Derringer's forehead, feather-light. Her worried turquoise eyes flashed to Leandra's hazel ones.

"I don't know," Leandra admitted. Stark came flying from the servants' rooms in the attic. "He was standing on the landing, bleeding all over, and then he looked down, and he... fell."

Martin made his appearance, distress creasing his pale brow. He saw the duke lying on the floor, swiveled his gaze slightly... and saw his brother. "Oh, bloody hell! You're supposed to be dead!"

"I've missed you, too," replied Gabriel, voice thick with sarcasm. "Perhaps someone could take Hart back to his bed? Hughes," he called, gesturing to the deaf footman, "ride for the doctor." Hughes carefully watched Gabriel's lips, nodded, and took off at a run.

Greville motioned everyone out of the way and lifted his tall friend with seeming little effort. He carried him back to the master chamber.

Leandra walked ahead of him, lighting candles all over the room. She gasped when she turned and saw the wreck of the room. "What happened?" Her voice trembled on the words.

Aurora put her arm around her, giving her a gentle squeeze. "We will find out, my dear. And he will be all right. He always is, you know."

Leandra sat down in the chair that Greville placed beside her husband's bed. She stared at Derringer's face, the loss of blood giving him an unnatural pallor, and struggled again with the strange puzzle of who would actually want to hurt him.

Greville stood a little to the side, staring at her. She could feel his eyes, boring into her. What was he thinking? Did it matter? She struggled to hold onto her composure, struggled to hold the tears at bay. Confusion was hard enough to endure. But the fear—the fear was unbearable.

Greville gave his head a brisk shake, his eyes falling away from her. Leandra witnessed the movement, her curiosity piqued.

"Is something wrong, my lord—Levi?"

He smiled, no doubt at her slip of the tongue. "No, Leandra, I was just thinking." He pulled a second chair up next to hers. "I was thinking perhaps I should call on an old… friend, of Hart's and invite him for a stay. Would you mind?"

She shook her head. "I have no objection. Will he be able to help find out who would want to harm Hart?"

Greville nodded but Leandra saw something in his dark eyes that put the lie to his claim. This friend may not be able to help, but at this point, it mattered little. Any help would be appreciated.

She stared into his eyes, searching for more reassurance, her own worry growing as she contemplated the very real threat to her husband's life. He'd been attacked in his own home.

Her companion's eyes widened, something giving him a bit of a shock. Unsure what to say, or do, she glanced away.

"Amazing," he murmured, dragging Leandra's attention back.

"What is amazing?" she asked, quirking an eyebrow at her companion.

"The fact that you seem to have caught the untruth in what I just told you."

"It was something in the way you did not answer my question verbally. Then you wouldn't look at me. You showed several signs that you were being less than honest."

"Were you this open and honest with Hart the first time you met him?"

"Of course," she replied in a tone that implied it would have been ludicrous to do otherwise.

Silence stretched. Leandra's attention returned to her ailing husband. He breathed steadily, the bleeding stanched for the moment. Her gaze focused on his face, roaming over the hard, angular features that lost little of their rigidity even in repose. Would he ever be at ease? Or did his life warrant such tension even while he slept?

A sigh bubbled up but she stifled it. He shouldn't matter so much to her, not already. She barely knew him and what she did know wasn't good. He was to blame for many of his own problems, she was sure. But for someone to want him dead... For someone to attack him in his own home... It pained her to contemplate the implications of such an action. It pained her more to realize he meant far more to her than was wise.

"I have it!" Greville declared, making Leandra nearly jump from her skin. He glanced at the still figure in the bed and lowered his voice. "My cousin's husband, Sir Adam

Prestwich, is a bit of a sleuth, if you will. He may be able to shed some light on this mystery."

"Would he be willing to, do you think?"

"If I ask him, I have no doubt. He doesn't care much for Hart socially speaking, but he would be willing to aid in the search for the person that wishes him dead."

"Dead?" she whispered, finding it very difficult to hear the word said aloud.

"Blast! I shouldn't have said that, Leandra, I'm sorry. Hart would have my head for telling you. But I have the feeling that you will find out anyway."

He paused and Leandra willed him to continue, despite her natural desire to pretend none of this was happening. Releasing Derringer's hand, she removed her spectacles, retrieved her handkerchief from her sleeve, and set about polishing the glass lenses. All the better to see Greville's tells. She settled them back on her nose and then settled her gaze back on Lord Greville.

He sighed. "Where do I start?"

"At the beginning," suggested Leandra firmly. "I want to know everything about this man and I want to know who is such a threat."

"I can't tell you who the threat is, Leandra. No one knows. Hart has been trying for years to discover the identity of the villain but to no avail."

"I see." She was right. Having her fears confirmed was not helpful.

The door opened and Gabriel walked in, leaning heavily on Hughes's arm. Leandra reflected that the man seemed to have taken the deaf footman for his own personal servant. If it made Hughes feel useful, all the better.

"Any change?" he asked.

Leandra shook her head. "He is as still as death." Her whispered words seemed to echo in the darkness of the chamber. It rebounded in her head until she wanted to scream. He couldn't die. Not now. Not when she...

"It can't be true," she murmured to herself. It was not possible to fall in love with someone one barely knew. Especially someone who had proven on more that one occasion that he was heartless, rude, and completely uncaring of others' feelings. He was a beast and she loved him.

"No, I don't."

"You don't... what?" Gabriel asked, his head cocked to one side in a way that reminded her painfully of her husband.

"Nothing," she muttered. She felt embarrassed heat climbing her neck and willed it away.

"He's not going to die, Leandra," insisted Greville gently. "Hart won't die until he finds out who is responsible for this. He is too stubborn and too ruthless to let the bastard just get away with it."

"Why does everyone use that word to describe someone who is evil and use it also to describe someone whose parents were not bound in wedlock?" queried Leandra, feeling a deceptive calm steal over her.

Gabriel laughed softly. "Does it matter?"

Leandra turned flashing green eyes on her husband's cousin. "It matters very much to one who is baseborn, sir. It matters very much when that person cannot help that her parents did not marry, or could not marry. It matters very much to me!"

Gabriel stared at her. Greville stared at her. Unbeknownst to her or the gentlemen, her husband stared at her. She jumped when long fingers curled around her wrist.

"Calm, Merri, calm. He meant nothing by it. He didn't know," murmured the duke. He coughed and found a glass of water thrust at him. He sipped at it gratefully, watching his wife the whole time. "I didn't tell him and I haven't spoken to Vi in nearly two years."

He shifted uncomfortably against the pillows, releasing Leandra's hand as he did so. "Now, could you all get the hell out of my room?" he grumbled.

Leandra shrank back as if struck. How could the man be so very rude to those trying to help him? "Very well, *your grace*," she told him in a carefully neutral tone. She stood to leave.

Her emphasis on his title informed him he'd managed to annoy her. Part of him rejoiced in this accomplishment. Annoyed was better than scared. He didn't like to see her scared.

Gabriel, escorted by Hughes, exited the room. Greville led Leandra to the door, whispered something to her and then remained behind.

Derringer's eyes narrowed. "Secrets with my wife, Vi? I'm surprised at you."

"Don't take that tone with me, Hart," replied his friend indifferently. "I have no secrets with her that I am not about to tell you."

The duke glared at him. The admission that he did, in fact, have secrets with his Merri made him want to tear Levi's heart out—even if the man *was* willing to share them with him.

"I have decided to ask Adam and Bri to visit and I discussed it with your wife. She is willing to allow it."

"And since Merri is master here, that is all the permission you need," retorted the duke. "You've told me, now you can get out."

"You are a bloody irritating patient, Hart," Greville told him with fond contempt. "You need help finding the bas… um, villain responsible for this." He gestured toward the duke's bandaged shoulder and ribs. "You do not seem to be progressing well in that."

"And how the devil can I when my time is spent searching for a cousin who has spent his time evading me and getting married to save a fortune that was mine in the first place? I haven't exactly had the time to search for someone wanting to kill me. Besides, don't you think society would rejoice to be rid of me?"

"Self-pity, Hart? Shocking."

"It is not self-pity, dammit! It is reality. I am not beloved in society, Vi. Everyone knows that. To a man they would love to see me dead. My father was not popular and King George himself hated my grandfather. I wouldn't be surprised if it was the king that ordered my grandfather's death. Would you?"

"The walls have ears," Greville warned.

Derringer snorted. "So let them listen. I care not."

"Adam can help, Hart. You know he can."

"Oh, yes, that stuffed shirt proved quite useful when you lost your daughter," retorted the duke maliciously.

Greville just barely reigned in his temper. "Because you are injured, I will let you live," he told him sharply. "Any more and I will thrash you to within an inch of your life."

"Cut line, Greville. I have no use for your threats or scolds. If you want to call in Adam, fine. If you call in Tiny, my wife will be worried unnecessarily and I'll have your head for that."

"How did you…?" asked Greville in stunned disbelief.

"I know you, Vi. You worry too much about me. Ask Aurora. She'll tell you what a cad I am and that you should cease wasting your time over me."

The earl snorted. "The devil she would. Aurora would have my head if I let you die, mark my words. Since you restored Rhiannon to her, she has nothing but praise for you."

"Bloody hell," muttered Derringer. "Tell her to stop, please." He tried very hard not to grin but failed. "She'll ruin my reputation."

Greville watched the duke thoughtfully. "I wonder what Adam would say to being called a stuffed shirt?" he mused aloud.

20

I⊤ was said one who listened at doors never heard good of themselves. Leandra knew the truth of that statement having had the habit of doing just that when she was a child. This time it was an accident and one she regretted. It shouldn't hurt but it did.

It wasn't as if she hadn't already known, she told herself sternly. The duke never lied about his reason for marrying her. She'd only hoped that he had at least come to care for her a little. Apparently, she was just an added burden when he had more important things to worry about.

Such as who was trying to kill him.

The thought made her tremble. Whether it was rage or fear, she didn't know. It was probably both. She was afraid the villain might succeed and she was furious that anyone would contemplate hurting her husband.

And she felt unutterably helpless. She clenched her hands and tried to compose her mind for sleep. It was early morning and the feeble light of dawn was creeping between the part in her bedroom drapes. It only made sleep far more difficult to achieve.

She must have slept at some point. Sunlight streaked across the room, straight to her bed and over her eyes. She blinked, turning her head away. She encountered two large blue eyes gazing at her in wonder. Pasting on a bright smile that she didn't really feel, she greeted Rhiannon Greville and tried to wake up.

"Hello, sweetheart."

Rhiannon smiled slightly. "Papa Levi bought me a new dolly," was the child's reply.

The response was effective in restoring much of Leandra's calm and natural joy, despite the events of the night just past. She struggled up against the pillows, popping her spectacles onto her face.

"Can I see?" she asked, smiling at the simple joy on the adorable child's piquant features. How she wished for a child of her own!

The little girl held up a very pretty doll with blond hair and blue eyes the same shade as Rhiannon's.

"What is her name?"

"I call her Moppet cause that's what Papa calls me."

"I see. Does she have another name as well?"

Rhiannon's brow puckered adorably as she thought about that. "Mama says her name is Lucy."

"That's a very pretty name," observed Leandra. "Where is your nurse?"

Her brow puckered again. Then she grinned. "In the nursery."

"And why are you not in the nursery as well?" Leandra couldn't resist asking.

"I wanted to show you my new dolly," explained Rhiannon as if the answer were quite plain to even the simplest of souls.

"Well, thank you for showing me, my dear. Now I must be up and about if I am to prevent the household from falling down about our ears."

She swung her feet from the bed and moved toward her dressing room. The clock informed her it was nearly four hours past her accustomed time to rise.

"Will the house really fall?" asked a tiny, fearful voice at her side.

Leandra paused to stare down at the little girl. She wasn't really surprised that she hadn't left. Who would want to stay cooped up in the nursery on such a mild autumn day? Perhaps she could take all the children out later to take advantage of the pleasant weather.

"No, I was speaking metaphorically," she told her now, keeping the idea of an outing to herself for the moment. She'd have to get permission from all the parents before doing anything and she didn't want to raise Rhiannon's hopes unnecessarily.

The child appeared to ponder her words carefully. Leandra used the opportunity to ring for her maid. Where was Liza anyway? She'd come and gone, that much was clear. The open drapes allowed in the sun that woke her and a pitcher of tepid water waited on her dressing table.

"What's metaphorically?" inquired Rhiannon, carefully enunciating the large word.

"Not literal."

Rhiannon thought about this while the duchess searched for a particular gown in her armoire. She finally found it and took it out, shaking out the wrinkles.

"What's literal?"

Leandra smiled. "Literal means true, I suppose."

An arrested expression crossed the child's tiny features. "Then you lied," she pronounced in accents of shock.

Puzzled over the little girl's strange reaction, Leandra opened her mouth to explain that it wasn't a lie, merely an exaggeration, but Liza chose that very moment to enter the room. Rhiannon sent the duchess one last look of reproach and darted from the room.

Liza glanced at the fleeing child then back at Leandra. "What was that all about, your grace?"

"She wanted to show me her doll." Leandra shot her maid a puzzled look. "Do you know much about children, Liza?"

"A little," replied the little maid with an air of curiosity. "My mama had ten, me being the oldest. Seven of us survived. Is this the dress you were wanting to wear today?" she asked, pointing to the wool gown draped over a chair.

"Yes," said the duchess. She sat down at her dressing table and allowed Liza to brush out her hair and style it in a simple chignon with a few loose curls framing her face. "I wonder why Rhiannon was so upset when she thought I was lying?" wondered Leandra aloud.

"Is that what had the girl in such a pother? I do suppose it were the fact that her mama lied so much to her husband."

Leandra turned in her chair, eyeing her maid severely. "What are you talking about?"

Liza took a nervous step back. "Lady Greville's maid did say as how her ladyship had that little girl out of wedlock and then married his lordship and did never tell him. He didn't know until the child were kidnapped by her real papa."

Leandra's mind raced. Aurora had admitted Rhiannon was her daughter but Leandra had simply assumed the child was Lord Greville's as well—it was a natural assumption. Apparently, she was not. It was equally apparent that the earl had already drilled into his stepdaughter how wrong it was to lie.

"Liza, you are not to speak of this to anyone, do you understand? I do not like gossip. It is hurtful and brings no good with it. Promise me, Liza."

"Yes, your grace. I promise, your grace," the maid responded in a terrified squeak.

"Good. Now I must finish dressing and see how his lordship is faring."

Liza swallowed with difficulty. "Cook says as how his grace is already up and about, your grace." She cringed at the no doubt furious look in Leandra's eyes. "I wasn't gossiping, honest."

"It's not that, Liza. I will murder that madman when I find him. He was stabbed just last night. What the devil does he think he's doing?"

Leandra's toilet was finished only moments later. She sped down the stairs to the drawing room where she assumed everyone would be. Upon entering, she found the ladies assembled in one corner of the room, two of the gentlemen entertaining them with Society gossip. In the far corner of the room her husband stood with Lord Greville and Mr. Gabriel St Clair, the expressions on their faces attesting to the seriousness of their conversation. She had trouble maintaining her temper as she stalked over to them where they stood near the window.

Derringer saw her coming out of the corner of his eye and his face lit up with unholy glee. "Unless I miss my guess," he told his companions, "my lady wife is going to finish the deed started last night."

Greville chuckled, agreeing with the duke's observation. Gabriel added his own observation that perhaps he deserved it. This made the three of them laugh.

They closed their mouths and placed innocent expressions on their faces as the duchess drew up to their group—which only made Leandra want to throttle them all.

"Just what the bloody *hell* do you think you are doing out of bed?" she demanded, keeping her voice low with an effort.

Greville's brows shot up at the intensity of her anger. With a muttered excuse, he and Gabriel fled what they were sure would become an awful row.

Leandra dimly noted their departure and heard him suggesting to the others that they take a stroll in the rear gardens. She continued to glare at her husband, who stared steadily back until the room emptied.

"Such language, my love. One would think you'd been hanging around the stables all your life," remarked Derringer. "Or me."

"That doesn't answer my question, your grace." She threw his title at him like a weapon and he stiffened imperceptibly.

"You do realize that as my wife you are of high enough rank to call me *my lord*, or *your lordship*, or *Duke*, or *Derringer*. You don't have to lower yourself to the ranks of an earl's bastard daughter."

Anger shivered through her. "Thank you for the lesson in proper deportment, *your grace*, but I *am* nothing more than an earl's bastard daughter!"

"You are behaving like a shrew," he informed her, ice coating each word.

"Is it shrewish to worry about my husband who was just *stabbed*, and *beaten*, a mere eight hours ago? You should not be up and about. You should be abed."

"Scratched, my blushing beauty, not *stabbed*. And hardly beaten," he drawled carelessly. "Just knocked about a bit."

His tiny bride growled at him in frustration.

Derringer's eyes lit with sudden speculation. The sight caused a momentary qualm in Leandra's breast. What was he up to now?

"I am well enough to wander around the castle, Merri," he soothed.

"How is that possible?" she exclaimed. "You were stabbed, Hart! Stabbed!" She completely ignored his earlier claim about his wound being a mere scratch.

"Would you like me to prove to you that I am well?" he asked, eyes intent on her face. He marveled at how green her eyes turned when angered. He'd seen emeralds with less vibrancy, less fire that were still magnificent specimens.

She studied his face for signs of fatigue, signs of hidden pain, but saw only his dark eyes staring relentlessly into hers, devoid of expression. "Very well," she replied reluctantly. "If you can prove to me, without a doubt, mind you, that you are well enough to carry on as usual, you may do so."

She wondered how he planned to prove it beyond the shadow of a doubt.

He wondered where she had gotten the mistaken impression that he would obey her whether he proved it or not.

Taking her hand firmly in his own, Derringer led his wife from the room and to the back of the house. He led her up the servants' stairs and down long winding corridors that Leandra had never before traversed. He finally stopped outside the door of his own chamber. Without a word, he led her inside, shutting and locking the door behind them. Releasing her hand, he locked the door leading to the sitting room between their apartments, pocketing both keys.

Leandra watched all this with growing alarm. Surely he didn't mean to...? Not now! Lord, what was he thinking?

Derringer was thinking that he'd waited long enough to bed his wife and she wanted proof that he was well. What better way to prove it?

When he advanced on her, Leandra found herself backing up. The gleam of desire in his eyes had her truly alarmed...more of her own reaction than his. And what if he further injured himself? She would feel it was her fault.

"Hart, listen to me," she implored as he continued to literally back her into a corner. "You cannot possibly mean to do this. It would be the greatest folly. It could kill you," she said desperately although she had no actual fear that it would.

This ludicrous statement made him pause. He cocked his head to one side, regarding her one dark brow quirked, then smiled. "But what a way to go," he remarked devilishly.

With those words, she knew there was no hope of dissuading him and her own sense of humor rose to the fore. She smiled at the look on his face, then laughed. He traversed the rest of the distance between them in three quick strides.

Before she could say or do anything, he was kissing her with a single-minded passion that threatened to rob her of her wits, her breath, maybe even her life, she thought, dazed. His hands went into her hair, scattering pins everywhere and she found her own arms stealing up around his neck. His hair was tied back in the usual tail and, seemingly of their own volition, her hands untied the knot in the black silk cord. She ran her fingers through his silky black hair and groaned at the feel of it slipping through her fingers. She had wanted to do that since she'd first laid eyes on him, she realized.

Derringer lifted his head just enough to see her face, his hands still threaded through her dark brown locks. Her eyes were closed, her lips parted slightly and swollen from his kiss. Her hands had slipped down to his shoulders, using him as support. His shoulder protested but he grinned at her reaction regardless.

Finally regaining some of her scattered wits, Leandra opened her eyes. She saw the look on her husband's face and felt her lips twitch up in amusement.

"I wonder," Derringer said seductively, one hand leaving her glorious mane of hair to move slowly along her neck, over her shoulder and down the front of her gown. She gasped as his hand closed over her breast. "I wonder," he repeated slowly, but he didn't go on.

She could barely think with his fingers making smooth circles over her breast. He seemed to realize that she was not in a state of mind to ask him what it was he wondered. He didn't seem to require a reply. "I think you do," he said. She was sure she heard surprise in his words but before she could comment on this, he slipped one arm around her waist and scooped her up against his chest.

"Don't tell me you haven't been wanting this, Merri," he said huskily, carrying her to his bed.

She didn't deny it. And as his lips met hers in another demanding kiss, she knew it would be everything that was wonderful.

21

ALTHOUGH the duke managed to suitably prove his point, he wondered if he might really die, as he'd jested earlier, when he collapsed, rolling slightly to lie at his wife's side. His breath came in staccato gasps, his heart trying to beat from his body.

He was laughing… and thinking that if he did die, he'd have proven just how stupid men could be.

Leandra, dazed at what had just happened, smiling and nearly laughing herself, smacked him lightly on his uninjured shoulder.

"Abuse!" he croaked out, another pained laugh escaping. He grabbed at his sore ribs, amazed he'd actually managed to successfully bed his wife when just breathing hurt like the devil.

Thank God—or somebody—that he had a high tolerance for pain.

Leandra turned to gaze at her husband. It was wonderful to hear his laugh, even if it was so painful for him.

She reached out and brushed a lock of silky black hair from his cheek, her fingers skimming his warm flesh. Not too warm, thankfully, she reflected. It would be terrible if he were to develop a fever.

Derringer let his head flop to the side, his laughter finally spent. His smile remained, however. Looking at his wife—in truth now—he couldn't help but smile.

He caught her hand when she would have pulled away, twining his fingers with hers. "Did I prove my point, lovely one?" he asked lightly, placing a kiss on her knuckles.

His duchess, smiling hugely, nodded her head. A pink haze crept over her features and she dropped her eyes, embarrassed... realizing she was naked as the day she was born. With a gasp, she pulled the bedsheets up over herself.

Derringer shook his head in mock reproof. "I'll never be able to properly corrupt you if simple nudity makes you skittish as a colt."

Leandra responded in quite the most adult manner she could—by sticking out her tongue.

The duke leered at her. "Is that an invitation?"

His bride rolled her eyes heavenward and edged off the high bed, the sheet wrapped securely around her. Derringer propped himself up on an elbow, ignoring the vehement protesting in his ribs. He watched as she scurried around, replacing the clothing that he had so recently removed from her delectable person.

As much as he regretted the necessity, however, there was something he had to discuss with her—and he was not looking forward to it.

"Tell me," he began curiously, "why is Vi here?"

"I invited him," she stated simply, not bothering to look up. She was trying to pull up her pantalets without dropping the sheet first. The duke was very interested to see who would win the battle.

"Why?"

Leandra frowned at him, pausing in her dressing to meet his eyes. "Why not? They are your friends, are they not?"

"Yes, they are. That still doesn't explain why you invited them."

He saw her shrug and, staring up into her face, he saw a stubborn look settle in her eyes. "Do I need a reason, your grace?"

The use of his title annoyed him and he had no doubt that annoyance showed in his eyes. At least he could easily tell when she was angry with him, he thought wryly.

After a moment, she asked, "Should I ask them to leave?"

Derringer sighed, shoved a hand through his dark hair, and shook his head, firmly repressing the twinge of pain in his much-abused shoulder. "No, Vi will be of some use to me, I think. And it was only a matter of time before he showed up anyway, demanding to know why he keeps hearing about my near-fatal accidents."

The blood drained from the duchess's face. "Near-fatal *accidents*? What *near-fatal accidents*?" Her voice was a trifle shrill and even she winced to hear it.

Vaguely, Derringer noted the panic in her tone but he was distracted by the fact that the sheet had won the battle, pooling at his wife's tiny feet. He sighed a little, wishing he could drag her back into bed. But he knew his shoulder and ribs were not up to it—even if other parts of him were more than willing.

"I exaggerate, sweeting," he told her with as much conviction as he could muster, which was significant, considering he'd been in so many accidents that he'd lost count. The need to keep her safe and unconcerned was paramount.

"You, exaggerate? But you don't! Exaggerate, I mean," she protested, still adorably unaware that she stood before him in her altogether. "You were attacked in your own home. It's clear to the veriest lackwit—and I assure you, I am not—that someone desires your immediate departure from this world."

Derringer stifled a smile and gestured toward her. "Merri, my love, perhaps you should pick up your sheet. I can't concentrate with so much bounty before me."

She snapped her mouth shut and bent to retrieve her covering, presenting the duke with the alluring sight of her curved backside. Her husband groaned.

Hearing the sound, Leandra straightened and asked, "What is it?"

"Muscle spasm," Derringer said, straight-faced.

Her expression implied disbelief. Securing her covering snugly around her and tucking the end in so both hands were free, she slipped on her pantalets. Her chemise took a little more effort but she managed.

The duke's shoulder started to protest vehemently, so he dropped back down on his back, noticing idly that he'd actually made the damned wound bleed again. He distractedly pressed a hand into the bandage, ignoring the pain that lanced through his upper body. He watched his duchess dress. She was quick about it, he thought with some disappointment. He had actually missed most of the spectacle. Comes from having to do for oneself, he reflected.

She moved to sit beside him on the bed. He took her hand and pulled her close, saying, "Merri, I should not have said anything. I didn't mean to frighten you. And there is really nothing to worry about."

She pulled roughly away from him, jarring his shoulder and making him inhale sharply. Leandra was too incensed to notice. "What do you mean there's nothing to worry about? Are you daft? Someone is trying to kill you. It was attempted last night and God only knows how many times before that, and you tell me there's nothing to worry about? What kind of simpleton do you take me for? Ugh! You make me want to scream!"

As she talked, Derringer's eyebrows raised ever so slightly. His little wife was turning into a shrew and he thought he rather liked it. Her anger made her face light up and her eyes turned that deep emerald green he found so fascinating.

And in the face of her discomposure, he realized that she just might do something foolish like try to protect him or hunt down his villain herself. That was out of the question. He had no desire to lose her when he'd only just found her.

A horrifying realization shook him. Lady Greville was in the castle. Derringer nearly groaned aloud. If she got wind of it—and according to Greville it was already too late for that—these two harebrained females would probably try to take matters into their own hands. He had no doubt the two women were already thick as thieves and that could only mean trouble.

"Merri, if you get involved in this, I swear I will beat you."

She reared back, mouth falling open in outraged shock. "Well, I like that! I express my worry for my husband and he threatens to beat me." She mumbled something under her breath that Derringer surprisingly didn't catch.

"What was that?" he asked silkily. He pushed himself upright, sitting against the pillows. He drew a blanket over his nakedness even as he reached out and took hold of her wrist none too gently.

"I said, your grace, that you are a damned nodcock," she told him fearlessly, chin tipped at a stubborn angle. Her eyes flashed. "You are completely attics to let if you think that for one second I am just going to pretend nothing is wrong."

Fascinated by his wife or not, Derringer was losing patience. "Such language, Merri? I'm surprised at you. Where did you learn such gutter talk?"

Leandra tried to hold back as he drew her closer but he was much too strong for her. His eyes glinted with anger. Had she pushed him too far? He threatened to beat her and she knew with a sudden sicking feeling that it was more than just empty words.

But she refused to sit around like a good little wife while her husband was murdered in his bed! And so she informed him before he could scatter her wits again by kissing her or touching her or... or... looking at her.

Derringer pulled her forward until she was forced to kneel beside him on the bed. He sat up straighter, bringing their faces within inches of each other. "And just how would you protect me, my little Valkyrie?" he asked, a thread of amusement coloring each word.

His lips waited only a hairsbreadth from her own. Coherent thought fled from her brain at his nearness. His eyes searched hers with mocking contempt and somewhere in the back of those inky depths she saw desire held rigidly in check.

A smile touched his lips. Anger flared in her breast. The cad knew what he was doing to her! If he thought seducing her would change her mind about doing what she could to protect him, he was vastly mistaken!

"Your grace—" she began, but he cut her off.

"Merri, if you call me that one more time, so help me God, I'll…" He stopped talking as if suddenly unsure exactly what he would do to her—which was exactly the case.

"You'll *what*, Lord Derringer?" she dared to ask.

"I'll lock you up until you're old and gray, Merri, see if I don't."

She laughed. "Is that a threat, Hart? I'd have to say I prefer the one where you'll beat me. It is far more in keeping with your dastardly reputation, you know."

"Leandra, you have no idea to what lengths I am willing to go in order to see my will done. I would suggest you not tempt me to prove it to you."

He still held her wrist in a steel grasp, a touch of pain shooting up her arm. But for some unknown—and possibly suicidal—reason, Leandra decided to test her husband. Would he really hurt her?

"I realize you are speaking of my desire to protect you rather than what I choose to call you. You will not stop me from trying to keep you from harm, Hart. You will not."

Visions of Leandra, bleeding, dying, even dead, rose before his mind's eye. And all because of her feelings for him. The pain these imaginings caused robbed him of breath, choking off his air. He reacted without thought, his free hand curling around her slim white throat.

Squeezing just enough to scare her senseless, he gritted out, "If you dare to get the least bit involved, Leandra Derringer, I will beat you black and blue every day for the rest of your life. You will beg for death by the time I get through with you."

Derringer barely understood his own actions and judging from Leandra's reaction, neither did she. Her body tensed, fear and unease coloring her eyes a deep brown. She tried to pull away but Derringer wasn't ready to let her go, wasn't ready to relinquish the fear that held him.

Struggling for control, struggling to hold the horrifying images at bay, Derringer finally forced his fingers to open. Red streaked her pale throat. He wanted to soothe her pain, reassure her, tell her he'd never hurt her, but she darted out of his reach.

Derringer sighed and leaned back against the pillows. He heard his chamber door close. Why did he feel the need to master her? She was sweet, unassuming, meek, and submissive. But he'd since learned that she was a veritable demon when it came to protecting those she cared about and he knew without her telling him that he was one of those she cared for. He couldn't let her risk her life for him, a cad and a ruthless bounder. It had seemed right at the moment to prove what a lost cause he truly was.

22

ONCE in the relative safety of the corridor, Leandra paused, leaning back against the closed door of her husband's chamber. Breathing grew difficult as she struggled against incipient tears. The tears won and she sagged, defeated, to the floor. Each breath ripped through her chest, tears streaming from burning eyes. Her fingers crept over the tender flesh of her neck. What a horrifying end to such a beautiful experience!

She allowed herself only a few moments, moments that felt like hours, to give in to her anguish. Tears spent, she pushed to her feet, smoothed some of the wrinkles from her gown, tied her hair into a knot without the use of pins, and took a deep breath. It would never do for the servants to see her in such a state. A duchess, even one as unconventional as Leandra, had to maintain a certain dignity. This was what she fought for as she descended the stairs.

Lady Greville stood on the second floor landing. Startled, Leandra paused, a hand automatically going to her hair. Despite her attempt to restore order, she knew her appearance was that of a woman freshly tumbled. She couldn't care. The disillusionment clattering through her brain was no doubt reflected on her face but she didn't have the will to control it at the moment. It was like a bucket of icy water had been dashed in her face. She was finally made to realize that her husband was a scoundrel and she had only herself to blame for not believing him.

Aurora took one look at her face and asked, "What did Hart do?" She tactfully refrained from mentioning Leandra's tangled hair and wrinkled gown.

The duchess opened her mouth to reassure her guest that it was of no import but found herself saying instead, "I wonder what caused that stain."

Aurora's gaze swiveled to the dark spot on the wall that snagged Leandra's attention. Her brow furrowed slightly. "I don't know. I admit I never even noticed it before." She moved closer to it. "How very odd. Look at this."

Leandra stepped up next to Aurora and stared at the spot the countess indicated with one delicate finger. "Do you see what I see?"

The large stain was located on the dark paneling of the wall. But near the floor, it had gotten on the carpet. Near the edge, along the wall, was a strip of white. Just under the stain, the white was stained a dull burgundy color.

"Wine?"

Leandra shook her head. The very slight paling of her face was the only indication that she was disturbed by her next words. "I think it's blood," she suggested with amazing calm. The picture she had found in the children's book seemed suddenly blazoned in her mind. "In fact, I know it is."

Aurora straightened to her full height, staring at Leandra in concern. "How can you be so sure?"

"Follow me. I'll show you."

The two ladies turned in the direction Leandra had just come from and for which Aurora was previously bound. The duchess entered her room and crossed to the nightstand. She pulled a worn leather book from the drawer and removed a folded piece of foolscap. Wordlessly, she handed the drawing to her new friend.

"That's how I know."

Greville studied the picture minutely, then handed it back to Leandra. "It certainly is detailed," he commented, his bland tone at odds with the sharp look in his eyes.

Aurora wondered at his oddly disinterested air. "But what do you think? Can it be Hart's mama?"

The earl shrugged. "I never had the chance to meet the woman. Hart was only six when she died, you know. I didn't even know him then."

Leandra was equally baffled by Greville's apparent unconcern. She shared a look with Aurora. Then she smiled. "Thank you for your opinion, Levi."

The ladies turned to walk out but paused when Greville called them back.

"Can I borrow that drawing, Leandra? I would like to discover who drew it, if I may."

Leandra handed it over, although she was loath to part with it. "Please don't show it to Hart."

"I hadn't planned on it."

As soon as the ladies were gone, Greville went in search of Gabriel St. Clair. If anyone knew what the picture represented and why, it was the one man who could truly claim a closeness to the Heartless duke.

The earl found Gabriel standing in the east garden contemplating a statue of Venus in spite of the chilly weather. As Greville got closer, however, he realized the man wasn't even looking at the statue but somewhere beyond it at the stone wall cutting off the castle's occupants from the rest of the world.

Greville approached him, inquiring after his health, and asked what held his attention. Gabriel pointed at a small groove in the wall about three feet from the ground.

"We were eight. Hart found his father's pistols and we decided to try them out."

"You were aiming at the wall?"

Smiling, Gabriel corrected, "No, we just weren't any good then. I was aiming for the statue, which I see has been replaced, and Hart was aiming for a bush that used to grow there." He pointed to a spot a little to the right of the ding in the wall. "We both missed. My shot nearly went into Hart. His went into the wall."

Greville laughed. "And your father?"

"Quite so. We should have been aiming at him."

"That's not what I meant."

The one-armed man shrugged, sighing. "I know. And I shouldn't have said that. You were perhaps wondering what he did when he discovered what we had done? He beat me until I could barely move, then he publicly whipped Hart. I think that was when Hart decided my whole family would have to go. Whatever it took."

Silence.

Then, "I was wondering if you could explain this."

Gabriel took the drawing. He stared at it for a long time. "Where did you find this?" he finally asked.

"Leandra had it. I don't know where she found it."

Gabriel nodded once. "I recognize my aunt, of course, and the landing. The boy is definitely Hart, although it could be me. Are you asking me if there's any truth to the picture?"

"Yes, actually. I know the late duchess died in odd circumstances."

"I suppose it could be true, if that's supposed to be Hart. Otherwise," he shrugged, "it is just an excellent representation of a rumor."

Greville was dissatisfied with this response. It appeared Gabriel was hiding something. He knew more about it than he was letting on. "Who do you suppose drew it?"

Gabriel shrugged again. "It is excellent but rather disturbing as a subject. I wouldn't even know where to start looking."

He walked away after that and the earl watched him leave. He wondered if Derringer remembered what had happened. Perhaps someone else had witnessed it and was trying to alert the duke to the truth. But what possible good could come of him remembering such a thing after all these years?

After one more day in his bed, the Duke of Derringer had had enough. Leandra had not been in to see him once in the past thirty-six hours and while he really couldn't blame her, annoyance held him hostage. She could not have told Levi of his rough handling of her. Had the earl found out, Derringer was positive he'd not be able to rise from his bed so soon. At the least, he'd be facing the man come dawn one day soon. Part of him was disappointed. He deserved a bullet.

Rising and carefully flexing his shoulder, the duke dressed in his customary black, giving little thought to the process. Plans took form in his mind but he wondered what he should do first. A gallop on Satan was his first choice but he was sure his shoulder and ribs couldn't possibly handle such rough treatment—especially after the jostling they received making love to his wife, he thought with a smirk. Seeking out Leandra was another idea but he was unsure of his reception. He wasn't quite ready to die.

It was nearing the dinner hour but Derringer refused to join his guests. He knew it was only a matter of time until Adam Prestwich showed up with his wife and children and he wanted to be alone as much as possible. Damn, his home was becoming a nesting ground for every looby in the kingdom!

Deciding Satan would cause him less damage than his wife or friend, he headed down the servants' stairs. He intended to exit the castle by way of the kitchen door but voices in the Great Hall slowed his progress.

He knew his wife's voice instantly. The memory of gentle remonstrances, soothing tones, and delicate laughter slammed through him.

But he could hear fear in her voice now. He could hear the fear although he could not make out her words. His destination changed in that moment, hearing her fear. He moved toward her voice. If someone were threatening her in her own home, he'd throttle the impertinent bounder.

It did occur to him that he had done just that and he even admitted to himself that he deserved nothing short of death for his treatment of his gentle wife. But he couldn't seem to rid himself of the haunting images of Leandra's death. If she was hurt while trying to protect him, he might as well be the one holding the knife.

As he drew closer, he realized she was talking to Greville. This development caused him to halt in his tracks and unashamedly listen to their conversation.

"You have to do something," Leandra insisted. "I can't take this anymore. If he leaves the castle again, he will die."

The earl placed an arm around her. For comfort, Derringer was sure, but he still wanted to knock the man down for touching her in any way.

"Leandra, he is still safe in his bed. You have nothing to fear. Adam will be here soon and I'm sure he can help."

"But Lee was making such odd comments about him last night. And after what Hart told me about Lee going to France with that… that man, I worry about the implications of his comments."

Lee? Harwood had something to do with this? Interesting.

"It is quite likely that your brother is babbling nonsense just to upset you. I have noticed he does not feel kindly disposed toward you."

Leandra's next comment was too low for Derringer to hear. Greville answered her in a low voice, she replied and Greville's voice was just a tad louder with his next words.

"I'll kill him for you. Better yet, I'll tell Hart."

Leandra reached out to stop the earl from storming away. Derringer itched to rearrange Harwood's angelic face based solely on principle.

"Levi, you can't. He has enough to concern him at the moment. I will deal with Lee. He has never actually hurt me and I don't expect he will with my husband under the same roof. Please."

Greville appeared to seriously consider telling her no. Then he bowed politely but told her clearly that if the Earl of Harwood continued his insulting manner, the duke would be informed. He left her alone in the Great Hall.

Derringer considered approaching her at that moment but decided against it. He knew the only way to lure out his enemy was to be out and about not arguing with his wife over his right to murder her brother. Somehow he doubted Harwood was the source of his troubles, however.

Satan was happy to see him. He stamped angrily in his impatience to be out. Derringer soothed him with a calm word, then saddled the beast himself, carefully checking the saddle and bridle to ensure they hadn't been tampered with. A trifle melodramatic but this was the point to which his life had come.

After assuring himself that everything on his estate seemed for the most part, normal, Derringer returned to the castle. He didn't want to but his wishes were moot. Sharp pains stabbed through his shoulder and neck while his ribs vehemently protested too much activity. Besides, his desire to see his wife was overpowering.

As he rode home, he pondered the chances of his receiving her forgiveness for his unpardonable behavior. If she were intelligent, she'd tell him to the go to the devil and live in the newly renovated dower house.

But what if she took his apology to mean that he was willing to allow her to risk her life finding his attacker? Would he then be forced to actually witness her demise, horrible and bloody as he imagined it would be? He shook his head. His apology would have to wait until he captured the villain responsible. Then he would simply grovel.

Satan stopped nearly causing Derringer to lose his seat for the first time in twenty years. He grabbed reins and mane to retain his balance, darting quick little glances in all directions. Something wasn't right. He could feel it just as surely as the mighty animal beneath him.

The giant black swung his head to the right. His nostrils flared and what sounded amazingly like a growl came from his throat. Derringer's gaze followed the same direction. He caught a sharp movement near a tree. Something glinting in the late afternoon sun like... metal.

The duke kicked the horse just as the gun exploded. Satan screamed and took off like a shot. Derringer managed to hold his seat while keeping his head low in case of a second shot. His thoughts were all on retaining his seat and staying alive.

The pair cannoned into the stable yard. Amid shouts of alarm and sharply asked questions, the duke brought the frightened animal under control and slid from his back.

When a groom stepped forward to remove the saddle, Satan bared his teeth. Derringer stepped back a pace, watching as the boy expertly groomed the stallion. He saw the boy frown at his hand and run it along the horse's hindquarters—and get nipped at for his trouble.

The duke started forward, speaking soothingly as he did so and copied the groom's actions. His hand came away bloody. The bullet had grazed the poor animal, which accounted for his headlong flight home and his bad manners now.

Derringer cursed long and fluently. The eyes of the boy widened to immense proportions at his inventiveness.

The duke swung around suddenly and shouted for every stable hand to congregate around. As soon as even the smallest boy was present, Lord Derringer began in the silky tones that meant he was severely displeased.

"If any one of you sees a suspicious person—someone unknown to you or to one of your fellow servants—on this estate, bring that person to me. If you see anyone, bring him or her to me. If they resist, *shoot* them and then bring them to me. I will have everyone know that this game of cat and mouse is over. I want the north woods searched. And I mean searched. Under every rock, in every hole, behind and up every tree. And I want to personally speak with anyone who has any information about who shot my bloody horse!"

This last was shouted. To a man, the servants bowed, swearing to do his bidding exactly. After leaving specific instructions for the head groom as to the care of poor Satan, Derringer stormed into the castle.

It was unfortunate that the Earl of Harwood happened to be crossing the Great Hall at the exact moment the duke entered his home. Considering how angry he was over the injury to his horse added to his conviction that Harwood had something to do with at least half of his current problems, it was impossible for Derringer to just ignore the man. Maybe he could have restrained his desire to actually lay hands on the earl but he rather doubted it.

Harwood never saw it coming. He greeted the duke with a smile that Derringer supposed was meant to be friendly. But all the duke saw behind the cherubic features was a lecherous mind and a devious spirit. His fist connected with Harwood's face, the force of which sent that man to the floor.

Savage glee shot through Derringer at the sight. Part of him acknowledged that he'd wanted to do just such a thing since the moment he first saw the man, but part of him wanted vengeance for Leandra, for the years of mistreatment she endured at her family's hands.

He stood over the fallen earl, hands clenched at his sides. Harwood shook his head, one hand fingering his bruised jaw while the other supported his body in its reclined position. Derringer watched, eyes narrowing as a conversation he'd had with his wife the day they'd met sprang to the fore.

Reaching down with his uninjured arm, the duke lifted the smaller man from his seat on the marble tiled floor. Holding him at eye level, he inquired silkily, "Where is your father's will, Lee?"

The earl's eyes threatened to pop out of his skull. "Father's will?" he repeated stupidly.

"Yes, lackwit, your father's will. Generally it is a piece of paper, maybe several, with words written on them in a nice legal hand. You know, words that outline the extent of a man's wealth and to whom he wishes to leave it upon his passing. His will. The one you stole and the one I want."

"I have no idea what you are referring to, your grace."

"Please, Lee, I thought we had agreed we were friends. I insist you call me Hart."

The earl trembled at the vague menace in the duke's low voice. "Will you put me down?" he then asked with a timidity that Derringer instantly distrusted.

He did, however, put him down. He threw him down, in fact. Harwood hit the floor hard enough to make him grunt in pain.

Derringer waited impatiently as the other man gingerly rose to his feet and dusted himself off. He straightened his neckcloth and brushed down his waistcoat and jacket. It finally took a low, menacing growl from Derringer to regain the man's attention.

"Where is it?"

"I am afraid, my lord, that you are vastly mistaken if you believe I have my father's will. I do not, in fact. He did not leave one. It is well known that he did not."

The duke did not like at all how confident the man sounded. It was probably true that the will was not in his possession. But Derringer was willing to bet his life that one did exist and that the late earl was far too shrewd to leave it where his avaricious wife or son might find it.

Which only meant that Harwood had perhaps left all of his wealth to his illegitimate daughter. Everything that wasn't entailed on his firstborn son, that is. The Duke of Derringer smiled. A treasure hunt was just what he needed to distract his mind from the threat that loomed over him... and his desire to apologize to his wife.

23

Leandra's eyes threatened to pop, her chest constricting at the sight of her husband, his one good hand twisted in her brother's shirt front, Harwood's feet dangling inches from the floor. She wasn't sure what she felt at the sight, awe at the sheer power Derringer displayed or pity that her brother fell afoul of her husband. Perhaps a mix of the two.

Something made her ease further back into the shadows cast by the grand staircase. Should she try to rescue her brother? He looked dangerously close to disgracing himself.

Her innate desire to forestall bloodshed propelled her forward. Before she could take a single step, Derringer dropped his captive, Harwood's backside coming into violent contact with the marble floor. Leandra was too far away to hear anything other than her brother's grunt of pain.

She wanted to know what they were discussing. She glanced back toward the drawing room to make sure no one else was coming. Then, she crept up far enough to hear.

The comment about there never having been a will caught her by surprise. She'd assumed it was merely lost or misplaced, but Harwood seemed quite certain it had never existed. But that would mean her father had lied. He never lied.

Derringer's expression slipped into something Leandra could only call savage delight. Why would Harwood's comment about there never having been a will cause such a reaction in her husband? An uneasy feeling crept over her skin.

She turned to leave. Derringer appeared quite through with her brother so her presence was not required. She slipped around the newel post, intent on making her escape before catching her husband's eye. Just as she reached the door to the drawing room, an arm of steel snaked around her waist and pulled her back against a hard body.

"Merri, Merri, I do believe you were eavesdropping," the duke breathed in her ear.

She sighed lightly when his lips briefly touched that sensitive area right below her ear. She fought the quivering sensation in her middle, reminded herself of his treatment of her after introducing her to the delights to be had in his arms.

Turning slightly to look up into his mocking black eyes, Leandra said, "I assume you require me for something, your grace?"

His reply made her ears turn pink.

Derringer released her with a mocking grin but took her hand. Without so much as a by-your-leave, he led her to his father's study and made her sit.

"How much did you hear?" he asked blandly.

Leandra watched him warily as he sat on the edge of the desk, hands braced on either side of him. If he suspected she had heard more than she ought, would he again threaten her with physical violence? Or would he make good on his prior threat to beat her?

"Come, Merri, I promise I won't bite," he cajoled. "Unless you ask me to."

Her natural poise came to her rescue in the face of this outrageous remark—this outrageous remark that caused an almost pleasant tingling in her skin. With a determined effort she managed to keep her thoughts and feelings from her expression. She hoped.

"I overheard Lee tell you that Papa never made a will."

"And do you believe him?"

"Of course not. Papa told me he left a will. He said I would never have to fear poverty. He said he would always take care of me, even after his death."

A twinge of desperation entered her final words, desperation and grief. She hated the weakness she displayed but she missed her father so much.

"Does your brother make a habit of lying then?"

She shrugged, her blank features telling Derringer nothing of her inner thoughts. He hated how he couldn't read her all the time like he could most people. If her silence was due to fear of him, he couldn't know. She hid fear as well as anything.

He did, however, catch the emotion behind her comment in regard to her father, a reaction that was to be expected under the circumstances. She had been deeply attached to the late Lord Harwood.

Though the duke *had* expected a little more emotion when faced with the likely perfidy of her brother.

Pushing away from the desk to pace before her, Derringer offered, "Perhaps he does not make a habit of it but deems it necessary in these circumstances, honorable, even."

Leandra sat up straighter, eyes widening, fingers clenching in her lap. Anger flashed through her eyes, almost lost behind her thick spectacles. "You mean, keep it out of the hands of the bastard?"

It was the duke's turn to shrug. "If you will. What I want to know is why he thinks it best to disregard your father's wishes."

"Lee pretended to love Papa but I always doubted his sincerity. He had a way of appearing so innocent that I had trouble believing him. Others seemed to see him only as he appeared. Papa never seemed to see through him, though."

Derringer very much doubted that. He had met the late earl once or twice and the man had never struck him as particularly obtuse. He had, in fact, appeared quite cognizant of his family's shortcomings. It was this that made Derringer positive that a will did exist and one that most likely left everything to the earl's one truly loving child.

A child whose existence Derringer was unaware of until he rescued her at an inn, where she'd managed to end up after her loving family tossed her on her ear. What a tiny world they inhabited.

His next comment, however, revealed none of his ruminations to his wife. "Perhaps your father was dense enough to believe in his only son's honor."

Leandra stood. Derringer watched outrage ripple over her face and form, tension settling on her shoulders like a dark mantle. With a token curtsy in his direction, she quit the room, nose in the air in the best grand duchess manner he'd ever beheld.

The duke was so surprised at her abrupt exit that he just stood there. It was only after she'd gone that he realized how rude she'd actually been. He smiled.

The Earl of Harwood was very careful to avoid Lord Derringer over the next few days, a circumstance that pleased the duke. He was unsure if he could avoid laying hands on the man again.

But Martin St. Clair seemed to be avoiding Derringer as well. This oddity so perplexed the duke that he sought the man out to question him over his behavior.

"Is there something troubling you, cousin?"

Martin shrugged, a smile touching his lips at Derringer's show of concern. "No, why do you ask?"

The very tone in Martin's voice, something bordering on contempt, made the hairs on Derringer's neck stand on end. There was also something almost chaotic in his cousin's eyes that caused an uneasy shiver to snake down his spine.

The feeling passed almost immediately, Martin's face clearing of all expression. Surely he'd imagined the strange look and the strange effect it had had on him.

"Then I would suggest you take your position seriously in future. I haven't the time to hunt you down when I have need of you."

Derringer walked away with the feeling that his cousin was glaring daggers at him. This completely outrageous feeling was eerie enough to make him glance behind him. Martin indeed watched him, but his face showed nothing more than blank inquiry.

The feeling followed Derringer out to the stables, however.

After assuring himself that Satan was mending well, Derringer returned to the castle. His bellow upon entering was answered with as much speed as he could wish. Every servant was soon before him.

"Excellent. I am glad to see that despite infirmities of all kinds, none of you appear hampered by them. My congratulations." He saw his wife enter the Great Hall with her stepmother and sisters followed closely by his aunt and cousins.

With a mocking bow, he addressed his next words to his family. "And my guests as well. How convenient."

"What is this about, your grace?" asked Leandra with a touch of impatience.

"It is not your place to inquire into my doings, Lady Derringer," he returned, disliking the rush of annoyance at her reaction.

Such humiliation in front of servants and family was enough to cause Leandra's eyes to darken. Without another word, she turned and left.

"Everyone is dismissed," growled the duke. "All family members will please adjourn to the drawing room." Without waiting to see if anyone complied, he stalked after his wife.

He entered her sitting room to find her pacing in obvious agitation. When she heard him, she turned and glared. "What do you want, your grace?"

The first response that popped into Derringer's head was "You." He refrained from saying that, however, and settled for, "I want to know why you left before I dismissed you."

Leandra stared at him incredulously. "I can't believe you! Of all the... you insufferable boor!" She marched up to him, shaking a tiny fist in his face. "I am not your servant, Hart. I will not be treated as one. You have no right!"

"Have I not, Merri?" His voice was silky, dangerous. As much as he found his wife in a temper most arousing, he was angered by her show of bravado. "I seem to recall you needing help most desperately when I found you."

"And I seem to recall that without me you'd be poor as a church mouse!"

"I could have had anybody, Merri. You were convenient."

Leandra was silent for a heart-stopping moment, the casual hurtfulness of his comment robbing her of breath. Then she lifted her nose a notch and replied, "Very convenient, your grace. I am, however, tired of being considered nothing more than your *convenience*. I am leaving."

She moved to go around him but he stopped her. "You are going nowhere."

"The devil I'm not!"

One black brow arched in surprise. "You are calling the devil into this? I'm shocked."

"You will not charm me into staying, Hart, any more than you will order me to. I'm done trying to prove that you're worth saving."

24

THE words were already said. There was no going back in time to rescind them. The damage was done. And if Leandra had known quite how much damage she'd done, she would have stayed and attempted everything in her power to make it right.

But she didn't.

"Have you been trying to save me, Merri?"

She made no reply to his horrified query. Instead, she walked away from him.

Derringer watched her leave and wondered why he'd ever made the idiotic mistake of falling in love. All his experience of that emotion had not ended well. And Leandra was more proof of that.

And he was. In love. Completely, irrevocably, head-over-ears in love with his own wife. He didn't know when it happened or how, but he admitted the truth of it.

So he did the only thing he could to prove it. He let her go.

Ten minutes later found the Duke of Derringer in the drawing room with his and Leandra's families. He looked them over with acute dislike, wanting nothing more than to throw them all bodily from the castle… tower. In some obscure way, he blamed them for his recent falling out with Leandra.

Taking up a defensive stance near the hearth, Derringer announced, "Just as soon as my servants have packed your things—which I estimate to be in less than five minutes"— glancing at the watch hanging from his waistcoat—"you will all depart Derringer Crescent. We will, of course, be sorry to see you go and all that rubbish, but I fear your welcome has long since been worn thin. Thank you." With a bow that lacked any mocking, the duke walked out on a sea of shocked expressions.

Gabriel followed his cousin into the hall. "Hart, wait!"

The duke stopped and turned, his left eyebrow raised in silent inquiry.

"What was that all about? And where is Merri?" asked Gabriel as he caught up with Derringer.

Save for the lowering of his brow, the duke's expression didn't change. "It doesn't concern you and please refer to my wife with more formality."

As he turned to continue on his way, Gabriel caught his arm and swung him around. "Just what the devil is that supposed to mean? You act as though I have committed some indiscretion with Lady Derringer."

The duke stared at his cousin's hand where it lay on his arm in the way that usually indicated his displeasure to the offending creature. Gabriel, however, was not afraid of Derringer as others were. He merely shook the duke's arm when no answer was forthcoming.

Derringer looked up and sighed. He had never had secrets from his cousin before, why start now when he had finally proven beyond a shadow exactly what a cad he was?

"If you must know, Gabe, Leandra has decided to take her glorious presence from my home and I find I am sick of playing gracious host to her blasted family, not to mention yours. If you and Martin would like to stay, you know you are welcome to. But," he shook his head, "I need to be alone."

The door to the drawing room opened to disgorge Greville and his wife. Aurora took one look at the duke, marched over, and glared up at him. "That was badly done, Hart, and well you know it. How could you be so very rude? Do you know that poor Michaella is in tears at the thought of leaving Leandra here with a monster like you?"

"Lady Michaella is crying?" asked Gabriel. Without waiting for an answer, he disappeared back into the drawing room.

"And what do you have to add, Vi?"

"Nothing, Hart. I agree that you have every right to ask us to leave. But," he said pointedly with a look at his tiny but furious wife, "I also think you could have been more polite about it." He shrugged. "But I also know that's not really you."

"Where is Leandra, Hart? Why didn't she come with you to extricate your unwelcome guests?"

"You will be pleased to know, Lady Greville," Derringer snapped, "that dearest Leandra has finally made an intelligent decision. She's decided life without me in it is far preferable."

Aurora paled slightly. "You jest. Please tell me you jest."

"I do not. Now, if you will be so good, I wish to be alone."

"No, Hart, I want to speak with you about this."

"Vi, when have I ever bowed to your wishes?"

"Never. But you will start now."

The determination in Greville's voice convinced Derringer that he would stop at nothing to get his compliance. "And if I don't?" he challenged anyway.

Greville smiled. "I'll thrash you. Or let you die. The choice is yours."

Derringer did not trust his friend's look. He supposed if Greville thought it necessary, he would simply step aside and let whomever it was that desired Derringer's death to have at it.

"Will you leave me be if I assure you it was my fault and the best thing for her to do is leave?"

"How was it your fault?" inquired Aurora. A look of disbelief crossed her features. "Did I just ask how it was *your* fault?" She shook her head at his mocking expression and continued, "Allow me to rephrase that. What did you say or do to make her leave?"

The duke shrugged with apparent nonchalance. "Nothing she didn't already know." He was secretly ashamed of his behavior with Leandra but he'd be damned before he'd admit it to even these, his closest friends.

He was saved from a closer examination by the exhumation of the drawing room. The rest of the family poured out and Derringer took a step back. "You are welcome to stay, of course, Vi, but I want everyone else gone."

Everyone assembled in the hall watched the duke stride away. Just as he was about to make good his escape through the front door, Stark opened it to admit Sir Adam Prestwich. Derringer groaned.

"Get out, Prestwich. I don't want or need your help."

"That's a fine attitude, Derringer," scolded the vibrant beauty that was Adam's wife, Lady Brianna. "You know very well this is one problem you can't solve on your own."

Without further ado, she pushed the duke out of the way and entered the castle. Following closely in her wake were her children, six-year-old Callie, two-year-old

Jessamyn, and the baby, eleven-month-old Lucien, was carried in by a chubby nursery maid.

"You brought them all?" asked Derringer. He glanced at the smiling baby boy and felt an odd pull that he refused to explore or even acknowledge. He addressed the baronet once more. "Why did you bring your whole family?"

The look of incredulity on Adam's face made Lady Prestwich laugh. "Do you think he could have stopped me, my lord duke?" she asked sweetly. "I assure you, he could not."

Her husband shrugged. "I choose not to argue with her. If she gets involved more than I would like, I'll tie her up."

Lady Brianna's expression reflected uncertainty at this calm announcement. That he would do it was not in doubt. Derringer got a twinge of malicious pleasure from this.

"Mrs. Stark!" The housekeeper bustled forward, a smile of welcome on her round features. "Put my new guests somewhere." Then, having decided he'd had enough of unwanted company, the Duke of Derringer made good his escape.

Greville glanced at the new guests and then at the old guests. He frowned. "Mrs. Stark, I know you would never disregard his lordship's wishes but please rescind the order to eject them."

The woman frowned right along with him. "I could never do that, my lord." She waved her husband over.

"Stark, his lordship requests that we rescind the order to remove his grace's unwelcome guests."

"Indeed, my lord?"

"I have my reasons, Stark."

The Starks glanced at each other, saying nothing yet communicating as only a longtime married couple could. Then, decision made, Stark returned his wooden expression to Lord Greville. "We trust that your lordship is fully aware of the risk you are taking?"

The earl smiled. "I am."

"Very well then, my lord." A flurry of activity began in which Stark managed to make the change in orders known without drawing his grace's attention. The efficiency was a sight to behold.

That taken care of, Greville came forward and greeted his cousin and her husband. "I apologize for our host's rather rude welcome, but…" He shrugged.

Aurora said a few things to Mrs. Stark and then took little Jessamyn by the hand and led the newcomers away. Prestwich stayed behind.

"I never expected better, Vi, believe me. Is there some place we can speak privately? Something has happened that perhaps you should know about."

25

THE lateness of the year brought darkness early, the sun descending though night still lay hours away. Leandra gazed through her bedchamber window, watching the sun begin its descent, streaking reds and golds across the sky. She saw nothing. Liza scurried around the room behind her, packing a valise at Leandra's request. No tears marred her round cheeks, no wrinkle disturbed her pale brow.

She felt nothing. She refused to consider her husband's hateful words, to recall the contempt in his face and voice. Tears were scorned in the face of her injured pride. It was outside of enough that he'd managed to shatter her heart, dismantle her world, and otherwise destroy everything she'd come to believe about love and marriage. He couldn't have her tears too.

She didn't know where she would go, however. Her allowance was enough she could go anywhere in the country but she hated the idea of using a penny of her husband's money. On the other hand, how was she to get away if she did not?

"Oh, bother."

Liza looked up, pausing briefly in the act of folding her mistress's underthings. "Your grace?"

"Nothing, Liza. I've just remembered something. Don't bother with the valise. I may not need it quite yet."

The duchess rose to her feet and retrieved the childish book of spells she had hidden in her nightstand. As she pulled it out, she inadvertently knocked out one of the late duchess's journals. It fell to the floor, an ominous crack sounding. Leandra clenched her teeth and bent to pick it up. As she did so, she noticed a very small piece of foolscap protruding from between the cover and the vellum carefully glued to it. Her eyebrows rose slightly at this and she gently removed the protrusion.

It was folded only once and written in the same hand as the journals. Why would Derringer's mama hide it instead of writing it in her book with the rest of her feelings and secrets?

Leandra gripped the journal, recalling some of the shocking things the woman had revealed in her private writings. She'd felt only a twinge of guilt at reading them, but nothing prepared her for the lack of compunction the late duchess felt at playing her husband false. At least she had waited until the birth of her son to dally, Leandra thought with unaccustomed cynicism.

Dismissing Liza firmly, Leandra sat down at the little writing desk in the corner of her sitting room. With a tiny bit of guilt for yet again invading the privacy of another, she unfolded the missive.

The writing was the same, she noted upon closer inspection, but it appeared rather forced, hurried, agitated. Two discolored spots in the paper indicated the possibility of tears. A shiver of unease snaked through her body.

Her eyes passed over the missive, widening with each word. By the end of the first paragraph, she was visibly shaken. By the end of the second, tears gathered in her eyes. And by the end of the third and final paragraph, her tears dried and a feeling of dread pooled in the pit of her stomach.

Leandra crossed to the bellpull. A moment of tense waiting was rewarded with the arrival of Liza. "Quickly, Liza, where is Mr. St. Clair?"

"Mr. St. Clair, your grace? In his grace's study, I believe."

Leandra fled her room and nearly ran to the study on the ground floor. She wished a trifle crossly that the castle wasn't quite so big, but brushed it aside with her customary sensibility.

Customary sensibility? Where exactly had that particular quality fled to when she had been faced with her husband's usual incivility?

Shaking her head, her goal uppermost in her mind, Leandra missed a pair of midnight eyes that watched her movements suspiciously—and a trifle sadly.

Derringer's eyes narrowed. What had his unwilling bride in such a pother? With the grace of a jungle cat, he stepped into her path.

Leandra, of course, could not avoid the imminent collision with Derringer's muscular form. He wrapped one arm around her waist and twitched the paper from her clenched fingers.

"What is this, soon-to-be-absent Lady Derringer?"

Despite the lie in the words, she retorted, "None of your business, your grace."

Derringer glanced briefly at the bit of handwriting that was visible. His black brows rose. "Is it not, my unwilling-companion-in-life? I do believe this is my mother's hand, unless I'm very much mistaken. Am I mistaken, Leandra?"

The stern note in his voice warned her of the wisdom of a candid answer. "Perhaps it is."

"Then you were looking for me, I suppose?"

"No."

Derringer leaned his head back, keeping her firmly locked in his embrace. "No? Then who were you looking for, Lady Doesn't-want-to-be-a-duchess?"

Leandra's brows drew down at his annoying appellations. "I was taking it to your cousin Martin, since it regards his brother."

The sudden tension in the arm around her sent a chill through Leandra.

"His brother?"

"Yes, your grace, his brother, Gabriel St. Clair."

"I see. And what, pray tell, does this mysterious letter reveal about my dear cousin, bride-of-my-heart?"

Leandra was not fooled by the softness that touched the endearment. He could not possibly mean anything by it, she knew. It was inconceivable that he had any feelings for her whatsoever considering he threatened her and then told her exactly what he thought of her.

"If you want to know, read the damn letter yourself, Lord Heartless!" she snapped. She wrenched herself from his grasp and tried to escape but he stopped her by the simple expedient of catching her hand.

"Let me go."

Derringer sighed. "Leandra, we have to talk and I don't mean to let you leave me until we do. Can you not at least grant me a few moments of your precious time, my heart?"

Before she could respond to this astounding, strangely humble request, Martin St. Clair walked into the corridor. His pale blue eyes passed from Derringer to Leandra and back to the duke with a vague hint of inquiry. He said nothing, however.

Derringer released Leandra and stared at his cousin. "Can I help you, Martin?"

Leandra noticed the dangerous silky tone that her husband employed when he was angered. Was Martin as cognizant of this fact?

If he was, he didn't reveal it. His face was suitably blank as he replied, "I was just coming in search of you, Hart." He eyed the paper in the duke's hand with an intensity that disturbed Leandra. Derringer noticed as well and shoved the note into the pocket of his black leather breeches.

The look of odd interest left Martin's bright eyes and he once again glanced at Leandra. Derringer, rather than taking the hint that Martin wished to speak to him alone, offered, "Perhaps you would like to talk to my wife instead? I understand she's looking for somewhere to go."

The duchess turned shocked eyes on Derringer. Of course he would assume she had nowhere to go. But did he have to inform his cousin of her imminent departure? Or imply that she was looking for... a protector, for lack of a better word?

The duke laughed at his cousin's astonishment. "Never mind, Martin. I do believe she is of two minds on the subject."

Leandra had, indeed, been of two minds. But after his assured belief of this, she once again decided it would be best to leave based solely on obstinacy.

"Go back to my study, Martin. I'll be with you shortly." Derringer turned to his wife as soon as the door to the study closed. "Have you nothing to say, my bride?"

"You assume much to think I would stay with you, your grace. You threaten my life, you tell me I am nothing more than a convenience, and you mock me before servants, family, and friends as often as possible. Why on earth should I even consider staying here?"

"You are my wife," he stated simply, unemotionally.

"Scarcely," she retorted. She immediately regretted her words. The implications were obvious and she knew her husband would hear the longing she'd failed to hide.

"Merri, my love, is that frustration I hear?" He took a step closer, his expression turning wolfish. "I have been neglecting you, have I? Should I remedy that oversight?"

Despite every effort to the contrary, Leandra felt a blush climb her cheeks. "Never!" she said. It came out, however, as little more than a breathless whisper.

A devilish twinkle lit Derringer's eyes. "You sound quite as though you desire my attentions, oh, worshiped one." He stepped closer still, shortening the distance between their bodies to a mere inch or two. "Do you?"

"No." Again, it was the merest sound.

"You lie."

Before she could think or react, her husband captured her head with one hand and pressed his mouth to hers. Desire flared as his lips moved over hers. Her arms crept around him, her longing for this man overcoming all the warnings her head presented.

She shouldn't love him, indeed she should cut him from her life with the greatest relief. But she knew as he made love to her lips, drew her closer until their bodies were pressed intimately together, she was as hopelessly lost as she'd feared. She would never love another as she loved him.

And she could never truly give up on him. Somewhere in there, somewhere buried deep was a man loving and kind. All she had to do was find him, coax him out.

The sound of someone clearing his throat finally broke them apart. Even then, their eyes remained locked. Leandra stared into troubled eyes, dark as pitch, clouded with a question she dare not consider at the moment.

With a will of iron, she whispered, "That was unfair, Hart. I am a green girl, as you very well know."

The strange vulnerability in his eyes disappeared, replaced with mocking contempt. "What do you want, Prestwich?" he asked, his eyes never leaving his wife's.

"I daresay it would be best if we spoke alone, Derringer."

Leandra turned and beheld an attractive gentleman nearly as dark as her husband. His eyes, however, were an odd gray-green color and held a note of pity in their depths. She found herself oddly resentful of his assumption.

Drawing herself up to her full height—which brought the top her head somewhere in the vicinity of her husband's chin—she inquired in the best duchess tones she could, "And, who, if I may be so bold, are you, sir?"

Laughter flashed through Prestwich's pale eyes. Derringer saw it. He was amused himself by his wife's quick rise to the ranks of the peerage in attitude as well as name.

Prestwich resisted the urge, however. He smiled rather pleasantly, bowed respectfully, and introduced himself. "I am a friend of your husband's, your grace," he added with a cynical look thrown Derringer's way.

"I very much doubt that, Sir Adam," returned the duchess. "My husband doesn't have friends. If he ever did, he has long since alienated them through his boorish behavior."

The duke shrugged when the other man leveled a questioning look on him. "I'm like an open book, Prestwich. Easily read."

The baronet snorted at this. "In a pig's eye," he muttered.

Leandra smiled despite herself. Prestwich caught it and shrugged. "I am truly a friend whether his unholy lordship chooses to recognize that fact or not."

"I believe you," Leandra murmured. "I will leave you now." She dropped a slight curtsy out of respect and walked away.

"You do have a habit of trying to destroy your life, Derringer," remarked Prestwich thoughtfully.

The duke stared at him, saying nothing.

26

"And I don't know why you insist that I stay out of it, Adam. This affects Levi, too, you know."

Sir Adam Prestwich glared at his wife. "We are dealing with a possible madman, Brianna Prestwich. Not some schoolboy out for a lark."

"A *possible* madman?" she interjected, snapping up the one unknown in her husband's statement.

"It is impossible that he be other than completely unbalanced. Remember," he added darkly, "you are not pregnant now. I will beat you."

Bri released an annoyed sound that Adam might actually have called a growl—had his wife been an animal. "Very well, Adam, you win. I will not get involved in apprehending the villain."

The baronet's eyes narrowed. "You will not get involved in the investigation, either."

This time she really did growl. "I hate you."

Prestwich laughed outright. "No, you don't. You love me and that's why you are so upset that you feel obligated to obey." He stepped close enough to wrap his arms around her. "Promise me, Bri."

"I promise nothing."

"Very well." He dropped his hands back to his sides and walked to the door. "After so many years of marriage, one would think she'd learn," he muttered to himself. Turning, he added, "I will just have to lock you in here until you do."

Lady Brianna's scream echoed off the stone walls of the castle corridors as her husband firmly locked her in. He just laughed.

"And people call *me* heartless," a deep voice mocked.

"You are," Prestwich assured him. He walked away and the duke fell into step beside him.

"True. But I wonder how long that room will actually hold a woman as determined as your bride. Care to lay a wager on it?"

"Very well."

"Leandra's locket says your lovely wife will join us for dinner tonight without apologizing or groveling or whatever it is she has refused to do."

Prestwich eyed the other man with dislike. "You would bet a piece of your wife's jewelry?"

"No, Prestwich, I would not, despite my heartless ways. I am informing you that I have discovered a way you may be of some assistance."

"Indeed?" the baronet drawled. "How so?"

"If I win the wager, you have to get Leandra's locket back for me. Her stepmother refused to let her take it when she was forced from her home and I want it back."

"And if you lose?"

The duke shrugged, stopped walking, and looked into Prestwich's eyes. "I will tell you everything I know about the person or persons trying to kill me and let you and Vi proceed as you see fit."

"And you will stop tormenting your wife?"

"My wife is my business, Prestwich. You'd do well to remember that."

Prestwich snorted. "I accept your bet on one condition."

"Name it."

"You are not to assist my wife in any way."

"And you are not to deter her in any way other than locking the doors to her bedchamber and locking her window."

"We're on the fourth floor."

"How well do you really know your wife?"

The duke was not surprised to see his unwanted guests had not only failed to leave, they seemed more determined than ever to stay. Never before had he had the dubious honor of being surrounded by those closest to him, friends and family. These were the people he could trust with his life.

So which one wanted him dead?

He shrugged. It suited his purposes that they remain, so their reason for doing so mattered little.

Instinct told him the gold filigree locket gracing the younger Lady Harwood's throat belonged to Leandra. He meant to have it before the little harpy departed.

But, just to be sure, he asked his wife to describe it. This interview went as he expected considering their rocky relationship of late.

"Describe it? Whatever for?"

Derringer frowned at her suspicious tone. "Curiosity," he told her with a careless shrug.

"I have no need, I daresay," she replied. "As you are a man, I venture to say you have noticed with what ample charms my dear sister-in-law is endowed. You have but to look higher to see the exact locket given me by my father. She wears it to spite me and yet cannot know exactly what sort of pain she causes."

The duke smiled. "As I suspected. I thank you for your information, madam wife," he said with a courtly bow. "Shall I see you at dinner? We have far too many guests for you to gracefully withdraw I am afraid."

"Then why do you bother to inquire after my attendance? It appears as though the decision was never mine to make."

"Husbandly consideration?"

Leandra's left eyebrow quirked at this. "Indeed? Why do I feel the need to disregard such a suggestion? Perhaps because a considerate husband would never threaten to beat his wife for caring about him, or humiliate her before guests simply to make sure she is aware of her place of lesser worth for being born a woman."

The duke made no reply, offered no apology, indeed his very expression did not even change from the mask of vague interest he'd worn throughout her diatribe. It made her want to strike him.

"Have you nothing to say? A defense of some sort would be appropriate now, I should think. Anything to justify what you have said and done to intentionally hurt me." She shook her head angrily when he opened his mouth. "No, do not. I care not what your excuse is. I care not how you feel, your grace. Leave me, please." She turned away, his dismissal clear in her rigid posture.

"Merri, I—"

She swung around, fury engulfing her diminutive form. "Do not call me that! Never call me that! My father loved me. He called me that. It is reserved for my friends, Lord Derringer, and those that love me. You have made it all too clear that you feel no such emotion for me so I would greatly appreciate it if you would refrain from taking such a liberty."

Derringer stared at her. He was so completely shocked that he stood there blank-faced while she clenched her small hands into fists and actually screamed. He blinked once and reached for her as she dissolved into wrenching sobs.

She shrank away. "No! Don't touch me!" Each word was separated with much feeling and intense loathing. Her eyes sparkled like emeralds, as hard and unforgiving.

The duke's heart felt like a lead weight in his chest. He had lost. He admitted it. It was too late. But he could still retrieve that which was rightfully hers.

With one last pain-filled look, Derringer left her to her grief.

Leandra dried her face only to burst into tears again. It was just too much. She was ashamed of losing control of her tongue and her emotions. But being in love with a man as loathsome as the Duke of Derringer had finally pushed her too far. Where was that man she glimpsed so very briefly from time to time?

He was still there, she admitted. But her hurt feelings over his well-known rudeness would not allow her to see him in any kind of objective light.

With an effort, Leandra managed to get herself under control. She washed and dried her face at the washstand in her dressing room and rang for Liza. Dinner was soon and she wanted to be dressed as befitted her station.

Granted, looking well had always acted as a sort of armor for a woman since times immemorial. This thought rested comfortably in the back of Leandra's mind an hour later as she descended the stairs for dinner in a dark blue dress of shimmery satin with an overdress of silver net.

Hesitating on the landing, she took a deep breath. How could so much have happened in one day?

Her husband stood outside the doors of the drawing room, awaiting her arrival. His breath caught at the sight of her. She was like a midnight sky covered in stars. Her dark brown hair was swept up away from her face with silver combs encrusted in diamonds and sapphires and allowed to hang loosely down her back. It caused the most painful ache in his chest to realize that he had lost a brilliant piece of heaven because he was too used to having his own way all the time.

He would have given her every farthing of his inheritance if he thought it would help. But she was not minded as other women seemed to be. She didn't care for wealth and power. It was one of the main reasons he loved her.

She paused before him, her poise once more a part of her. With a graceful curtsy, she murmured, "Good evening, your grace."

Derringer bowed, his heart breaking at her formal, emotionless tone. Her insistence on the improper form of address saddened him. How he wished she'd stop emphasizing her belief that she was so much beneath him on a social scale. How he wished he could tell her she was above him and everyone he knew, regardless of title.

"You are beautiful tonight, your grace," he said, meaning every word.

He offered his arm to escort her into the drawing room, as manners deemed proper. She looked steadily at his face, glanced at his arm, and finally gingerly placed her hand on it.

It was enough to make a grown man cry. The duke thought for a moment that he might disgrace himself in just such a way. But he managed to swallow the lump in his throat and smile down at his tiny bride.

She stared hard at the floor. He wondered if perhaps there was some kind of insect or something that had caught her attention when he noticed her shoulders tremble.

The duke removed her hand from his sleeve and, instead of entering the drawing room, he took her down the corridor to a small, little used salon.

Turning her to face him, he said, "I wonder if you might let me say something."

Leandra looked up, tears in her eyes and on her cheeks. She brushed them impatiently away, angry that she had allowed her emotions free reign again. "What, your grace?"

Derringer sighed. "I was wrong."

She blinked, stared at him silently for a long moment, blinked again, sniffed, and then released a mirthless laugh. "You almost convinced me, your grace. Excellent attempt."

She turned to go but found her way impeded by her husband's grasp on her arm. She looked up at him. Would he beat her now?

"I am in earnest, Lady Derringer. I was wrong for threatening you, wrong for belittling you, wrong for telling you that you were unimportant to me. I was wrong. I would beg your forgiveness if I thought I deserved it, but I do not. You would be far better off without me in your life and I daresay would welcome the respite."

Leandra mulled this over, fighting back a fresh onslaught of tears. He seemed so very sincere. His black eyes were sad, his expression somber, and his bearing held a note of defeat.

She couldn't just give in, however, no matter how much her heart and soul cried out for her to do so. It was suicide to trust such a man.

"Why did you threaten me?" she asked instead.

Derringer tensed. Every time he thought of that incident, he was tortured by new visions of her horrible death. In fact, he'd started having nightmares about her falling down the stairs. The same stairs that...

"Hart! What is it?"

The duke shook his head, trying to clear the cobwebs from his brain. What was that all about? The same stairs that... what?

Leandra shook his arm, reached up and shook his shoulder, and then slapped him lightly on the cheek. She didn't understand what was happening, why he looked so distant, so frightened. What distressed him so?

Derringer looked down at Leandra with a perplexed, distracted air. It was such an odd recollection that he still couldn't grasp exactly what it was about. Her slap across his face snapped him out of it. His eyes widened considerably in surprise.

When he realized that she was very nearly embracing him, he did the only natural thing he could do and wrapped his arms around her.

Leandra tried to frown but was tempted to laugh. "I was not offering you anything other than comfort, your grace."

"You called me Hart a minute ago and I promise I am very comfortable." He leaned closer and placed tiny, nibbling kisses along her neck and behind her ear.

A giggle escaped before she could stop it. Her husband released her with a smile and held out his hand. "Shall we go in to dinner, my duchess?"

She hesitated. "Hart, what happened just now? You seemed to be miles away."

He tried to shrug nonchalantly but was afraid he failed in the attempt. "I honestly do not know, my dear. It was nothing."

Her eyes narrowed behind her spectacles. "Nothing? I saw an injured child once with less fear in his eyes than I saw just now in yours. How can that be nothing?"

It is said that one cannot change overnight. This universal truth had little to do with Derringer. He had only been striving to change for a few hours. His annoyance levels were increasing dangerously, mainly because he was frustrated by his own inability to understand what had just happened.

But, remarkably, instead of snapping at her, he said, "I don't know what happened, I don't understand any more than you, in fact, I am through discussing it."

Leandra wisely heeded the warning tone in the duke's voice. She had no desire to bring about another onslaught of his sharp tongue.

She took his arm and together they joined the others.

27

DERRINGER nearly burst out laughing when the redoubtable Lady Brianna, loving and... hmm, obedient wife of Sir Adam Prestwich entered the drawing room with all the magnificence of a queen. He strode over to greet her before her husband had the chance.

"My dear lady, you have no idea how welcome you are," he told her, bowing over her hand.

Bri gave him a startled glance. "Why?" she asked, green eyes narrowing in her stunningly beautiful face.

"I believe I will allow your husband to tell you that if he so chooses. Meanwhile, please join us for dinner."

Prestwich joined them, frowning, clearly suspecting that the duke had something to do with Bri's escape from her apartment. "Well, my lady? How did you do it?" he inquired, his voice soft but intent.

Before Bri could form a response, Derringer inserted dryly, "She picked the lock on the window and climbed down the ivy, Prestwich."

Adam looked his wife over carefully. "How do you know that?" There were no telltale marks or tears on her lovely gown of lemon yellow silk and her hair appeared to be in perfect order. He looked at the duke.

Derringer smiled at Bri, a bit of his old glee in the discomfort of others peeking through. She seemed to plead with him to hold his tongue, but he was nearly as worried about her getting involved with his problems as his own wife. The last thing he needed was the death of two or three ladies on his conscience.

"I think perhaps this should wait, Prestwich," the duke said lightly. "Very bad *ton* to murder your wife in a duke's crowded drawing room, you see. Not sure even I can get away with that."

Prestwich was livid; anyone with eyes could see that. Derringer patted him on the shoulder in a friendly gesture of understanding just as Stark entered to announce dinner.

Leandra presided at the foot of the table entertaining her dinner partners. Gabriel St. Clair sat on her right side and Lord Greville on her left. She was talking to Greville about nothing really when she suddenly remembered of the letter she had found in her predecessor's journal. She glanced at Gabriel who laughed at something Michaella was saying. Had Derringer even read the note, or had events prompted his forgetfulness as it had hers?

"Lady Derringer?"

Leandra turned a bright smile on Greville. "Why so formal, my lord?"

"Because I have said your name several times with no response. What is going on in that very fertile mind of yours?"

"I don't know why I should tell you, Levi. A woman in this day and age has very little left to her other than her thoughts. I think I prefer to keep mine to myself."

"If I suspected you of getting involved in something you shouldn't, Leandra, I would feel obliged to put a stop to it."

"I don't think I care for your tone, sir."

Greville sighed and lowered his voice. "This situation with Hart is dangerous, Leandra. I think you know that. He would be destroyed if you were to get hurt trying to protect him."

"Is that not a decision for me to make, my lord?"

"No, Lady Derringer, it's not," Greville told her adamantly.

There was a lull in conversation just as those words left the earl's mouth. Everyone turned surprised eyes on the couple at the end of the long table. The duke's expression was faintly inquiring but he said nothing.

Leandra smiled and shrugged. "Simple misunderstanding," she murmured.

The duke cocked an eyebrow but returned his attention to Aurora on his left.

The gathering in the drawing room after dinner proved entertaining to nearly everyone present.

Derringer watched Adam Prestwich as he managed to inveigle Harwood's empty-headed wife into willingly giving up her locket. This was done off to one side of the spacious room, out from under the eyes of everyone else. Derringer made sure the rest of his guests were entertained elsewhere, leaving Adam to charm his victim.

The duke noted Leandra chatting with Aurora, Michaella, and Bri, while trying to get his cousin Kathryn to open up a little. She was paying Adam no heed whatsoever, he was pleased to see. He returned half his attention to Greville while still watching Adam.

The baronet proved to be very adept at negotiation and soon had the young woman willing to part with all of her jewels if he wished it. Adam assured her he only desired her locket and she handed it over.

"Thank you, Prestwich," said Derringer as the other man joined him. "I appreciate it."

Adam grunted. "How did she do it, Derringer? I have racked my brain all night and the answer eludes me."

The duke laughed, drawing the eyes of some close to them. "When you retire, ask your bride to undress before you."

Adam opened his mouth to protest, thought better of it, and shook his head.

"And if you can't even determine how your wife escaped her room, I'm not sure I believe you will be of any help apprehending my attacker."

Adam made no reply to this and walked away to join his lady.

It wasn't until later that night that Derringer recalled the note he had taken from his wife. He sat down behind his father's desk in the study and pulled it from his pocket. He read the short missive once, twice, and a third time before the words really sank in. Then, his eyes blank, the duke rose from his seat and left the room.

Gabriel was awake, reading a book that the duke remembered from their schooldays. He walked over and tossed the paper onto the bed. "Read that and tell me what you think," he commanded curtly.

Gabriel was surprised at his cousin's tone but forbore mentioning it, reading the note instead. His eyes grew wider and wider the further he read until he finished and fixed his blue gaze on Derringer. "Is it true, do you think?"

"It is the duchess's hand, I've no doubt. Why she would lie about such a thing, I don't know. So how can it be other than true?"

The other man shook his head. "It must be. But how the devil did she manage to keep the servants quiet about this? Someone must have been here at the time. Someone must have known."

The two men looked at each other in surprise. "Mrs. Stark!" they said at once.

The duke would have left right then to question the housekeeper but Gabriel stopped him. "It is too late, Hart. Wait until morning."

"Don't you want to know now? I do."

Gabriel said nothing for several seconds. "Do you realize someone wanted me dead in France?" he finally asked softly.

"Of course they did," scoffed the duke. "Those French bastards wanted as many English dead as possible."

Gabriel closed his eyes for a moment. When he opened them again, he said, "Yes, you are right."

Derringer stared at Gabriel for a minute before leaving. He was suddenly very much aware that his closest friend and relative kept secrets from him and he was very much afraid they might be to that man's detriment.

Leandra woke slowly from a deep sleep plagued by bittersweet dreams. As a result, part of her refused to wake while the other part refused to remain asleep. She went in favor of waking over sleeping and stretched her arms far above her head. Her hazel eyes flickered open, focused blearily on an object dangling before her face. She blinked several times before she realized what it was.

"My locket!"

Stretching out her hand, Leandra reached for her precious possession only to have it jerk back out of her reach. Startled, and not quite awake enough to realize it was obviously being held by someone, she screamed.

"Lord, Merri! Your screeching will wake the dead, love."

Leandra paused mid-scream. "Hart! What are you doing?" She retrieved her spectacles from the bedside table and plopped them on her face. Derringer's face came sharply into focus, his dark eyes rife with laughter.

"Why, returning your property to you, my dear lady. What other possible reason might I have for invading my wife's bedchamber?" he asked in all seriousness.

She blushed, as he knew she would. "Thank you, Hart. How ever did you convince her ladyship to part with it?"

The duke smiled. "That is, I think, a secret I will take to my grave, duchess."

The thought that immediately crossed Leandra's mind made her glare at her husband. "I suppose you enjoyed it, too," she said darkly.

"It was entertaining, I admit," he replied with a pointed look at her.

"I'm sure it was, your grace. Well, you can leave and return your reward to your whore!" She was so angry she thought she might spit. She settled for throwing a pillow at him.

Derringer laughed, catching the missile. "A whore she may be, Merri, but she isn't mine. I don't know that anyone would actually lay claim to the woman."

"She's not? Then how…?"

"Have a little faith in me, my blushing bride. I am not so lost to propriety that I would take a mistress under my wife's very nose."

"Are you not?"

He shrugged. "Well, maybe I am. The point is, I didn't, I haven't, and," he reached over and grasped her chin, forcing her to look him in the eyes, "I won't bring a mistress into our home."

The duchess studied his sharp features for any signs of duplicity and, finding none, ventured to ask, "Why not?"

Derringer sat back, stunned. "I promise to keep my amours far from home and you want to know why?"

She released a breath and admitted, "No, actually, I don't. Never mind. What are your plans for the day, your grace?"

His brows drew down. "I am probably wasting my breath, but why am I 'your grace' all of a sudden?"

"For the same reason you always are, I suppose," she replied with a careless shrug. "I am annoyed with you."

"If I inquire as to what I've done to incur your wrath, would you tell me?"

"You just told me you will, one day, take a mistress. Should I be relieved you have at least promised to keep the woman from my sight?" Her fingers clenched in the bedclothes. "Was that reassurance meant to be comforting?"

"You would like a promise that I will never take a mistress?" He leaned back, studying her tense features. "And why would my word mean anything? I am not known for keeping my word, nor am I known for bowing to the whims of another."

"Except me, Hart," she murmured, her voice almost lost in her sigh. "I do take you at your word and you made it all too clear that you chose me because I needed help."

She bit her lip, lost in thought. Derringer waited, curious despite himself, wondering at the odd sensation that prompted him to assure her that he'd never stray. How could he promise such a thing? He didn't trust himself and could hardly believe she would.

Her lips parted, his gaze settling there, suddenly wanting nothing more than to end the conversation with seduction, make her forget for a time. Make him forget. Forget that someone wanted him dead, forget her life was very likely in danger because of him, forget he wanted more from this marriage than he felt he could offer, forget that she deserved better than him.

"Fidelity is not a whim."

So unexpected were her words that he looked at her blankly for a moment before changing the subject entirely. "Your family has gone, by the by. They departed earlier this morning."

His wife struggled up to glance at the clock over his shoulder. "Oh, good Lord, it's gone ten o'clock already! Why didn't Liza wake me?"

"Perhaps because I threatened her with dire retribution should she dare."

"Oh, Hart, you didn't! That poor girl is probably scared half out of her mind."

"You really do have a low opinion of me, my love."

"How could I not?"

"Good point. I concede defeat."

He sat on the bed regarding his bride steadily. She grew uncomfortable and started to fidget.

"What is it?" she asked, her eyes narrowing. "You look at me as though pondering something."

He shook his head a little as if coming out of a trance. He looked down and fingered the locket that he still held. Raising his gaze and the necklace, he extended his arm, dangling it before her again. "You have not thanked me, Merri," he murmured.

She tried to take the bauble but her husband drew it back. "Thank you, Hart," she said, wariness trembling on each word.

"That's not the kind of thank you I had in mind, *wife*."

Her face paled a bit, then flushed bright pink. "You can't possibly mean... no, I refuse to believe you would expect..." She shook her head at her own words. "Of course you could. You are the Duke of Derringer, after all."

His reply was an impish grin.

"What do you expect of me, Hart?" she whispered sadly. "Forget all that's been said and done between us and behave as though everything is well? Take you into my arms and body without a thought for the fact that you'd as soon see the last of me? How can you possibly expect so much of me for a simple locket, even one as important to me as the one you hold?"

Traitorously, her body was more than willing to give in to his seduction—and he hadn't even touched her yet. But memories of his lovemaking were enough to make her heart beat harder and her skin tingle.

Her husband sensed her contradictory emotions. She could see it in the glitter in his eyes and the way he hesitated before touching her cheek with one long finger. Her eyes closed against her will and she breathed a little sigh.

"It would be so easy, Merri, to just let go. Why do you resist what you want so desperately?"

Her eyes snapped open. "Why do you?" she countered.

Derringer sat back, eyes roaming her features intently. "If I were to seduce you now, would you still walk out of my life forever?"

She had no answer for him because she honestly didn't know. She looked away, staring down at her hands. "I don't know," she whispered. "Making love will not solve our problems. It may suspend them for a time but they will creep up, probably worse than before. But…"

When she didn't continue, he prompted, "But…"

She met his eyes, her own filled with frustrated, hurt, and angry tears. "But… I find it nearly impossible to consider leaving now. If we were to… make love, I would probably never be able to leave your side, despite any problems that arise." Her shoulders lifted in a tiny shrug, a defeated little movement that said far more than her words.

The ruthless side of Derringer urged him to seduce her. But something she wasn't saying held him back. He suspected that while she wouldn't leave him, she may never forgive him for using her lack of control to gain his own ends.

Dropping her precious necklace in her lap, he rose to his feet and walked to the door. "I will await you in the stables if you would care to join me for a ride."

The ruthless side of him growled in unreasoning anger at his ready capitulation.

A half-hour later, Derringer paced back and forth before Odin's Offspring. The horse nickered every time the duke paused beside him but Derringer was too lost in dark thoughts to notice.

While he wanted to ruminate about his wife and her words to him, he forced his mind to contemplate somewhat weightier matters instead.

He wondered how the letter written by his mother was connected with the attacks on his life and why. His fortune was immense, true, but if someone thought with the title came power, they were in for a rude awakening should they succeed and actually acquire it. Most of his "power" was in rumor, the stuff of legends and myths rather than hard fact.

Martin would inherit should Derringer perish. But according to that damned paper, it was...

"Hart, I am here now. I am sorry it took so long."

Derringer looked his wife over critically. Her rust-colored habit complemented her hair and complexion, while the little shako on her head sat at a rakish angle completely at odds with her somber expression.

She approached him and he braced himself for her reaction. A part of him expected violence but her demeanor did not suggest she was ready to murder him. As usual, her features were impossible to read.

His shock was complete when she grasped his coat and pulled, bringing his body down to an uncomfortable angle, more of a level with her. He cocked his head to one side inquiringly but she firmly took his face in her hands.

With a secret smile playing about her full lips, she whispered, "Thank you for my locket, my love." And she pressed her lips to his in full view of every stablehand and outdoor servant the duke employed.

And Derringer, being Derringer, picked his wife up off the ground and turned her chaste salute into something far more intimate.

They were both breathless when he set her down, amidst the cheering of their outdoor staff. Her rueful smile was endearing and he couldn't stop a wicked grin from tilting his own lips upward.

"We could go back to bed," he suggested, only half in jest.

"We could," she agreed. "But I was so looking forward to riding with you."

The duke released a short bark of laughter, laced with genuine mirth. "Isn't that what I was just suggesting?"

Her brow furrowed in confusion. The look of supreme innocence she gave him made his lips twitch.

Determinedly suppressing the urge to tease her some more, he shook his head slightly, saying, "Never mind, lovely Merri, never mind. We'll ride." Unable to resist, he added in an undertone, "Now and later."

It was another twenty minutes before they were actually ready. Leandra had realized she'd forgotten her gloves and rushed back inside to fetch them instead of sending a servant—what the bloody hell were they there for if not to serve?—and she was only just then returning.

And she seemed to positively exude excitement.

"And what, may I ask, has you in such a mood?" he asked testily, the extra wait having worn his patience to the breaking point.

Leandra smiled brightly. "The sun is shining, the birds are singing, and for the moment, all is right with the world."

The duke grunted in reply, glaring at the grinning stable boy who held the reins of two saddled horses. "Give me those, you cheeky brat," he commanded. The boy laughed and handed over the reins of the horse Derringer preferred to ride when Satan was not available.

Leandra was helped into the saddle and handed the reins. Lady whinnied at her in greeting, nipping at her skirts. "Hello, my dear girl." Leandra extracted two sugar cubes from her pocket and fed them to her mount, Lady stretching her neck back to receive the treat.

Derringer watched this impassively. "Are you ready?" he asked.

In answer, his wife smiled and kicked her horse into a gallop, heading for her favorite place, the rocky cliff overlooking the sea. Derringer followed suit after a rebellious snort from Odin.

Leandra had barely a head start on her husband but Lady proved her mettle by outdistancing the other mount within a few minutes. As soon as she reached the cliffside, she pulled up to wait for her husband. He soon joined her, scowling at her in annoyance.

"Just what the devil possessed you to ride like that?" he demanded.

Leandra laughed, the wind ruffling her hair where it escaped her pins. "Have you never wanted to fly, my lord? To spread your wings and soar like an eagle?" She gazed at him, awaiting his reply.

Derringer stared at her in amazement. How could she be sad one moment, happy the next, and then return to her usual calm serenity?

"I have not, madam."

Leandra gave him an unreadable look. "And what has you in such a pucker, Lord Derringer?" she asked.

"The sun is shining, the birds are singing, and for the moment, all is right with the world," he mocked.

"Hart, if you wish to behave like a child, please do so when you are not around me." And so saying, his darling bride spun Lady around and headed back to the castle.

The duke watched her go, half-amused, half-annoyed. She really did look magnificent on horseback, he thought in surprise. But then, to him, she looked magnificent all the time.

A sound caught his attention. Derringer turned his head and gazed out to sea. He didn't like what he saw.

28

GABRIEL sat alone pondering what he had learned from the late duchess's written confession. He wondered what the duke would do about it and how long it would take him to determine what it all meant.

Gabriel already knew. As soon as he had seen that note, he had known. Everything became suddenly clear. Why Derringer was being attacked nearly every time he set foot from the house; why he, Gabriel, had been under similar attacks nearly all his life. There was only one other person he knew of that was privy to this sensitive information.

As Gabriel was setting off to pay Lady St. Clair a visit, Derringer was asking Leandra what she knew of her brother's recent activities.

"As I have already told you, Hart, I know nothing. Lee has never confided in me and his wife certainly has no use for me. I don't know why you should think I would know anything about it."

"I merely wonder if perhaps you could give me an idea as to why he may be skulking around my yacht."

"He's what?"

"I saw him down at the bay just now, skulking around my boat."

"Perhaps he is merely admiring it?"

Derringer shot her a look of reproach. "He's not even supposed to be on my land, Merri. They all left this very morning, remember?"

Leandra shrugged. "I do not know how you think I can help you, Hart. Lee was always skulking about when he thought no one was looking; I'm not surprised he still does that. I doubt he's up to any good. Do you think he's dangerous?"

"Yes," he replied. "He associates with Fraser D'Arcy. He's dangerous."

Leandra stared at her husband. He appeared very worried about her brother and she wondered if he thought Harwood had something to do with the attack. She voiced this thought.

"He may, although I can't imagine why. Excessive hate seems far too outlandish for reality and I can't recall ever having so much as met your brother before this. D'Arcy and I, however, are in the way of being old... acquaintances," he concluded darkly.

Leandra, who had entered the house a bare ten minutes before her husband and gone straight to her sitting room, sat down in her favorite chair with a bump. "He means to kill you then? Have I no say in this, think you?"

"What would you say, my beauty? 'No, you may not kill my husband, if you please.' He would laugh before running you through for getting in his way, Merri. The man has no conscience."

"Funny, I seem to recall the same being said of you, my lord duke."

Derringer sat in the chair opposite, leaning back with a crafty smile on his face. "Oh no, my merry dove, I have a conscience. I sometimes choose not to use it."

"Could that not be considered worse?"

He cocked one black brow. "How so, my sweet?"

"You can control where and when to employ that part of your mind that determines right and wrong. D'Arcy, on the other hand, cannot. He simply does not have one. Which, Lord Derringer, is worse?"

"Should I vote in my own favor or vote for the man that tortured a child once just to hear her scream?" he retorted brutally.

Leandra snapped her mouth shut, biting her lip to restrain her horror. That such a monster was allowed to remain free was sickening.

"He will be taken care of, Merri," Derringer soothed. He should not have said what he did but she had a way of bringing out the beast in him.

Her eyes snapped. "Why has he not already been 'taken care of'?"

"I have not yet had the means to do so, my bloodthirsty siren."

"I mean, why has he remained free? Why has he not gone before a magistrate?"

"The child was a low class orphan, love. She had no more rights than a mongrel dog." His voice held traces of bitterness. "Such is the way of the world. One man, no matter how many vermin he rids the earth of, cannot change a damn thing."

Leandra fell silent, watching her husband carefully. He watched her as well and she was unsure what changed but she suddenly felt breathless and excited. To distract her wayward thoughts, she looked away and studied her shoes as if she'd never noticed them before.

Derringer nearly laughed at his wife's expression. He did smile when she looked at her shoes. "Would you care to know how my investigation is going?"

She snapped up the offered distraction. "What investigation?"

"Into the recovery of your father's will, of course."

"You have found it?" she asked in disbelief.

"Merri, Merri. Your lack of faith wounds me to the quick, my love."

Leandra scowled. "I apologize. Have you found it?"

"If I didn't know better, I'd think you were anxious to discover how rich you are." His tone was deceptively mild.

"Perhaps I am," she retorted. "Perhaps I am anxious to end this farce of a marriage and get on with my life."

Why, oh, why had she said that? Leandra saw the darkening of her husband's face and knew she was not going to get away with such a statement. She wondered what imp had prompted her to say it, arousing Derringer's anger. She was very much afraid it was not only his anger that was aroused, however.

"Farce, Merri? How so?" he asked in that silky, infinitely dangerous tone.

Leandra stood and backed toward the exit, the one door leading to freedom. "Did I say farce, Hart? I don't know what I was saying. I must have been thinking of… something else."

He followed her to the door, matching every step she took, stalking her like a panther. She shivered when she made it to the door, reaching for the handle behind her. She turned it and practically fell into the corridor. She swung about, prepared to run for safety but her arm was lodged in something like steel. She turned her head, gazing up into the mocking eyes of her husband.

"Going somewhere, Merri?" he inquired as though asking about the weather.

"I have to check with Mrs. Stark about something," she fabricated with impressive speed.

"Indeed? Well," he said, drawing her resolutely back into the room, "Mrs. Stark will just have to wait. And damn the consequences."

Gabriel wandered around the chilly countryside, pondering what he had learned, which was precious little. His mother had, of course, known about the late duchess's revelation. She disclaimed knowing anything, however, about Derringer's near-death experiences and seemed completely shocked that Gabriel may be going through the same.

There had been something in her manner, however, a furtiveness, a suspicious look in her eye that had caused him considerable alarm.

It was near Leandra's cliffside that Gabriel bumped into the Earl of Harwood. Literally.

"The devil, man! Watch where you are going!" snapped the earl. Then he realized who it was and Gabriel was curious to note how the man's complexion paled.

"Lord Harwood, I did not expect to see you out here," responded Gabriel amiably.

"I was merely getting a view of the countryside hereabouts," Harwood replied quickly. So quickly, in fact, that Gabriel knew he was lying. What did this man have to do with the attacks on Derringer? Instinct told Gabriel that Harwood was a key element in all this, though he couldn't, for the life of him, determine how or why.

"Indeed?" Gabriel looked around. "There is not much to see here unless you are waiting for a boat to come in."

Harwood shook his head emphatically, his cherubic countenance turning a dusky shade of red. "I have no reason to be doing that, have I?" he said with a smile.

"Then why are you here?" Gabriel stood looking down on the shorter man, his face as dangerous as Derringer's and uncanny in its resemblance to that man.

Harwood stuttered something unintelligible and hurriedly took his leave.

Gabriel watched him scurry away and frowned. The man had been skulking about for a reason. What was it?

As he turned to walk away, a man stepped out from behind a tree nearby. Gabriel never saw him. He was struck down with a stout cudgel and hefted over a stouter shoulder.

It was amazing, Leandra thought later, how one could actually fear something that could turn out so completely wonderful.

But then, her husband had looked anything but gentle when he forced her back into the room a few hours prior. He had seemed determined and perhaps a little angry. For that, she really couldn't blame him. She had pushed him too far, she knew, with her complaints about the consequences of their actions and leaving him. It was her desire for him that made her goad him into taking her and her fear that had kept her from admitting that she was deeply in love with him.

She turned slightly to gaze at her sleeping husband. His black hair was spread out on the pillow, his breathing deep and even. She stared at him for a long moment, content, happy. While she missed her father a great deal, she knew that had he lived, she would have ended her days in spinsterhood if she hadn't married some man who was willing to take her on for the dowry her father was willing to pay.

Reaching out a hand, Leandra gently brushed a lock of hair from her husband's brow. He came awake, every muscle tensing as if waiting for attack. His hand trapped hers where she touched him and she bit back a startled cry of pain.

Derringer released her, dragging her up with him as he sat, holding her close. He said nothing and just held her until the initial fear subsided. Her own tension faded, her body easing against his.

"What has happened to you, my dear," she murmured into his chest, "to cause such fear?"

Derringer stiffened. "I am afraid of nothing, Merri," he growled.

Leandra sat back and looked up into his dark eyes. "You fear many things, Hart. Everyone, man, woman, and child, has fears, worries, and anxieties. It is normal. The strength is in letting someone share those with you."

He stared at her. "You make it sound so simple."

"I didn't mean to," she said. "It is most difficult, I assure you."

Derringer released her and pushed one hand through his hair, frowning as he did so. He was completely fed up with wondering when the next attack on his life would take place. He was not afraid for himself anymore, and that scared him more than anything else did. Leandra needed him and he realized that life without her was not worth living.

But there was no way, despite her entreaties, that he could confide in her. He looked at her, watched the emotions flit through her hazel eyes and at that moment, he smiled with a trace of genuine happiness.

"What?"

"I just realized," he murmured, drawing her back into his arms, "when you are completely incoherent with passion, your eyes turn the most beautiful shade of blue."

Derringer emerged from another steamy session of lovemaking strangely restless. His wife knew no such restlessness, having dropped off to sleep almost before he'd rolled away from her. His body screamed for a respite, just a bit of rest, but his mind refused to calm.

He, of course, knew why. He wanted an end to the madness that plagued him. It was very nearly over, he knew, and all he had to do was put himself out there where he could once again be vulnerable to attack. Then, he'd either have the villains responsible or he would die like his father had—young and under suspicious circumstances.

He looked down at his sleeping wife and thought he had never seen anyone quite so beautiful. Her long brown curls lay in disarray over her naked shoulders, partially masking her face. Her beauty wasn't of the obvious or of the popular sort. Her clear skin, honest, open features, and acceptance of her own strengths and flaws made her something out of the ordinary. To Derringer, the obvious and the popular beauties paled in comparison.

Desire flared, the desire to love her again, to show her how much a part of him she'd become. Consideration for her held him back. He'd made demands on her innocent body that she barely understood and, he realized now, she'd complied with innocent desire and complete trust. In him.

His desire of a moment before died, fear taking over. Trusting in him for any reason could get her killed.

The duke pressed a kiss to Leandra's brow. She murmured something in her sleep, a smile curving her kiss-swollen lips. Derringer felt a painful lurch in his heart. He silently rose from the bed and dressed, his movements hurried. Returning to the bedside, he stared down at her for a long moment. Leandra sighed in her sleep. He pulled the blankets up over her tenderly.

"I love you, my heart," he whispered.

Then, the Duke of Derringer disappeared.

29

LEANDRA didn't wake until the following morning, her stomach making its dissatisfaction known. The rest of her body remained satiated, memories of the previous day warming her from head to toe.

She stretched like a cat, reaching for her husband. Her hands encountered nothing but air. Heart lurching, she opened her eyes. He was not there. In fact, the bedsheet's cold caress on her fingertips revealed it had been some time since he'd been there.

The duchess sat up, forehead creasing in deep thought. She reached for her spectacles, losing her grip on the bedclothes. A blush climbed her cheeks though no one was there to see. She jerked them back into place over her naked chest. Then she plopped her spectacles on her nose and got out of bed.

If she was to find out what had become of her husband, she couldn't loll about in bed all day reliving the glorious night in his arms.

She paused as a smile of remembrance curved her lips. Then she went to her dressing room and rang for Liza.

Unease crawled Leandra's spine at the sight that met her eyes in the breakfast room. The sensation increased at the noticeable absence of Derringer and Gabriel. Michaella, who'd decided to stay after her family's ejection from the premises, bit her lip as if fighting back tears, her features unnaturally pale. Lord Greville had a worried look on his face and Sir Adam appeared almost angry. The other two ladies stared at Leandra with carefully blank expressions, the most suspicious of the expressions she beheld.

Leandra motioned for the gentlemen to return to their seats and sat in her customary spot at the right of the head. She looked expectantly at Greville. "Well, sir? Why all the long faces?"

The earl flushed and looked down at his empty plate. Aurora placed a tiny hand on his arm and whispered something Leandra couldn't catch.

Leandra turned her gaze to Adam Prestwich. "Where is Gabriel?"

Michaella burst into tears and fled the room.

The duchess rose as if to follow, but Lady Prestwich restrained her. "Gabriel is missing, Lady Derringer. He didn't come home last night and one of the gamekeepers said there was blood near the cliffs."

"Which cliffs?" Leandra asked blankly.

"The ones overlooking the Strait," answered Adam. "Harwood has been seen creeping around there and I am afraid he is suspect."

"Well, of course he is," Leandra asserted. "He is, after all, in need of my father's will and Hart happens to have it."

This little piece of information silenced her companions. Wordlessly, the duchess signaled a footman to bring her breakfast and ate with all the absorption of a starving waif. Everyone waited until she was finished and had risen to leave before they erupted with questions.

"When did he find it?" asked Greville.

"Where was it?" asked Bri, Lady Prestwich.

"How did he get it?" asked Aurora.

"And how did he manage to keep it a secret?" asked Prestwich. He paused. "Wait, never mind," he said, shaking his head. "I must have forgotten for a moment who we were discussing."

Leandra smiled. "I believe he has had it for a few days at least, Levi. He has yet to tell me where he found it, Lady Prestwich. And I think you know him well enough to know how he got it, Rory." Her gaze fell on Prestwich. "I realize you spoke before thought, Sir Adam, but I will answer anyway. He said nothing because he was hoping to torment my brother with it."

Nothing was said to this revelation. Then, "The more I get to know you, Leandra," inserted Greville, "the more I believe you and Hart were made for each other. I wonder, could you tell us where your brother, or whomever is responsible, has taken Gabriel St. Clair?"

As her husband was still very much the heedless man he had been when she first met him, Leandra did not overly worry about him until dinner that night. She would not have worried even then but for the disappearance of Gabriel just after she had discovered that note penned by Derringer's mother. There were far too many pieces falling into place for any of the recent happenings to be mere coincidence.

It was not until two days later that Leandra realized her husband might not return. She was near the study when she overheard Greville discussing the duke with Prestwich.

"I know it is something Hart would do, Adam, but I can't see him not saying anything to Leandra. He's in love with her, you know."

Leandra's heart picked up at this, hope warring with common sense. As much as she wanted her husband's love, she was not going to assume she had it, no matter who happened to think it was true.

In Prestwich's reply she could almost hear his look of disbelief. "Derringer? Is he actually capable of love, Vi? And even if he was, why would feeling that tender emotion suddenly change his manners?"

Leandra nodded her head. It was true and she was actually fascinated to realize that she didn't expect him to change. She loved him and that was all there was to it.

A thread of annoyance entered Greville's voice. "I would normally agree with you, but hasn't your own experience with love made you realize that things are not always so simple?"

Prestwich grunted. "This really has nothing to do with a missing duke, has it?"

"No, but I think even Hart, as callous and unfeeling a monster as he is,"—Leandra had to stop herself from marching in and boxing Greville's ears—"would never send this. Even as a jest."

Leandra wanted very badly to push open the door a little more so she could see what it was they had. Something in their manner alerted her that they were not going to tell her what was happening, so she did just that. Except, she threw open the door, catching the gentlemen unawares. She gasped when she saw what the earl held.

"Oh, dear God!" Her huge eyes flashed from one man to the other. "What happened? Where is he?"

"Leandra—" began Greville, rising from his chair.

"No! Do not *Leandra* me, Lord Greville. I will know what has happened or I will flail you both alive!"

Prestwich's eyes lit with an unholy glee much like Derringer's would have done, while Greville took a hasty step back. The duchess glared at both of them for a moment, then, reasserting her usual unruffled calm, she sighed. "I think you both know that I will not simply walk away without some explanation. I can be quite as stubborn as Hart, I assure you."

Prestwich took the object from the earl's grasp and held it out. "I'm sure you know what this is, your grace?"

Leandra took it from him, tears forming. Her husband's hair, the long hank tied with a black riband. The silky black strands slipped through her fingers, the same silky strands she'd slipped her fingers through only days ago. Why had it been cut off?

Prestwich appeared to read her mind. "There was no note with it, Lady Derringer. We do not know if someone else sent it or Hart himself."

"Why," Leandra began in a dangerously soft tone, "would my husband do something so reprehensible?"

Greville chose to intervene. "You know Hart, Leandra. I do not think he would do this to you but he has been known to do some fairly… well, despicable things in his lifetime. I just can't think what he thinks to gain by this."

"He will gain nothing, gentlemen, because he didn't do it," stated the duchess with confidence. She moved across the room and sat behind the large desk still strewn with paperwork. She stared down blindly at a piece of vellum as she continued. "Hart was very adamant about his appearance. I've yet to discover why exactly, but he would not do anything to mar it." She looked up at Greville as if for confirmation. He nodded in agreement since it was quite true. Looking down again, her eye was caught by something in a paper on top of the desk.

"What is this?" she asked.

Prestwich stepped closer. "It appears to be a normal order for the departure of a ship."

"But who ordered the departure?"

"If it is one of Hart's, Leandra, it had to be him," offered Greville. "I know he is the only one with the authority to do so."

Leandra studied it with the gentlemen looking over her shoulder. "It appears someone is trying to set sail and according to this, it should be right now."

"Captain Taverner will not leave without this order," remarked Greville.

"Would he realize it is forged, do you think?" inquired the duchess with a grim look.

"Is it?" Prestwich peered closer. "How do you know?"

Leandra smiled. "I have seen enough messages from my husband to know how he signs them." She pointed at the D in Derringer. "He does not make that little tail there.

He always starts his signature with a wicked slash. This was done by an amateur," she remarked meditatively.

Brushing a few other documents aside, she discovered two more such orders, the signature on each closer to the duke's than the previous, as though someone practiced until they got it right. That could only mean an order went out on which the forgery was close enough to remain undetected by the captain.

"So what does all this mean?" asked Greville. "Someone wants to set sail enough to forge Hart's command. What has that to do with Gabriel and Hart disappearing?"

Leandra went very still, heart stuttering in her chest. She remembered the words of a certain letter word for word, the words of Derringer's mama. In a voice devoid of expression, she asked, "Where is Martin St. Clair?"

30

In the following weeks, Leandra began to lose hope. Her worry increased with each passing day. They had no news of her husband, nothing to lead them to his whereabouts or even if he still lived. Each morning she woke, as wearied as if she'd only just dropped off to sleep.

Then one morning she woke, clutched her stomach, and cast up her accounts in the chamberpot. Logic might have suggested she was simply sickening for something but instinct declared otherwise. She was increasing.

While she prayed for her husband's safe return, she rejoiced in the knowledge that she carried his child. She threw herself into planning for the child's arrival, adding in the preparations for the many holiday celebrations in the not-to-distant future.

It was in the midst of her planning that Leandra found a moment to wonder over Martin St. Clair's disappearance. From what she could tell he'd not been at Derringer Crescent for some time. Leandra would have pondered the situation sooner had she not been so caught up in her own problems.

Prestwich and Greville returned to London to see if perhaps they could find more information. Leandra heard nothing from them for some time. And when she did, it was only more mystery added to the conundrum that already was her life.

Sir Adam Prestwich strode into Greville's townhouse in Berkley Square exactly three months after the Duke of Derringer's disappearance. He strode to the bookroom in the back of the residence, not even bothering to knock. Greville didn't look up as Prestwich entered and sat in a leather armchair opposite the desk behind which the earl sat.

"What have you found?" inquired Greville. He frowned at the letter he held as he waited for Prestwich's response.

"Tiny," Prestwich said, referring to a friend of Derringer's. "Ran into the giant while scouring the East End for clues. He gave me this." Leaning forward, he tossed a folded sheet of foolscap at Greville. "Said we're not to worry about the missing duke and he added that we keep the duchess safe. Oh, Tiny also sends his regards to your lady wife."

Greville grunted and accepted the paper. "What else?"

"Big John Hancock heard a rumor about a black devil being sent back to hell but I attributed that story to his flair for the dramatic."

"Do not be so sure. You read this?"

"I did but the Captain's writing is not easily understood. I surmise whoever took Gabriel also took Derringer. You think they still live?"

"I hope so, based on Taverner's convoluted mutterings, but I don't think they will be for long. Look at this."

Greville searched his desk for a moment, locating what he sought in a copy of *Debrett's Peerage*. A folded sheet of vellum fell out, settling on the desk before him. He handed it to his companion.

"Tracing your lineage?" quipped Prestwich as he took the sheet of vellum. His smile disappeared when he read the rather shaky handwriting on the sheet. "Where did you get this?"

"Leandra. She found it in Lady Derringer's journal, hidden in the flyleaf. What do you want to wager Martin St. Clair and his mama know about that?"

"I thought you had given up gaming?" Prestwich remarked in an offhand manner, his attention almost entirely focused the paper he held.

"Only when it's not a sure thing."

"What I want to know," Prestwich said, ignoring Greville's assurance, "is why either one of them are still alive."

"I wondered that as well. It certainly would have been in their best interest to kill them both, dispose of the bodies, and claim the title and inheritance."

"You are positive Martin and Lady St. Clair are behind this, aren't you?"

"Absolutely. They are the only ones who stand to benefit by their deaths."

"What about our new king?" Everyone knew how the royal family felt about the Dukes of Derringer, past and present.

Greville thought about it for a moment. "No, this doesn't have Prinny's feel to it. Cutting off Hart's hair was not his style and we would have found the bodies by now. Prinny would make sure they were dead and make sure everyone knew it. And our recently passed monarch was never really in the right frame of mind to properly despise Hart. It is suspected he disposed of the previous duke, though."

"Interesting," Prestwich muttered, sounding as if he cared little for the machinations of the previous king. "Suppose Martin is the one responsible. What do you think he'll do when he finds out Leandra's *enceinte*?"

"I know. I've been thinking about that, too. We simply have to catch the scoundrel before he has a chance to harm her."

"Easier said than done, don't you think?"

"We're missing something," said Greville, ignoring Prestwich's comment. He stared hard at the desktop. His face suddenly cleared. "Harwood!"

"Leandra's brother?" Prestwich asked in disbelief.

"Of course. He is the one that links everything together. He is the reason Hart and Gabe are still alive. He needs them alive to get his father's will back. Once he has it, he will let St. Clair kill them."

Prestwich shook his head. "It doesn't make any sense. Harwood is a sniveling milksop. How can he force a St. Clair to bend to his will?"

"He must have found out Martin's plans and offered to help. Or, stupidly, he threatened to expose Martin's plans. In which case, we'll probably find his body as well."

"There's another missing piece to the puzzle in there somewhere," Prestwich insisted, tapping his finger on the desktop. "There has to be another person involved in all this."

"But who?"

Nearly admitting defeat, Greville returned to Derringer Crescent a week later to at least inform Leandra of what they knew.

She took him to her little morning room, where she was normally found, and bade him sit. She sat beside him on a pretty little sofa and asked what he had learned.

Instead of answering right away, he asked, "Where's Aurora?"

"With the children in the nursery. We spend most of our time there now, considering." She blushed slightly with pleasure at the thought that she would be having Derringer's baby. But, as always when this thought occurred, she was nearly overwhelmed with sadness at the loss of her husband.

The earl smiled. "I see. I wonder if you might be able to tell me anything about your brother's friends or associates. Adam and I are in a bit of a quandary."

"So you have decided Lee is involved. I wondered when you would grasp that."

"If you already knew, why didn't you tell us?" he asked, indignation pinching the corners of his mouth.

"I am a woman. Would you have listened?" She shrugged. "And I didn't know. I merely suspected. He is after my father's will and he knows my husband has it.

"As to his friends, the one that comes to mind first is Fraser D'Arcy. Monsieur D'Arcy visited Harwood House often and Hart mentioned seeing Lee in France recently with D'Arcy. He said the Frenchman was dangerous and quizzed me then about what I knew of him."

"Hart mentioned him to me. And I recall the man has a grudge against Hart. He may be the one that ties this all together."

"What else do you know?" she asked, her hand coming to rest on her belly in an unconscious gesture of protectiveness.

Greville shrugged. "Not much. We've received missives from Captain Taverner, but the man writes in a rather convoluted fashion. Adam and I had trouble making heads or tails of his message. But we determined that either Gabe or Hart, perhaps both, are still alive."

Leandra's forehead creased. "How did you receive word? Where is he that he can know of Hart and Gabriel? Where are they? Surely he knows that if he can tell you that they live."

"Derringer has an associate known as Tiny Boy. Adam found him. Tiny indicated he was on some sort of errand for his current employer. He handed Adam a message and walked away."

"Do you have it with you?" she asked. At his nod, she held out her hand. "May I see it?"

Greville handed over the foolscap sheet. "Perhaps you will understand it better."

Leandra opened it and studied it silently for several minutes. A slow smile curved her lips. "Captain Taverner either hates France with an undying passion or he would like us to know that he was made to sail to France, Vi. I do believe Monsieur D'Arcy is indeed our key."

Despite all objections, Leandra insisted on accompanying Greville to London. Smiling to himself, he wondered how his friend felt about finally meeting his match in sheer stubbornness.

"Adam has probably not uncovered anything new, you know," he told her for the tenth time. She only smiled and returned her gaze to the dreary countryside passing the carriage window.

Greville gave up. Aurora smiled at her husband, amused, he knew, at his own stubborn determination to sway Leandra's determination.

The rest of the journey was conducted in silence. Leandra pondered the chances of finding her husband while Greville pondered the chances of dissuading Leandra from doing anything stupid. Aurora regarded their mobile faces with amusement, as they were incapable of hiding their feelings at the moment.

Upon arriving at Prestwich's London residence, Greville found he was wrong, but in the worst way imaginable. Prestwich had new information but not something he wanted the duchess to learn immediately, if ever. So he glared at Greville and dragged him into his study.

"You gudgeon, why did you bring her here?" he demanded as soon as the door was closed and barred against entry by inquisitive females.

"You have spent little time with Leandra, Adam. That girl was determined to be here and in a few moments, she will be in this room despite that lock."

Prestwich grunted. "I wanted you to know before we tell her, Vi. This is the latest communication from Captain Taverner."

"Delivered by the redoubtable Tiny again?"

"No, it was tossed to me by an urchin as I left my club in St James's Street. He didn't even linger for payment, just darted into the crowd and disappeared."

As Greville unfolded the message, he wondered how the man was sneaking messages off his boat. Leandra voiced the question first and now Greville couldn't help but wonder the same thing. Would a dinghy go unnoticed leaving the yacht? Even in the dead of night, Greville was unsure how it could be accomplished. And the early spring weather—steady rain with intermittent breaks for a meager ray of sun—surely wasn't conducive to long periods in a small boat on the open sea.

Greville read the message carefully, by now familiar with the captain's way of communicating something important. He hit on the same thing Prestwich had. The man prosed on about the afterlife. "They're dead? Both of them?"

"So it would seem," confirmed Prestwich. "Which means that unless Hart made a will before he died, Leandra is at the mercy of Martin St. Clair. How long do you think she'll survive when he discovers she might be carrying the new heir to the title and estate?"

Leandra surprised everyone, even herself, by remaining patiently in the drawing room with Aurora and Bri. They chattered about children and Leandra wondered if perhaps her child would be the only link that she'd have to her husband. If he were dead…

She refused to think that. He had to be alive. Her hands strayed to her stomach, a protective shield between her child and the rest of the world. He had to be alive.

Aurora saw the action and reached over to squeeze her hand. "All is well, dear. They will find Hart and Gabriel and all will be well."

It was at this moment that the men joined them. They heard Aurora's comment and both groaned inwardly at the news they were about to impart. They had decided it would be best coming from Greville since he was closer to Derringer and Leandra.

"Leandra, can I have a word with you in private please?" he asked.

The ladies rose as one, Bri and Aurora hugging Leandra before following Prestwich from the room. Greville motioned Leandra to sit on the sofa and he took a seat beside her.

Taking her hand, he looked into her large, hope-filled eyes. Lord, how was anyone able to deliver bad news without feeling like the cause of it?

"I have news, my dear," he began. "Bad news." Her lip quivered. Sympathy tugged at his heart, prompting him to squeeze her fingers, thus giving him a moment to swallow the lump forming in his throat. "We believe Gabe is dead." Her eyes filled with tears and her hand tightened in his. "And Hart. The captain implied both were dead."

Two tears ran down her cheeks. She sniffed and removed her hand from Greville's. Wiping away the offending moisture, she rose to her feet.

"Well, that is a relief," she commented, much to her companion's surprise.

"A relief?"

Leandra turned to face Greville, nothing of her emotions showing in her round features. "In a way, yes. The past months have been... unbearable, Vi. Not knowing whether or not he is alive is much worse than knowing one way or the other. I can now move on with my life instead of enduring this terrible limbo."

Greville was too shocked by how well she was taking this life-changing news to notice the rather hectic light in the back of her eyes. He smiled and assured her that he and Aurora would help in any way possible.

"Thank you, Vi. And thank you for telling me. Will you give me a few moments, please?"

Seeing nothing odd in this request, Greville left her to her thoughts, thoughts that would have alarmed him horribly had he been privy to them.

Leandra fought tears, fought to stifle the urge to scream, shake her fist at the sky, curse God and all his angels. The fear changed, shifting into helpless rage. It was unfair that her life had come to such a pass.

The rage passed, dwindling to nothing more than a dull ache, a helplessness in the face of things out of her control. Clasping her hands before her, knuckles whitening from the pressure she exerted, she forced her mind to focus, forced herself to face the inevitable.

He was dead. She tried to tell herself that she could move on, that she could make do without his caustic presence to mock her at every turn. Her hands covered the slight bulge of her abdomen for a moment, and she tried to imagine how enjoyable, how peaceful life would be without the chaotic Duke of Derringer.

She failed miserably, dissolving into tears.

A half-hour later, she left the drawing room and approached the study. Raised voices filtered through the wood. Without bothering to knock, she entered the room.

Greville stood in the center of the room gesturing frantically and shouting at Sir Adam Prestwich. Prestwich stood passively, though clearly annoyed if his narrowed eyes were any indication. Aurora glared at both gentlemen while Bri gestured just as wildly at Greville. Her voice was nearly a screech as she strove to be heard above Greville's deep voice. Leandra would have found the tableau amusing had her world not just shattered beneath her feet.

Aurora became aware of her first. She signaled her husband, who fell silent and flushed with embarrassment. Prestwich turned sympathetic eyes on her and Bri rushed forward to hug her.

"I am so sorry, my dear. And no doubt Vi made a terrible mess of telling you. He is such a clunch sometimes."

"Is that what has everyone so upset?" asked Leandra.

"Well, no," replied Bri. She glanced at her husband uncertainly. Leandra noticed the look of warning on his face and wondered what it meant.

"I demand someone tell me what is going on." They remained stubbornly silent. "I enter a room to find a group of well-bred people behaving like children, all because of me, and I think I have a right to know why."

"I'll tell you, Leandra," Aurora offered, voice low and soothing. She ignored the warning looks from the gentlemen. "Bri and I read the letter from Captain Taverner and we are unsure he meant to imply that Hart is dead. The man writes in such an odd fashion that we have decided not to give up hope of finding Hart alive."

Leandra's brows lifted. "Indeed? I am relieved. What was the shouting about then?"

"Someone didn't think we ought to tell you," Bri said hotly, shooting a darkling look at her husband.

The duchess glanced at the baronet curiously. "Why ever not?"

"It matters little now," Prestwich replied, clearly annoyed with the whole display of temper to which he had just been treated. "Since we all know, now we decide what to do about it."

Greville inserted, "Perhaps we should call Bruiser and Tiny."

Prestwich sighed, rubbing one hand tiredly over his face. "Tiny is in France already, searching. When I told him the duke was dead, he looked at me with what I can only describe as pity and took his leave, informing me as he went that he would find *Heartless* and bring him back alive.

"As for Bruiser, do you know where he is? I went by Derringer's townhouse and the man wasn't there. Has he left his employ, do you know?"

Greville frowned. "I would not have thought the man would do so until all threat on Hart was diminished. Why wasn't he at the Crescent with Hart in the first place?"

"How do we know he wasn't?" Prestwich asked. His gaze swung to Leandra.

She shook her head. "I met no one named Bruiser. Is he someone my husband would have introduced?"

Both men shook their heads, though Greville hesitated. "With Hart, one never does know what to expect, though we think he would have introduced the man as his valet. You might not have believed him."

"Why not?"

Greville exchanged a look with Prestwich. "Bruiser does not look like a valet. He looks like the former pugilist that he is."

A silent "oh" formed on Leandra's lips.

The men continued, Leandra silent witness to their plans. Hope rose and mingled with fear in her breast. A strange excitement tingled along her spine. They would find her husband, return him to his rightful place, and punish the ones responsible. Though she'd be happy just to have him back.

"So when do we leave, gentlemen?" she asked, unable to help an eager smile.

Everyone in the room, as one joined entity, turned to stare at her incredulously. Prestwich was the one to reply. "What do you mean *we*?"

Leandra strode over to the chair behind Prestwich's large desk. She sat down and smiled all around. "It is my husband who is missing and I am determined to find him. If you gentlemen would like to accompany me, I will allow it. If not, I will be setting sail tonight for France."

"How do you even know he is still in France?" asked Prestwich.

"Where else would D'Arcy take him? The man thirsts for revenge and he will do it where he can feel the most satisfaction, and where he can dispose of Hart with very little trouble. Since the war with Napoleon, the French government will not be overly curious about the body of an Englishman turning up unexpectedly somewhere in their country. I doubt they would even report it." Her smile disappeared, replaced by a look of grim determination. "If Hart is alive, I will find him. Either help or stay out of my way."

Greville shared a look with his wife. He nodded. "Very well. We go. But I still think you should stay here with Rory and Bri. Hart will skin me alive should anything happen to you."

"Rory and I will take care of everything here," inserted Bri. "Some rumors have started concerning Derringer's disappearance and we will simply tell everyone the truth."

"Surely you cannot be serious?" Prestwich exclaimed, giving his wife an incredulous look.

Aurora smiled. "We will say he is off visiting relatives," she said. "I suppose that could be true, could it not?"

"Who will you get to help you in this?" asked Leandra curiously.

"The season is just starting and I know of a certain young man who will be very willing to assist us," Bri assured them.

Prestwich groaned. "You are not dragging Miles into this," he said. "Miles has too much responsibility already."

"Miles will love to squire us about, Adam," retorted Bri, her green eyes sparkling at some secret joke.

"Only because I pay him," muttered the baronet. "Very well. Use Miles if you must but please be nice to him. He has enough to endure from me."

31

DERRINGER attempted to straighten his aching limbs. He had been tied up for months and loosed only when he had to relieve himself and then for only a few minutes at a time. He dipped his head, his hacked off hair flopping over his eyes. Tossing his head back only served to intensify the hammering behind his eyes, a constant pain in the past months. His hair was the first thing to go, the removal of which convinced Derringer of the very personal nature of his kidnapping. It wasn't about money, it was about revenge.

Food was nothing more than a means to keep him alive and mostly conscious while they tortured him. They would visit to torture him and not return for several days. He could only assume they wanted him to heal a bit between sessions.

Physical torture, he knew. Physical torture, he understood. Physical torture, he could endure. Cuts, bruises, broken bones, all healed eventually. Such injuries were superficial, healing quickly to leave a scar as a reminder of the pain and nothing more.

If only they'd stopped at physical torture.

He groaned, flexing his fingers to restore some feeling. One hand was completely numb, trapped half under his body where he lay in the bunk. The rope binding him chaffed his wrists, a bead of moisture sliding over his palm. Blood, no doubt.

His physical weakness pained him far less than his emotional one. He knew the stupidity of forming attachments, the futility of negotiating with madmen, yet he did just that. He gave up the location of the late Earl of Harwood's will. He gave it up to save Gabriel, the will's location in exchange for his Gabriel's life, and they'd killed him anyway, tossing him overboard like so much refuse.

The pain of that loss sparked something in him, a similar pain, one so old he barely recognized it. His mother's passing when he was so young had seemed unreal at the time. He remembered seeing her lying in state, her beautiful features in silent repose. Peace lay easily upon her, as if she'd known it all her life. Yet he remembered not one moment in his parents' marriage that was peaceful. They tormented each other, but his mother always had a kind word for her son, a gentle squeeze, a distracted kiss on the head. He'd adored her in the way of a child in awe of his mother, awed by her beauty, awed by her distracted kindnesses.

Smiles she'd bestowed aplenty, but the smiles never reached her dark eyes. And now, in the midst of physical pain, the anguish of loss and the terrifying fear of death, Derringer remembered her dark, sad eyes, eyes so much like his own.

The loss of Gabriel touched Derringer in a horrific way. He wanted vengeance, a painful, slow death for the ones responsible. And he knew who they were. They didn't bother to hide their identities which only meant one thing.

They didn't plan on letting him live.

He had to survive. His shoulders tensed as he pulled against his bonds, sending more blood sliding down his fingers. If he didn't escape, Leandra would be in trouble.

His motions stilled, one thought freezing his blood. What if Leandra carried a child? How stupid he was to take her to his bed! Her life was already at risk, just through her marriage to him and now, if she carried a possible heir, she stood in the way.

He looked around the ship's cabin, searching for a weapon, a path for escape, anything that might help. He came up empty, as usual, but it was something to occupy his mind in the long hours between meals and beatings.

His morale was fading, his faith in his own ability to extricate himself from any situation dissipating like morning fog. But his desire for vengeance burned bright. While pretending Gabriel's death was the final straw, letting his captors think he was finally broken, he plotted.

The next step in their torture was cutting things from his body that would not kill him but leave him with little will to survive. Feigning that loss of will now might delay the inevitable. But he had to escape.

They had two of the three things they wanted: Harwood's will and Gabriel's death. All that remained was Derringer's death. Fraser D'Arcy wanted him dead as payment long overdue for that horrendous beating the duke had given him all those years ago.

But there was still one person missing in all of this. He knew the identity of the final captor, but he did not want to believe it. There were only two people who would benefit from his demise, only two who may have known Gabriel's real identity.

His aunt and cousin.

"So you are awake," inquired a new voice, a pleasant voice, soothing and low. Misleading.

He growled low in his throat, hating that his suspicions were realized. "Martin, release me now." He forced his body up into a sitting position on the bunk. It was not easy, his bruised, weakened muscles protesting, but he refused to face his captor while lying helpless. "Release me now and I won't kill you as slowly as you deserve."

"I hardly think you are in any position to be making demands, cousin," replied Mr. St. Clair calmly. "I now hold all the dice and you will do as I say, or you will die."

"You mean I have a choice? How magnanimous of you, worthless scum. Tell me, oh cowardly one, what must I do to ensure my survival?"

Martin moved across the tiny cabin in seconds. He struck out, snapping Derringer's head back with the force of his blow. The duke glared, a trickle of blood coloring his bottom lip, his coal-black eyes taking on a dangerous glitter.

"You had better pray whatever god you worship will save you, Martin, because when I am free, I will hunt you down like the dog you are and tear you limb from limb," the duke promised with unutterable calm.

A flicker of fear passed through Martin's eyes even though Derringer was quite unable to make good his threat at that moment. The duke's reputation was such that even tied up, immobile, those who crossed him still feared him.

Martin's blue eyes darkened and his slight form stiffened. "You would do better not to make threats, cousin. I can still kill you and I happen to know your friend D'Arcy wants just that."

"I assume that whatever you have planned, you will end up with my title. So what is it, dog? I disappear? My body is found somewhere quite soon, washed up on my own beach perhaps but too mutilated to be identifiable? You can't honestly be considering letting me live? If so, you are far stupider than even I gave you credit for."

Anger settled on Martin's normally placid features. The expression was so ludicrous that Derringer wanted to laugh. A split second later, however, he knew he had severely underestimated his cousin.

Fire streaked his face, from his jaw to his hairline. Shock paralyzed him, his eyes squeezing shut, the pain so profound he couldn't determine the cause. He opened his eyes and stifled his outrage.

Martin held a long, wicked looking knife up in the light of the lantern that sat forlornly on a small table. The shiny blade glinted and the duke caught the almost maniacal look that entered his cousin's eyes as he watched several tiny droplets of blood slither down the blade.

Derringer nearly growled. The miserable cur had actually cut him! From his chin to his hairline, judging by the ribbon of pain throbbing across his face.

Just what he needed, he thought. Yet another thing to make him appear a little less than human, inspire fear in even those few souls who didn't already know his identity.

"I have the strongest urge to skewer you on this blade," Martin murmured. A shiver snaked through Derringer's body at the strange tone in Martin's voice. "But I will resist —for now."

"What do you want from me, Martin?" inquired the duke, keeping his tone as neutral at possible. He ignored the steady pain in his face. He'd experienced worse.

"Other than your title, you mean? I want your wealth, of course... and, I think, your wife. Such a pretty, taking little thing she is, Heartless. I shall enjoy making her mine."

Derringer restrained his fury just enough to bite out, "And if she carries my son?"

The ugly twist of Martin's mouth at the suggestion struck Derringer as odd. Did he not realize the possibility was there?

Martin shuddered, extreme distaste coloring his normally even tones. "Such a waste. She shall have to die." His lips twitched at the corners as if enjoying some grand jest. "Perhaps I shall push her from the third floor landing. What think you, little duke? Her warm blood cooling as it soaks into the carpet, the same carpet that drank of your mother's lifeblood. How fitting for one whore duchess to die as her predecessor."

Crimson rage flashed in Derringer's brain. All he needed was to get his hands free so he could snap Martin's neck. Snap his neck and make him pay—finally—for her death.

The duke blinked. Martin's threat put an image in his head, an image of Leandra, dead, choking in her own blood. But Leandra's face faded, changed, became another woman's features, prettier, classical, etched in porcelain.

His mother. He saw her, lying on the landing, her blood strangling her as she gasped for breath. She reached for him, grasping his small hand, squeezing with the last bit of strength she possessed. When she let go, he didn't understand, not until he looked up and saw his father standing on the landing above.

The old duke descended, staring at his wife as he did so. His gaze shifted to his son, the silent boy who stared from his mother to his father and then up the stairs. He glanced at his sire again, suddenly knowing without a doubt that his mother was there because of his father.

And his father shook him, threatened him, ordered him to forget. And the boy Derringer was then knew fear for the first time in his life, knew his father would kill him as surely as he'd killed the duchess.

As surely as Martin would kill the new duchess.

The memory faded, Martin's face coming into sharp focus. The knife glinted as the other man turned it this way and that, watching Derringer the whole time.

"You remember?" Martin mused. "How was it, cousin, watching her life slip away? Did you revel in it? Did you feel... powerful? Was it exhilarating?"

The duke growled, yanking at his bonds. To think his cousin was so far gone, so detached from reality. It sickened him, the very thought. But there was nothing he could do about any of it, not until he escaped. If he could only get loose and get his hands around his cousin's white throat.

His exertions reignited the fire in his cheek, a warm trickle of blood sliding down.

Martin took a step back and smiled malevolently at Derringer. "Ah well. I will have to experience it for myself,

I see. Meanwhile, I, and the crew, require some entertainment, cousin. At your expense, of course."

"Of course," mocked Derringer. He would kill him. If he dared to lay a hand on Leandra, he'd torture him first. "What sort of entertainment do you want? I'd be happy to beat you to a pulp. I don't suppose you'd volunteer?"

Martin's thin smile was devoid of any real mirth. "D'Arcy will have that pleasure, cousin."

"I would be pleased to render the English duke—dead, I think."

Derringer glanced toward the door, his expression shuttering. "D'Arcy. As usual, it is not a pleasure to see you. It will be, however, a pleasure to best you yet again." The confidence in his tone rang out clearly and he saw the wiry Frenchman's face darken with anger.

"I will see you dead this night, Heartless," he bit out.

"Then I will see you in hell!"

D'Arcy turned and stalked out.

"I fear you have made him angry," remarked Martin as he cast a bored expression at the closed door. "You will probably die now, Hart."

"Indeed? You're all attics to let." He smirked. "I have bested that slimy frog before. I'll do so again."

Martin turned from the door, facing the duke once again. "I shall enjoy watching you die, cousin," he said in a soft, reassuring tone. Then he walked out as well.

Derringer leaned back in the bunk, weary and afraid he just might die in the coming confrontation. D'Arcy lacked Derringer's height and breadth but the Frenchman more than made up for that with his speed and willingness to use whatever dishonorable tactics were at his disposal. Derringer also knew in his own weakened state, he really didn't stand much of a chance.

Closing his eyes, he settled his mind into what he was about to do, determined to come out of it alive. He knew, deep down, that Martin could never allow him to survive, but his only chance of escape would come when he was actually loosed from his bonds.

And so, for the first time in decades, the Duke of Derringer prayed.

Martin paid a visit to the duke again that night. The man stood just beyond Derringer's reach. Another man stood in the shadows, his features hidden but his size declaring his identity. The man was too broad, too tall, and too quiet to be anyone other than Tiny Boy, a man Derringer often hired to act as protection. A man whose services could be bought, who would do what was asked of him if the price was right.

Who hired him and why? What did they want him to do?

A groan rose in the duke's throat. If he was expected to fight Tiny, he'd lose. Years ago Derringer and Tiny met, Tiny having been hired to kill Derringer. And Derringer barely survived that encounter. Now, in his weakened physical state, it was unlikely he'd survive, or even last very long.

On the other hand, perhaps Tiny's loyalty to Derringer would supersede whatever amount Martin paid him. One could hope.

Regardless, Derringer could make no assumptions. So he watched. He watched Martin and he watched Tiny.

He still had a part to play and never one to pass up an opportunity to vex an enemy, Derringer smiled, a patronizing smirk that brought a scowl fluttering over Martin's pale face. He pushed himself up to sit, cursing how slow he was to do so, then pushed himself to his feet, no easy feat with his hands tied behind his back.

"What do you want, cousin?" Derringer asked.

Martin St. Clair studied the duke for a long moment, pale blue eyes skimming over Derringer's tall, emaciated form. Then he smiled. "You really should be thanking me, you know," he finally uttered.

Derringer's face went as blank as a slate wiped clean. "Why?"

"Well, you should be thanking my father," Martin clarified. "It was he who made you duke."

His expression still revealing nothing, Derringer replied, "Indeed?" in an attempt to draw his cousin out on the subject. Although, he really didn't care what the man said. Derringer intended to kill him anyway.

"Yes, it was my father who damaged your father's boat." Pride crossed Martin's features, further supporting Derringer's doubts as to the man's sanity.

"I would ask why he would do such a thing, but I realize he wanted to be duke, so I will refrain." Derringer smiled grimly. "That would also explain why I've been fighting for my life since I was seven."

Martin took a step closer and the duke saw Tiny move behind the blond man. Interesting. What was Tiny's plan?

"Do you want to know another secret, Hart?" taunted Martin. "Your wife thinks you're dead."

"Is that supposed to surprise me? Or anger me?"

Martin lurched back. "You truly are heartless, cousin, if you care so little for the misery of your bride."

"She's a wife, Martin. Where I got her, there are a dozen more. Did you think I would get attached?"

"Only so much as you consider her your property," Martin smirked, leaning in again, allowing Derringer to feel his breath fan his cheek. "How will you feel, Hart, when I peel her gown from her breasts? When I expose her white thighs, sink myself—"

Derringer's head slammed forward, cracking into Martin's. They both stumbled back, the duke falling on the bunk while Martin landed on his backside at Tiny's feet. Derringer shook the dizziness away, his hair flopping over his eyes. He didn't see what happened next, but he heard it.

The sound of flesh striking flesh, a grunt, and silence.

Whipping his hair back, Derringer struggled to sit up, flailing about like a landed fish. He managed to uncover one eye, enough to see Tiny standing over Martin.

Blood pooled under Martin's head. A lot of blood. His cousin's eyes were open, staring at nothing.

Derringer's eyes met Tiny's. "You killed him."

"He needed to die," the other man answered, his voice oddly high for one so large.

"But I wanted to kill him. It was my right," Derringer complained, his vision swimming, his voice coming out like a plaintive child.

Tiny grunted, shoving Martin's body from his path in the small cabin. "If you want to whine, Heartless, do it at a later time. Now we leave." He strode forward as he talked, extracting a knife and making short work of the rope binding the duke's wrists.

Derringer flexed his fingers and shook his head. Black rimmed his vision, dizziness threatening to send him sprawling. "I don't whine." He raised his hands, gazing at the burns and scrapes marring his wrists. "Bloody hell, that stings!"

"Whiner."

"What are you doing here?" Derringer asked, ignoring the insult that would have gotten many a man injured, if not killed. "How did you know? How did you get on board?"

"Why are they keeping you on your own yacht, with your own captain?" Tiny countered, stooping next to Martin's body. "Rather short-sighted of them, is it not?" He rifled through the dead man's pockets.

Derringer stopped stretching his cramped muscles, eyes glued to Tiny. "What in hell are you doing now?"

"Taking his money."

"You have no need of money."

"He hired me to kill you. Well, D'Arcy did but I don't see him honoring that agreement." He glanced up. "Do you?"

The duke shrugged. "Not bloody likely. Take what you will, then. I care not." He gazed about, searching for anything he could use as a weapon. "D'Arcy hired you to kill me? When?"

"Months ago. I think this one" —gesturing to Martin's body— "told him to hire someone. They were together often and I laid low when this one was about. Couldn't take the chance he's seen me before." He stood, shoving a bulging purse into his pocket. He held out his closed fist.

"What is it?" The duke accepted the object. It weighed little, though it was large, like most objects of its like. "My ring. Not sure I want it back," he muttered, staring down at the signet ring, contempt curling his lip.

He strode to the door, barely noticing the uneven movement of the floor. He did, however, adhere to the dizziness, putting out a hand. Tiny took his arm and kept him upright.

"What news from home?" Derringer asked before his companion could open the door.

"Your wife is pregnant," Tiny informed him, "if the rumor mill is to be believed." He paused, a funny, crooked grin curving his lips. "Congratulations, Heartless."

The duke stared. "Merri's pregnant?"

32

"GERARD, my most faithful! You have brought the prisoner to me."

Derringer glanced at Tiny, stifling the smirk that threatened. Tiny shrugged, the motion jarring Derringer and reminding him of his weakened state. He stumbled, drawing a laugh from Fraser D'Arcy.

Derringer focused his eyes on the man, willing himself to stand on his own. His black eyes narrowed. D'Arcy was stripped to the waist, flexing his upper body in anticipation.

The duke looked over the man's sinewy torso and prayed he would be able to last long enough to give Tiny the opportunity to take care of the other men on deck. He had no hope of besting the man in the weakened state he currently suffered.

Captain Taverner stood off to one side, a blank expression on his face. Several sailors were laying bets. Derringer was relieved to note they were not any of his men. Martin and D'Arcy must have hired their own crew. What had become of his own men? Had they suffered the same fate as Gabriel? How had they gotten Captain Taverner over to their side?

Tiny let him stand and Derringer flexed his shoulders. He needed to focus, ready himself for the extreme pain he was about to experience. He met Tiny's eye and the man nodded imperceptibly. All was set then.

Derringer turned his black gaze on his opponent, stripping off his tattered black shirt. The light was fading fast and a chill wind kicked up from the north giving him goose flesh. The loss of weight made his ribs stand out, giving him the look of a weak, enfeebled vagrant—a misleading image to anyone who didn't know him. Cuts and welts crisscrossed his torso, front and back, some of them seeping blood as he moved.

He stretched his neck, his eyes never leaving D'Arcy's. Derringer hunched his shoulders the slightest bit, wanting his opponent to think there was extra weakness there. If D'Arcy underestimated the duke's stamina and threshold for pain, Derringer could prolong the beating until Tiny could subdue the crew, maybe even win.

"What are you waiting for, frog?" Derringer taunted. "Did you learn some honor somewhere?"

The Frenchman growled and made a lunge that the duke easily sidestepped even in his weakened state. Just as Derringer suspected, D'Arcy was laboring under the misapprehension that his victory was guaranteed. His overconfidence was Derringer's asset.

He continued to taunt the volatile Frenchman as they circled each other like jungle cats. "Are you so much a coward you think you can only best me when I am half starved?"

He lunged again. Derringer nearly missed avoiding a blow that would have killed him. He saw the unmistakable glint of a knife blade in the meager light thrown by the setting sun. A fleeting thought went through his mind that D'Arcy had cheated in every possible way, but it was nothing more than he'd expected.

"You will die this night, Heartless," growled the angry Frenchman. He lunged again, half expecting the duke to sidestep him as he'd been doing and was unpleasantly surprised when he didn't.

Derringer shifted just enough to get an arm around D'Arcy's throat, squeezing until he felt the smaller man gasping for breath. He caught D'Arcy's flailing arm and wrenched it savagely behind him, the knife D'Arcy clutched falling to the deck. The snap of the bone and the agonized scream of the injured man echoed over the water. Derringer tightened the arm around D'Arcy's neck until the Frenchman slumped unconscious on the deck.

No one was more surprised than the duke that it was over, that he had won, and so quickly. One never should underestimate an opponent, even one so weakened from abuse that he appeared close to death. Derringer could only imagine how he looked, emaciated, wan, trembling in his bare feet. Anyone would have thought he'd lose, anyone would have expected Derringer's body to fall to the deck instead of D'Arcy's. Derringer himself had expected no less.

The deck dipped on a wave, sending Derringer stumbling to his left. His head spun. He tried to look around, tried to see the faces of those surrounding him. Instead his eyes rolled back in his head and he joined D'Arcy on the deck.

Prestwich and his band of intrepid rescuers returned to Portsmouth mere days after their departure. Leandra's condition was to blame, her stomach unable to endure the constant motion of a ship.

They journeyed straight from Portsmouth to Folkestone, a certain urgency not allowing for a stop in London to apprise Aurora and Bri of new developments.

After several days of uncomfortable travel, they finally drove under the raised portcullis of Derringer Crescent. The front gardens flowered with early spring blooms, two fountains filling the air with the constant splash of water meeting water.

Leandra gazed about her in rapt wonder. Such drastic changes had occurred in the time since she'd taken up residence. Her heart filled with joy at the sight.

The loss of her husband had occupied her mind to the point that she noticed nothing around her. Now, tired, ill with worry and despair, and so close to giving up she could taste it, she saw the changes her servants had made, saw the instructions she'd given carried out. It gladdened her heart even if that gladness was tinged with sorrow.

Her husband should see his estate returned to its former glory. But she doubted he would. Her faith in his return had waned. All that kept her hanging onto the future was the child under her heart, a small piece of the husband she'd learned to love.

Leandra put on her best gown, an ivory silk trimmed with Brussels lace, tiny seed pearls sewn all over the bodice. Such a beautiful gown, she thought, stroking the soft fabric with a shaking hand. She'd never worn it, having taken one look at it and deciding to save it for something special. Liza had taken an hour to let it out a bit, allowing extra room for her pregnancy.

What made her decide to wear it now?

Liza wound her heavy tresses into a loose cluster of curls, pinning them securely and placing a seed pearl and diamond encrusted comb within the dark locks. A matching necklace of diamonds and pearls went around her neck and bracelets of gold around her gloved wrists. Her maid tried to convince her to carry a lorgnette, a beautiful eyeglass boasting diamonds and pearls, but Leandra declined, settling her spectacles firmly on her nose. After looking in the mirror, she had Liza put a dab of rouge on her wan cheeks to give her some much needed color.

Liza stood back, her pretty face a picture of awe. "You are so beautiful," she whispered.

Leandra laughed. It felt good to laugh. "Hardly that, Liza." Tears started to her eyes and she pulled her maid into an impulsive embrace. "But thank you."

She swept from the room but a sharp pain halted her at the door, nearly sending her to her knees. Breathing deep, she gripped the doorpost, fingers whitening, and stifled a groan. It soon passed. She straightened, smoothing her hands over her belly, then continued on down to the family dining room. She told no one of the cramping in her abdomen and as it was not repeated, she soon forgot about it.

After a satisfying meal of no less than four courses with innumerable side courses and a final course of chocolate trifle, the gentlemen decided to forgo their port in favor of joining Leandra in the drawing room. As Leandra left the room, smiling at something Greville said, she caught sight of an arriving party. She paused, curiosity and unease tingling along her skin. Who would drop in on her without warning, well after the dinner hour? Greville and

Prestwich halted beside her, their faces mirroring her concern.

The party shifted, parting to allow someone to fall to the front. Leandra's smile faded, falling away as this person approached with the help of a very large man.

She dared not believe her eyes as she beheld the beloved countenance of her husband, his cheekbones protruding unnaturally over his sunken cheeks, one side of his face crusted with dried blood. His harsh features wavered, her vision blurring before the onslaught of tears.

He stood before her. She stared up into his battered features, her heart aching at the sight of cuts and bruises, his dark eyes probing hers. Then he spoke. It was a pain-filled whisper that tugged at her heart, her pooled tears overflowing.

"Merri, my angel, goddess of my heart, you are beautiful."

After everything that had happened, Leandra Derringer could finally take no more. For the first time in her life, she fainted, falling gracefully at the duke's feet.

33

DERRINGER knew hell but nothing prepared him for the long, frightful night ahead. Nightmares plagued his sleep, his younger self watching his mother die, then his adult self watching Gabriel die, and finally his future self watching his wife die. He awoke, covered in sweat, heart slamming against his ribs.

A quick glance around the room reassured him. He was safe. His ambitious relatives could no longer harm him. Tiny had assured him they would plague him no more and Tiny was very thorough when it came to taking care of things.

A cold feeling of dread assailed him even as this comforting thought occurred. The clock by his bed, illuminated in a shaft of moonlight, stared back at him, informing him of the time but giving him no reason as to his unease. What woke him? Was it the nightmare alone? Or some other disturbance, something outside his unconscious mind?

A muffled sound caught his ear. Two doors and a sitting room separated him from his wife. He'd gone against his instincts, allowing his wife to sleep alone, in her own bed, convincing himself that she would rest better without his haggard presence at her side.

His eye was drawn to the connecting door, senses alert. He eased to the edge of the high bed, straining his ears for a repeat of the muffled sound. When it came again, it was louder, barely muffled at all.

He streaked across the room, thankful he'd been put to bed in his breeches. Two doors and a sitting room later, he strode into his wife's bedchamber.

Her scream rent the air just as he reached her side, a keening, agony-filled howl that froze his blood. Her arms pressed into the feather mattress, her back arching with the pain. The metallic tang of blood filled the air, Derringer's stomach clenching at the scent.

He found himself beside her before he even realized it, sitting on the bed. He gathered her in his arms. Terror clenched at his heart while he cursed his ignorance. He knew what was happening, the dim light of a fire allowing his eyes to see the dark stain spreading over her lower limbs. But he didn't know how to help her through it, how to ease the pain that threatened to tear her in two.

Would a physician know what to do? Possibly, but Derringer would have to leave her side, venture into the corridor, shout the castle down in an attempt to get help. Would it be too late by then?

Confused, frightened, and a little angry, he just held her. He held her until she stopped crying, stopped struggling.

He held her when she stopped moving at all and the only sound that could be heard was the sound of his own convulsive sobs.

Liza entered her mistress's room cautiously. She'd heard her mistress's screams and gone to Mrs. Stark immediately so that lady could send for the doctor. Liza had too many younger brothers and sisters, had seen too many difficult pregnancies to not be aware of what was happening as soon as Leandra screamed in the night. The housekeeper agreed with Liza's assessment of the situation and sent up a sleeping draft should Leandra need it. Then she roused a footman and sent him to order a groom to ride for the doctor.

As Liza looked around, she saw his grace in the bed with the duchess and her heart nearly broke. She clapped a hand to her mouth to stifle the sobs that tried to escape and knocked the tray she carried out of her own hand. It clattered to the floor, shattering the early-morning peace.

The noise woke Derringer, who had fallen asleep only minutes before the maid's entrance. He looked up at Liza, down at his wife, and couldn't stop a fresh torrent of grief. He buried his face in Leandra's neck and wept bitterly for the loss of his wife and child.

He wasn't aware of Liza's leaving the room. Indeed, he was aware of nothing but the agony that threatened to tear him apart. He didn't even hear his name whispered over and over until someone rudely shook him.

"What?" he roared at this hapless person. He opened his eyes and stared into hazel eyes turned dusky green with pain and a shared sorrow.

Scarcely daring to believe, Derringer sat up, touching his wife's ashen cheek with one long finger. She smiled wanly at him and opened her mouth to speak. But the duke forestalled her by covering her mouth with his in a kiss that spoke of love, passion, heartbreak, and relief. And somewhere in the depths was a profound grief over the loss of their child.

Leandra recovered slowly, which was no great surprise to anyone. She had just lost a child, a child she had for so long thought of as her only link to a man she loved more than life itself. Her grief consumed her and Derringer tried to help her through it as best he could. But he was grieving, too, and had little experience with helping others to heal.

Greville departed shortly after Derringer's return. Prestwich remained for a few weeks, determined to stay until he knew the duchess was out of danger. He knew his wife would never forgive him if he left too soon. But he was next to useless when trying to help a grieving female, a failing he openly acknowledged, and in so doing, was oddly more comforting than not. Mostly, he kept the duke from going stark-staring mad.

But the duke was at his wit's end regardless. He stalked the castle corridors, talking to himself, trying to work out a solution, one that would resurrect the lively beauty that was his wife. Something had to get through to her, wake her up from her sorrow, help her move forward.

Derringer sent for Michaella. He hoped his wife's sister would be able to help her. Besides, he had some very bad news that should only be delivered in person.

Lady Michaella arrived a few days after she was summoned. Derringer greeted her, taking her to his study. She sat down, pretty face blank, waiting. After ordering a servant to fetch the duchess, he paced before his sister-by-marriage.

The duke wondered how much this young lady had been made privy to during his absence. He'd been aware of a certain attachment between her and the man the world thought of as his cousin, Gabriel St. Clair. He did not look forward to telling her of his demise but he hoped that she and Leandra might be able to help each other.

"Thank you for coming so promptly, Lady Michaella," he began formally.

"Please, call me Michaella," she inserted quickly, a sweet smile curving her lips. Derringer could understand Gabriel's having fallen for this rose. She was completely unspoiled.

He bowed. "Michaella, then. And you will call me Hart, I hope. We are brother and sister, after all." Michaella smiled and nodded.

Derringer stared down at her. He felt like pacing but he knew this would not soften the blow she was about to receive. So he sat beside her instead. "Michaella, I wonder if you would permit me to ask you something very impertinent before Merri arrives."

Brows lifting in surprise, she replied, "If you wish."

"Are you in love with Gabriel?"

Her blush was answer enough but to his surprise she didn't hesitate in replying in the affirmative.

Leandra must not have been far when the servant found her. It was then that the door opened to admit Lady Derringer.

Doubt curled in Derringer's chest. He hoped the sisters could help each other through their grief. Neither lady had yet learned of Gabriel's death and Michaella was as yet unaware of her sister's loss. His loss.

He had no other ideas to try to help his wife and he was beginning to feel rather helpless—an emotion he quite simply could not countenance.

Standing as she entered, he offered her his seat beside her sister. A taut smile briefly curved her lips as she acknowledged his unwonted courtesy. He felt his own lips twitch in response. His Merri was still in there somewhere, beneath all that mind-numbing grief.

Assuming bad news was best delivered while all, including the bearer, were seated, he dragged the chair from before his desk and placed it near the settee upon which the ladies perched.

Derringer opened his mouth, then closed it and shook his head. "First, have you heard any rumors of my cousin, Michaella?"

Michaella blushed quite becomingly, darting a look at her sister. "No. I was rushed home soon after you… left."

He smiled. "No need to feel shy about mentioning that. It was a difficult time for us all," he remarked in the single biggest understatement of the century.

"Yes," she murmured. "I was sorry to leave Merri at such a time but I felt she was in capable hands with Rory and Bri. Much more capable." A smile trembled on her lips when Leandra reached over and squeezed her hand.

"Quite. You have not heard then that Gabriel is not my cousin?"

"Whatever do you mean?" she asked.

He sighed, clenching his fingers in an unusual display of uncertainty. "Gabriel was taken from our mother just after his birth and raised by my aunt and uncle. Gabe is my twin." He paused, drawing in a deep, rather unsteady breath. "Gabe *was* my twin."

It took but a moment for his listeners to digest what he was saying. Leandra gasped, a tear sliding down her pale cheek. Her sister released a shaky breath but did not cry.

"He is… dead?"

Derringer was very much affected by the empty look in Michaella's eyes but he did not show it. "Yes, he is."

The young lady's lips curved upward a bit but it was not a smile. It was more a grimace of acceptance, a look of acute awareness of life. Somehow, this was far worse than if she had screamed and wailed against the unfairness of fate. But at the same time, he had to admire her strength.

"Thank you for telling me, Hart," she said, her voice hollow, dead. She rose in one graceful movement. "I know how difficult it must be for you right now. Please accept my condolences on your loss."

"Lady Michaella—Michaella—he was as much your loss as mine. More so yours, I think," the duke observed, his voice barely above a whisper.

Michaella did smile then, a soft, heartbroken little twisting of her lips that slammed Derringer in the stomach. "We all lost something wonderful, Hart. The key is to live on with his memory strong in our hearts and minds. To wake up each day, thankful we are alive, and thankful we had the pleasure of knowing him. I am thankful for that pleasure, Hart, and I know I owe that to you." She went forward and bent to kiss him on the cheek. "Thank you."

Derringer watched her leave, unsure what to say to that. He'd neglected to tell her of Leandra's misery, too stunned by her words to do anything other than stare at her.

And ignore the memories clamoring for attention. His mother, his father, his brother and the added horror of his child's death fought for dominance, threatening to drive him mad. His wife sat silently watching him, tears streaking her cheeks. He had nothing he could say to her, nothing to ease the agony in her eyes, heal the ache in her heart. How could he help her? He couldn't even help himself.

The duke left her alone with her misery. Leandra closed her eyes, willing the tears to cease. She felt powerless against all the grief and even more so against the hurt she saw in her husband's dark eyes—hurt that she'd caused.

And so, with just a look from the person she loved most in life, the Duchess of Derringer died a little more inside.

34

THE duke's plan failed. Michaella was too shy, too withdrawn an individual to draw out the stubbornly silent duchess. She tried but when her attempts came up against monosyllabic replies time and time again, she gave up, weary and utterly defeated—and a little disappointed in her sister for being so selfish.

Life might have progressed this way for quite some time had not the duke finally decided it was time to move on. He loved his wife desperately, worried over her constantly, and was blindingly jealous of his own dead child who seemed to be the only focus she had in her life. He grieved for the child too but life had to go on and one had to grow away from tragedy to survive.

Three months after the child's death, Derringer marched into his wife's morning room where Leandra sat with Michaella. The ladies glanced up at him as he entered, their expressions faintly curious. Leandra sighed once and looked away.

The duke, while being heartbroken by this same attitude every time she saw him, felt his temper rising at the same time. "Madam, a word," he bit out.

Michaella squeaked in alarm and darted a look at her sister. She was worried about Leandra and although she didn't like the duke's tone or angry stance, even she had to agree that this grief of Leandra's was bordering on obsession and therefore unhealthy. So she turned to the duchess, who was staring at her husband as if he'd suddenly sprouted a third arm, and urged her to go with him.

Leandra rose to her feet and started across the floor. Derringer turned on his heel and walked out, assuming she followed. He did not stop until he stood outside her bedchamber. With a mocking gesture, he indicated she precede him into the chamber. With a questioning look, Leandra obeyed. She swung around with a start when he turned the key in the lock.

"Hart, what are you doing?" she asked.

The duke circled around her, giving her a long searching look. He opened his mouth to speak, then closed it. He seemed to be trying to decide something and Leandra wasn't sure she really wanted to know what it was.

He took two steps forward, backing her into the door. Leandra, startled, could do nothing but stare up at him as he placed both hands on the wood above her head, successfully blocking her in with his tall body.

Leandra swallowed with difficulty when she recognized the emotion blazing in her husband's eyes was not anger, but rather desire. How could he still desire her after…?

"Not acceptable, Merri," he whispered harshly, lowering his mouth to hers.

She had been wrong. Some of it had been anger, after all. But he did desire her, his kiss heating her from the top of her head to the tips of her toes, stopping off at some critical places in between.

Leandra gave as good as she got, arching into him, drawing him closer, begging with her body for the mastery of his. She craved his lovemaking, had been afraid for months that he'd never touch her again.

It was with a severe shock that she realized her face was wet. And something had changed in her husband's kiss. Pulling away, she wondered if she were crying, not the least surprised to realize she was.

What effectively stunned her was the fact that the duke was crying, too.

Feeling more tears well up and slip down her cheeks in the face of his obvious pain, Leandra choked on a sob.

His hands no longer lay flat on the door, but were holding her face, his forehead pressed to hers. She copied him, her hands framing his face, gently, her thumbs wiping away the tears.

He growled, in anger and frustration. Manfully swallowing the convulsive sobs that begged for release, he shook her a little, saying, "Dammit, Merri, tell me!"

She blinked up at him. "Tell you what?" she asked, her voice a harsh, tear-choked whisper.

He met her eyes. "What do I have to do? What will it take? What do you want from me?"

Her heart skipped a beat at his suffering. She could have asked him the same question, really. But she didn't.

Gazing up into shimmering black eyes, Leandra whispered, "Make love to me, Hart."

"Merri, my love, seduction was not what I intended," murmured her husband later. He wound a lock of her hair around his finger, seeming quite fascinated with the play of the late afternoon sunlight on the glossy dark strands.

Leandra smiled. "Indeed? You did not set out to seduce me, dearest husband? I must confess I'm disappointed you only wanted to talk." She pretended to pout.

Derringer leaned up on one elbow, looking down at her. Serious lines etched his face, a tinge of sadness curving his lips. She reached up, tracing one finger along his face, along the scar marring an already harsh countenance. How sad she'd been upon beholding his injury! To learn his own cousin was the cause, a man she'd once considered a friend, had only served to deepen her agony.

He didn't flinch away though his eyes closed, briefly, at her gentle caress. His lashes fluttered open, black eyes spearing her where she lay, half beneath him.

She tensed, knowing what was coming. "I am sorry about the baby, Merri. And I know how much you wanted our child."

She reached up to stop his words, still too grief stricken to talk about it. "Please don't, Hart. Not now. I can't—" Her voice broke on a sob.

"Don't you see, Merri? You have to. Prestwich told me that although you converse with him as if nothing weighs upon your mind, you would never discuss the baby. I know you don't speak to Lady Michaella about it. How will you grow away from the pain if you refuse to even acknowledge it?"

She pushed him away from her and sat up, hugging her knees to her chest. What an abrupt change from her mood of just moments before! Tears streamed down her face. "I don't want to grow away from the pain, Hart! I lost a baby. Your baby. I will never stop thinking about it, never stop remembering, grieving. Just let me be!"

She swung her feet toward the edge of the bed, attempting to escape her husband's demands but he snaked his arm around her waist before she could. "Leandra, this is cannot go on! I will not let you avoid me as you've been doing."

"I have to avoid you, Hart," she cried in anguish. "It's all my fault. Don't you see? If I had listened to you, to Levi, and to Adam, I would have been safe at home. The baby would be safe. I killed our baby! How can you ever learn to love me now?"

Derringer was so shocked at this that she was able to wrench from his arms and dart into her dressing room. He didn't follow. How did he miss that her despondency was due to guilt? The thought had crossed his own mind that perhaps it would not have happened had she obeyed his command to stay put. But he had just as quickly determined that the anxiety over the months of his disappearance would have been enough.

It was her final words that succeeded in propelling him from the rumpled bed. She believed he didn't love her? That he never could? How could she think such a nonsensical thing?

He found her huddled in a chair before the fire in the sitting room. Her shoulders shook with the force of her silent tears. She looked so tiny, so dejected that Derringer thought he might cry as well… again. He was becoming a veritable watering pot, he thought in disgust.

He approached her cautiously, like he would an injured animal. He reached down and picked her up, cradling her in his arms, and sat down in the chair. "Leandra, love, we really do need to discuss this, I think." She shook her head, still too distraught to speak. "You say it is your fault." She nodded. "All this time, you have been blaming yourself." Again, a dejected little nod. "And you believe I blame you as well." This time, she didn't nod. She sobbed harder.

"Oh, Merri, Merri," he said fondly, forcing her head up, forcing her to see his sincerity. "I do not blame you. I think it might have happened no matter what you did. I am surprised you did not lose the baby when you were informed I was dead."

Her tears stopped falling and Derringer gently brushed the moisture from her cheeks. She still said nothing, just gazed at him through huge gold-flecked eyes.

"As for the never loving you part," he said with a half-smile, "No, don't you dare start crying again, Leandra Derringer. Wait until you hear what I have to say." She sniffed once and dutifully held back the sobs that threatened. "I have a confession to make." Her eyes widened slightly. "It's true, I've been keeping secrets." He nodded at her, his lips twisted into a self-deprecating smile. "Despicable, I know, but there it is." And he stopped.

Leandra stared at him in disbelief. He had actually told her nothing. What great secret did he keep from her? Other than every other thing about him she'd only recently learned.

His smile grew and she felt the urge to hit him. "What secret?" she finally asked.

"I love you."

THE END

About the Author

Jaimey Grant, a pseudonym for Laura Miller, was born in Michigan in 1979. After a fun-filled childhood interlaced with moments of emotional trauma and an insatiable curiosity about the reasons people act the way they do, she became a writer.

Primarily a Regency romance author, Jaimey has also dabbled in fantasy of a non-romance variety. A comprehensive list of works and where to find them can be found on her website, www.jaimeygrant.com. There are more Regencies and fantasies in the works.

She currently lives in Michigan with her husband and two children.

To learn more about Jaimey and her work, visit any of the sites below.

Website: http://www.jaimeygrant.com
Blog: http://jaimeygrant.blogspot.com
Facebook: http://www.facebook.com/jaimeygrantauthor
Email: jaimeygrant@yahoo.com